God's Mafia

a novel by

Alfred Fortino

Lost Coast Press
Fort Bragg, California

God's Mafia © 1997 by North Central Properties

This is a work of fiction. Any resemblance to actual persons, events or entities is purely coincidental. All rights reserved. No portion of this book may be reproduced by any means whatever, except for brief excerpts for the purposes of review or analysis, without the prior written permission of the publisher. For information, or to order additional copies, please contact:

Lost Coast Press
155 Cypress Street
Fort Bragg, CA 95437
1-800-773-7782

ISBN No. 1-882897-09-9

Library of Congress No. 96-80309

Cover photo credit:	©Stock Boston / John Maher / PNI
Cover design:	Elizabeth Petersen
Book production:	Cypress House

First Edition

Manufactured in the USA

Acknowledgments

This novel would never have been completed without the commentary of my dear sisters, Marian Aquino and Betty Metz, as well as other friends.

I am particularly grateful to Professor Timm Thorsen, Chairman of the Department of Sociology at Alma College, Alma, Michigan, and Professor Stanley Chipper, retired chairman of the Economics Department at Indiana State University. They read every word of the manuscript and spent hours writing suggestions which were most helpful.

I had the great good fortune of drawing a singularly sympathetic editor in John Fremont of Cypress House. His help was instrumental in making a novel out of a notion.

I am obliged to the library of Alma College and to the Law Library of the State of Michigan whose respective staffs were always ready to help.

I also owe much to my secretary and administrative assistant, Brenda Mitchell, for her persistence in typing the manuscript many times over, both in the office and at home, unstintingly, always with a smile and with a pat on the back for me.   – *A.J. Fortino*

Dedicated to

My mother
Giovannina Scarcelli Fortino
a devout Roman Catholic

and

My wife
Mary Alice Damon Fortino
a dedicated Presbyterian

Introduction

This is a work of fiction. I must admit, however, that it was written as a commentary on the current prison system. The statistics cited in *God's Mafia* are not fictitious. The status of recidivism in this country can be ascertained by reading any text book or commentary in criminology or sociology. The rate of rise in the prison population, the number in prison, on probation or parole was furnished by the United States Department of Justice in August of 1995. Things have not improved since then.

The information on the compounding of rules and regulations and the growth of government was compiled by the author in December of 1992 for an article in the Michigan Bar Journal.

– A.J. Fortino

ONE

Paul Nagel entered the lobby of the Capital Hotel and went directly to the main dining room, where he was greeted by the head waiter. "Good evening, Mr. Nagel," the waiter said as he led the prosecutor to his customary table. "Your usual, sir?"

Nagel nodded and the waiter beckoned a busboy to serve the attorney a cup of coffee. Nagel checked his watch and stared at the front door.

As he sipped his coffee, Paul Nagel thought about his dinner companion, Janet Wingate. They both served on the governor's commission on poverty and welfare, although Janet was on the board as proxy for her boss, Tyrus Smith, chief executive officer of the Fairfield Bank. Heavily engaged in merger talks, Smith relied on Ms. Wingate, the bank's trust officer, to represent his interests. He trusted her completely, and she faithfully reported the commission's activities to him.

Nagel wasn't quite sure why he had been named to the commission. He held no political office. He did not work for a major company. He was only an assistant US Attorney in Crystal City, the state capital. Although he was not a political luminary, he was regarded as one of the foremost crime fighters in the state, perhaps in the country, with many court victories over organized crime. He had written and lectured extensively on the subject and was an authority on combating organized crime. Perhaps the governor wanted the commission to investigate crime in the poverty areas, particularly in public housing. Whatever the reason, Nagel was grateful he'd been appointed, not because he relished the spotlight but because he relished Janet Wingate. She, however, knew nothing about his feelings.

Alfred J. Fortino

As he waited for his dinner partner, he observed that these dinner dates were the only enjoyable part of the monthly commission meetings. He looked forward to sharing dinner with Ms. Wingate much more than he looked forward to the meetings of the committee. For the first time in his adult life — he was now 42 years of age — he had come upon a woman who intrigued him. He had dated on occasion, mostly at the insistence of his sister, Kathleen, who was happily married and thought he should be married, too. He'd never had time for dates or anything romantic. And now he couldn't keep his mind off an attractive tall blonde with blue-green eyes who reminded him of a classic Greek statue. Still, he could not picture himself married. His work was his sole and complete master, every waking hour of every day, seven days a week. He had at times been tempted to try a relationship. He had managed each time to resist the temptation.

Janet Wingate, widowed when her husband had died three years earlier in a plane crash, was sole parent of two boys, ten and eight years of age. She was in her hotel room preparing to join her companion at dinner. She, too looked forward to these dinners, flattered that such a well-known, highly respected person wanted to have dinner with her each time the commission met. There were many rather important people on the commission with whom he could spend the evening, but apparently he preferred her company. She too was fond of him. What aroused her interest was that he had recently established a trust fund with her bank to benefit Bryan Dibble, a high school student from Fairfield paralyzed from the waist down as a result of a football injury. Nagel apparently didn't know the youth but had read about the case and started a trust to provide for the boy's college education. What had particularly impressed Janet was that Nagel had made it a part of the trust agreement that no one but Janet was to know he was the boy's benefactor, not even Bryan or his family. When she had asked him the reason for the secrecy, he had said that he could not stand publicity. Publicity would spoil the gift, because it would make a hero out of him and seem a publicity stunt, a cheap bit of deceit he would not permit himself. In Janet's mind, that made for quite a guy. If only he would make their relation more than a Dutch-treat dinner every month or so. During the past year, Janet had begun to long for male companionship. Paul Nagel was the only man who had even slightly interested her. She hoped this evening he might "make a move."

As she reached his table, she noticed he had changed suits since the commission meeting. He rose and helped her to her seat, and the waiter served coffee without being asked. "How's Bryan doing?" Nagel asked.

"Just fine. He is such a joy to be with that I make it a point to see him once a week. We've become good friends."

"How is he doing in school?"

"Very well. He'll have no trouble getting into college. I am having trouble answering his questions, though. This secrecy stuff is making it difficult." Janet paused, then brightened "You'd really enjoy knowing Bryan, and he'd enjoy knowing you."

Nagel shook his head. "I could never do that."

"You can't face someone you're helping?"

Nagel did not answer immediately. He fumbled with his napkin as he sought to place it on his lap, then picked up his coffee cup and sipped. "I can't explain," he said. "I would be terribly embarrassed." He did not look at her.

"Why?" she asked partly in supplication, partly frustrated.

"I can't explain it." He raised his eyes to hers and smiled humbly.

Janet smiled and said sadly but affectionately, "The great Paul Nagel, the terror of the mob, the tough prosecutor can't face a boy whose future he has made possible."

"You can put it that way," he responded, hoping it might end her line of interrogation.

"I don't understand it Paul. You do something wonderful for somebody and you won't admit it to anyone, not even to your beneficiary, probably not even to yourself. It doesn't make any sense."

Paul spoke slowly, carefully. "Even trying to explain it makes me feel terrible. I do it because I must do it."

"Are you trying to play God?"

"Oh no! God has nothing to do with this, or with me."

"If you must do this, and God doesn't compel you, who does?"

"Janet, we're all selfish. I'm no different. We're all hypocrites. Everything we do is for ourselves, for our benefit, for our aggrandizement. All the things we talk about in committee, all the people who give to charity, to the poor, It's all hypocrisy. It's all a big grandstand play. We try to make ourselves heroes. Everybody thinks we're great stuff. As for the weak and the poor, what do they get? A pittance. It doesn't do a thing for them except keep them weak and poor. But we big philanthropists, we are saints! Look, I'm as vain as anyone. I love being praised and acknowledged as a success. I like to give speeches and write papers. I like to testify before legislative committees. My ego is as big as anybody's. But when I can help somebody without anyone knowing about it, I redeem myself. Does that make any sense to you?"

Janet was thunderstruck! So that was it! That's what it was all about. What a guy! What candor! For a moment she said nothing.

Nagel smiled again. "You've become my confessor," he said sheepishly.

"Oh, Paul, only in your eyes, in your mind, is a recitation of good deeds a confession! My God, Paul, you are upside down. How many other good deeds do you want to confess?"

Paul Nagel shook his head. "I know where I stand, Janet. It's the world, not I, that's upside down."

"And where do you stand, Paul? To whom are you accountable?"

"Must I tell you more?" He agonized. "Don't you understand that I need to keep this to myself?"

"Why, Paul? Don't tell me you don't believe in anything. Who keeps score on you? Obviously, it is not God."

"You can be tough, Janet. Frankly I don't know. Maybe it's my mother. She's dead, but she's with me everyday."

"You don't believe in God!" Janet's voice was sympathetic, but she did not know whether she was sorry for this man or falling in love with him. She knew she had a new feeling for him even if she was having difficulty identifying it. Only minutes ago she had acknowledged an admiration for him and hoped she might get to know him better. Now she knew him better, or did she? She still didn't understand him but she was much more interested! The next move, if there was to be one, was up to him.

God's Mafia

During the rest of the meal they talked about the day's meeting. Paul reiterated his displeasure with private charities, particularly those which received more than their beneficiaries. They talked about what should be in the governor's report. The dining room was almost empty when Janet announced she simply had to get to sleep. She had a big day at her office the next day.

Nagel escorted her to the elevator, then left the hotel, picked up his car and drove to his apartment. As he traversed the rain-dampened streets, he muddled over the evening. Who was his score-keeper? Only Janet would raise such a question. He had never thought about it, but he had answered truthfully. His mind reached back to his childhood, to the mining town in West Virginia, to the dismal, dark days and long nights which he and his family endured. His mother Nadia was in the center of the nostalgic portrait, his father Joseph and his sister Kathleen were in the background. It was Nadia who had fed and cared for them, who had inspired her children to excel, who had prompted Paul, driven him to excellence. She told him not to follow the lure of the mine; he must become a lawyer, a good one. He must improve the lot of the common man within the system. It must be done there, she had insisted. The way of the socialists and communists was a false one, a hopeless one, she told him. She had worshipped John L. Lewis, had fed workers on the picket lines, but her son could do more by working within the system. She tutored him and Kathleen even though she herself had never finished high school. She scoured the little library in their town. And when the family got an old Ford, she drove to the library of the University of West Virginia to get books for her children. Yes, she was his scorekeeper and always would be.

But what about Janet? He was thinking about her more and more. He had tried to resist, but now it would be even harder to do so. She was the first woman ever to claim even part of his attention. A still-small voice within him warned that this posed a dangerous situation. He felt both threatened and enthralled! Was this what happened when a confirmed bachelor fell in love? It was all rather disconcerting.

TWO

When Nagel arrived at his office on Monday, his associates Tom Wicker and Anthony Draefus were waiting for him. He had barely seated himself when Wicker said, "We've just received a blockbuster of a case from Washington. It's a RICO deal, but it's not like anything I've seen before. It's the most unusual con-game I've ever come across. Washington wants us to break it up immediately. A dossier came by special courier Friday. Our paralegals took one look at it and rushed it to me. Tony and I reviewed the file this morning. The AG hasn't seen it yet, but we got a call from a Deputy in his office and were informed that one of the FBI agents who investigated the case will be here this afternoon to discuss it with you. We wanted you to get a taste of it before he arrives." Tony jumped to his feet to join Tom, who rose as he was speaking.

Nagel waved them back to their chairs. "Are we supposed to drop everything we're working on? We've got important actions pending."

"Whatever we have here is nothing compared to this," Tony said. "Apparently this racket has been going on for a long time and is really picking up steam now. It's already making a lot of money for the racketeers and growing exponentially. It's hidden behind a perfect cover, with a lot of people being fleeced out of a lot of money." Draefus had the file in his hand and was getting excited. Wicker continued the story:

"The racket was brought to light through a plea bargain with three defendants who, in exchange for the information in this file, entered pleas to reduced charges in three drug busts. They have a fantastic story about ex-convicts who have hit upon a scheme to recruit people about to be released from prison. They provide recruits a job in return for 7.5% of their net income! And, get this, a Catholic Priest and a Presbyterian Minister in Fairfield, go to the prisons to interview candidates. If the prisoners appear malleable, they are promised jobs and even training and some rehabilitation at no cost to them. The clerics provide cover to the operation which is called the 'Ecumenical Society.' The money goes to this so-called religious society and is used by the insiders to finance businesses that on their face appear legitimate. The so-called 'Board of Directors,' ex-convicts all, are millionaires with their own individual businesses. They tap into money from the Society where ordinarily, they wouldn't be able to get credit at any legitimate bank. The Society holds no church services and does no charitable work. All it does is take money from the employees and use it for their respective businesses. They now have $20,000,000 in the trust department of the Central Bank in Fairfield, about thirty miles from here. Headquarters are located in New York City. No money deducted from an employee's pay is ever paid back."

Nagel asked, "What if someone refuses to pay?"

"He loses his job or his financing," Draefus replied.

At three that afternoon, FBI agent Harold Sutherland joined Nagel, Wicker and Draefus. Wicker began interrogating him without introductory pleasantries. "Why is the money in Fairfield and the headquarters in New York?"

Sutherland smiled. "We don't know the answer to that question. We have guessed that it would be impossible to hide such an organization in Fairfield. In New York, it's just another company in an old building. We really haven't figured it all out, but the operation is clearly a rip off.

"Our information comes from the three men we convicted. They've told us that secrecy covers absolutely everything and everybody — that we're unlikely to learn anything from anybody else. If we tried to interrogate any board members, they'll probably claim the Fifth.

"That's why, we've focused on the priest and the minister. According to our witnesses, they're the leaders. We haven't made any attempt to interrogate them, although we have initiated an investigation into tax evasion and criminal records. Nothing remotely suspicious has surfaced. These characters have no record of any kind."

"Why focus on these two?" Draefus asked.

"If you want to try more, who would you pick? Five of them, ten or 20? We'd be looking at separate trials, varied verdicts and years in court. But that's up to you. Our opinion is that if we can convict the leaders, we'll bring down the whole operation."

"Are you confident that the priest and minister are the heads of an organization engaged in criminal activity?" Nagel asked.

"If our witnesses can be believed, these two are the gang leaders."

Nagel wasn't convinced. "It just doesn't add up. Why would they rake in millions without changing their life styles?" Nagel asked.

Sutherland had a ready answer. "Mr. Nagel, scams like this have been used by so-called ministers of the gospel since the middle ages.

"What we have here is a clear case of extortion prosecutable under RICO. The victims pay money out of fear that if they don't pay they'll lose their jobs or be out of business. The operation is a clear violation of the *Racketeer Influenced and Corrupt Organization Act*, which was passed to stop ill-gotten money from flowing into legitimate businesses. On top of that you have a conspiracy to finance the drug traffic. The 'holy men' knew they were dealing with convicted drug peddlers when they loaned money to them.

"What's more, the court has held that we don't need to show the preachers got anything. Being parties to criminal violations or acting as part of a conspiracy to violate the law is all we need."

Nagel flipped through the pages in the file "Many associations have members who pay dues," he observed. "This has been going on for a long time. They take prisoners, determine that they're employable, enroll them in an organization and provide jobs for them. Seven and a half percent of an average income of $25,000 is $1,875 per year. What's extortionate about that? It is not an unlawful debt. It may be a bit stiff as a fee, but that doesn't make it criminal."

Sutherland was becoming disgusted with Nagel but kept his cool. "That's the genius of this whole thing. It sounds so pious and legitimate! But it is really a typical protection racket. The Mafia is not extortionate either. They don't want to kill the goose that lays their golden eggs. They just want a good sustaining income. If you've got five, six or ten thousand victims you've got several million dollars a year coming in.

"Even if they're only skimming $100 a year, it's still extortion. The statute requires no minimum amount to make the payment extortionate. All that's required is that money be paid under threat of loss of money or property.

"You've got a board of directors who have become millionaires as a result of money fleeced from people who cannot help themselves, who cannot say 'no.' It's a protection racket all right, one of the best disguised rackets ever invented."

Draefus who had been listening closely, said, "Paul, think for a moment about the real implications of this case. All a racketeer has to do is pick a religious name for his organization, find some vulnerable targets and set up business. Can you imagine what the big boys would do with this concept if we don't shut it down right now?"

"Does this Ecumenical Society have any branches? Is it a part of a larger religious group or of any charitable organization?" Nagel wanted to know.

"There is no similar organization anywhere we know. This society is just a name attached to a racket," Sutherland said trying to be polite.

"Do we have indication of any ties to any known crime families?" Nagel asked him.

"We have no proof of any affiliation," Sutherland replied. "Even if this is strictly amateur, how long do you think it will take before the pros take over?

"It doesn't matter what was in the minds of the defendants. What matters is whether the victims perceived their intent as extortion and whether the circumstances were such as to make that perception a reasonable one. We think that the circumstances in this case can reasonably be construed to constitute extortion. Fact: a lot of money has been deducted from the paychecks of people who must have those paychecks to survive. Fact: if the victims don't pay they lose their jobs. If that isn't extortion then I don't know what is."

"With regard to intent," Nagel observed after Sutherland's explanation, "we have a sure fire way to establish it: wire tap."

Sutherland smiled. "We've done that. I have the tapes. We got a court order in the narcotic cases." He reached for a case and pulled out a tape player with the tape already in place.

A voice, which Sutherland described as belonging to the minister, said, "Murray, Fitzgerald and Martino have all pleaded guilty to selling cocaine. Apparently they worked together. I don't know whether they peddled in the street or sold it wholesale. In Murray's case, this is his third strike. Fitzgerald has been arrested once before. It's Martino's first time. Murray and Fitzgerald plea bargained. They were facing steep sentences, and I think they talked to get reduced sentences."

"That was Hamilton," Sutherland said. "The next voice is that of Father Leahy."

Father Leahy: "Murray could have gotten life. We can be pretty sure he and Fitzgerald made a deal."

"This next voice is unidentified."

Unidentified voice: "How did you learn this?"

Hamilton: "There was a very brief note in one of the New York papers and the office in New York made some discreet inquiries through some reporter friends."

Unidentified voice: "How many times have I warned you about Murray? You trust anybody and everybody. How much do they know?"

Father Leahy: "They know the organization and they know some of the directors. They probably don't know many members — no more than five or six. Fortunately, they never really participated in the organization. Murray's been with us 15 years, Fitzgerald ten and Martino three. None were directors or attended any conventions."

Hamilton: "The real problem is, will others panic and start talking?"

Unidentified voice: "What can we do about it?"

Hamilton: "I don't see that we can do anything."
Unidentified voice: "We've got to do something. We can't let $20,000,000 and years of work go down the drain. We must fight."
Hamilton: "What good will that do? There'll be more publicity which will certainly bring us to the end. It's best to do nothing. Maybe Murray, Fitzgerald and Martino will simply serve their time and nothing more will happen."

After a few polite inquiries into Hamilton's family's health the tape ended.

"What does that say to you?" Nagel asked Sutherland.

"That there is a big secret and the secret is a criminal conspiracy. I see no other interpretation for that conversation!"

Wicker broke the ensuing silence. "Paul, this is your call. I'm sure that Thornton, the local District Attorney, as well as the AG in Washington are looking to you to try this case. It's a challenge which the government cannot duck. Sooner or late the whole country will know about this operation and the press and everybody else will claim that the government did nothing about it. We must ask for a grand jury."

Sutherland spoke directly to Nagel: "Washington is expecting you to crush this operation without delay."

THREE

Fairfield had a population of 20,000 people. The Reverend Malcolm Hamilton had been the minister at the Fairfield Presbyterian Church for so long that very few could recall the name of his predecessor. Father Patrick Leahy had been pastor at St. Mary's Catholic Church for twenty five years. It was most unusual for a Catholic priest to be in the same parish that long. He was loved and admired not only in his parish but throughout the community.

Hamilton was a slight man, five feet seven inches tall and weighing no more than one hundred forty pounds. Leahy was a giant, six feet four inches tall, two hundred fifty pounds. He had been an All-American tackle at Notre Dame University. What was extraordinary was that these two men had become personal friends. Leahy was often a guest at the Presbyterian Manse presided over by the minister's wife, Vera.

The Fairfield Coffee Shop was where the local gentry met. Ben Schwartz, a wealthy Jewish scrap dealer and Frank Walker, an attorney whose office was in the same block, were regulars, and the two clerics were a close friends with Ben, close enough to travel together to athletic contests, concerts and other events throughout the US.

At eight o'clock the previous morning, Leahy and Hamilton had asked Schwartz to meet with them away from the coffee shop crowd. "We need to talk to you right away," Father Leahy said, and Ben agreed to meet them at his office in the scrap yard at nine o'clock in the morning.

"Why all the secrecy?" Schwartz asked when they got together.

Hamilton said, "We're meeting here because my home is bugged and we're afraid Pat's place is also wired. My wife found the device in my den yesterday. We did not disturb it. Question: 'What do we do now?'"

"We've got to assume the government is not satisfied with convicting Murray, Fitzgerald and Martino," Leahy said. "I think it's time we convene the Board of Directors and make some decisions. However Malcolm and I think we are being watched all the time. We thought we'd speak with Nelson while you went to the meeting."

"Let me call Nelson," Schwartz suggested. "I'm sure my phone isn't tapped."

Robert Nelson was executive director of the Ecumenical Society in New York. Nelson agreed to call a special meeting of the board at the New York office in seventy-two hours. Schwartz flew to New York, took a taxi to the run-down office building and rode the elevator to the fourth floor. There was no name on the door in front of which he paused, only a number: 427. The door was locked, but Schwartz had a key. Opening the door he walked into a shabby office where six women typed at six desks or calculated sums on old-fashioned adding machines. There were no computers or phones on any of the desks

One of the women greeted him. "Mr. Schwartz," she said, "Mr. Nelson is expecting you." She led Ben to a small back office where Nelson was waiting for him. "Hello, Ben. Come in. We need to talk fast. I'm expecting the board members to come in about an hour."

Schwartz sat down and noticed that the room was bare, devoid of any decorations, bare walls, bare floors, just like the outer office where the women worked. There was no reception area as such.

"When I called the individual board members," Nelson commenced, "each told me that some of their employees had read about the defection of the three and were very much disturbed. The biggest concern is how the employees will react when there is more publicity."

"It may be worse than they think," Schwartz said. "The government has Father Leahy and Reverend Hamilton under surveillance. We are afraid the next move will be against the Society."

"That would be disastrous," Nelson responded. "Most employees have enjoyed fifteen to twenty years of prosperity. Some of them are millionaires. Bursting the bubble now would be a disaster for them."

"To say nothing," Schwartz added, "of our loss. We have accumulated over $20,000,000. The government can confiscate that in a minute. Why would anybody want to talk and risk losing everything?"

"To avoid prison. They may think they can get a break like Martino, Fitzgerald and Murray did when they talked."

Within the hour the board members appeared, including Velma Smith, who owned three beauty shops; Barbara Ross, who owned five candy and confectionery stores; Janet Lombard, who owned a manufacturing firm specializing in women's clothing; Frank Bustamente, a beer and wine distributor; Robert Manta, a manufacturer of men's clothing; Werner Kaiser, a construction company owner; and José Fuentes, who owned seven super markets. All were ex-convicts!

Nelson opened the meeting. "You all know about the three who have squealed. Today you are going to hear more bad news. You all know Ben Schwartz. He will tell you about it."

Ben addressed the board. "The government is giving us trouble. They have statements from Murray, Fitzgerald and Martino implicating the Society. They bugged the home of Reverend Hamilton and the parish house of Father Leahy. They have talked to the bank where our assets are held. Any day now they may issue a complaint against all of us. It is possible that only the members of the board will be indicted, but everyone could be implicated."

"That's nothing new for any of us. We've all been in court before." Werner Kaiser spoke as though reconciled to his fate. "It's been a great ride. We've made a lot of money. I'll admit I've never had it so good, but if it's over, it's over."

"It's not that simple," Barbara Roth put in. "As a director you have personal liability that goes beyond your holdings in the Society."

"We have no interest in the assets of the Society. We don't own any of it. If it is lost it's no loss to us," Manta observed.

"Just who is damaged?" asked Bustamente. "I don't see that anybody has lost anything."

"We've been taking 7.5% of people's income for over 20 years. If that has to be repaid it will take more than $20,000,000," Wilma Smith pointed out.

"So, what do we do, if anything?" asked José Fuentes.

"We make sure nobody else talks," Schwartz answered.

Everybody agreed that silence was the order of the day. No action was taken by the board as a matter of record.

As Schwartz made his way back to Fairfield it occurred to him that nobody had bothered to ask just what the charge might be. He was sure that the sale of drugs was illegal. But those sales were absolutely unauthorized and beyond the functions and objective of the Society. The next job was to get some legal counsel. It was imperative that they should know what law or laws were being violated.

Immediately on his return home Schwartz summoned Leahy and Hamilton and made an appointment for the three of them with Frank Walker.

Walker greeted his friends with apprehension. Unless they wanted to arrange a football or baseball trip this had to be something serious. He was quite sure it did not involve any trip.

Ben Schwartz spoke on behalf of the others. "For thirty years Pat and Mal have been part of an organization engaged in helping others. That should not be too surprising. It is called the Ecumenical Society. It has been kept secret all these years but recently three members who borrowed money from the organization got into the drug trade. They have pled guilty in return for a reduced sentence. Now the district attorney and the FBI are after the Society. They have bugged the homes of these men and they have them under general surveillance. Nothing has happened to date but we thought we should get some advice."

Walker could not believe what he was hearing. How could this be? These good friends in this little town. "What's going on?" he asked. Father Leahy and Reverend Hamilton remained silent as though they were ashamed.

"I know this may shock you because this matter has been a secret operation for all these years," Schwartz replied. "There is an Ecumenical Society that was created by these two men. I've had a part in it as well. Moreover, the whole thing must remain a secret,"

"How do you expect me to advise you if I'm not to know what's going on?" Walker asked.

Schwartz did all the talking. "I guess we want to know what rights a private citizen has when the government starts bugging his home and tapping his telephone and generally spying on him."

"I suppose," Walker answered, "that one could file a petition in court to raise the question point blank. However, if you do that you will have to tell the government what it wants to know. It's a no-win situation as far as you are concerned."

Father Leahy now spoke up. "That doesn't sound right to me, Frank. I've always understood we have a right to privacy. According to you there really is no such right."

"That's true when drugs are involved. The combination of an on-going enterprise and drugs creates a situation where RICO kicks in and under RICO your right of privacy is considerably reduced."

"What's RICO?" Leahy asked.

"It's an acronym for *Racketeer Influenced and Corrupt Organization Act.* It was adopted by Congress in 1970 to get to organized crime, and it gives the government very broad powers to investigate and conduct surveillance. It is intended to reach operations which seem legitimate but are really fronts for racketeering."

"We have nothing to do with drugs," Father Leahy said firmly.

"There are circumstances which make the government believe that drugs are involved. That's all they need. Tell me more about this Ecumenical Society."

"We can't tell you any more," Reverend Hamilton replied.

Walker became stern. "Gentlemen, you are here seeking legal advice. What you tell me is as secret, as confidential, as statements made in confessional. I can't help you if I don't know the facts. You know that."

"Yes, we know that," said Hamilton. "We also know that what you want to hear from us was learned by us in a pastor-penitent relationship and we cannot tell you that."

"A pastor-penitent relationship with three people who have already talked no longer binds you."

"There are 6,000 other people who are in the same relation with us."

"Six thousand penitents who have been in your confessional?"

"Not in a confessional but in that relationship."

Father Leahy took up the cause. "It is not so much the relationship as it is that to reveal the information would ruin thousands of people."

Walker was now completely mystified. These friends were making no sense at all. There was a long silence. Finally, Reverend Hamilton spoke: "I guess we have the answer to our questions. We can't stop the government from spying on us. Thank you, Frank. Please send me a bill for this conference."

With that Leahy, Hamilton and Schwartz quit the office and left Walker in a confused state. He was worried for his friends.

A week later Walker's secretary announced that a woman named Janet Wingate had scheduled a two o'clock appointment that afternoon.

"Your name is familiar," Walker said when the lady came into the consultation room and stood before him.

"I'm Reverend Hamilton's daughter," she announced.

Walker stood up and extended his hand. "I'm very glad to meet you," he declared. "Please have a chair. What can I do for you?"

"I'm not sure you can do anything," Janet replied. "But I need to talk to somebody. You've been recommended to me."

"Don't I know you?" Walker asked.

"I'm the trust officer at the Fairfield Bank. I'm sure I've talked to you on the telephone and we have corresponded on trust and estate matters."

"Of course," Walker exclaimed. "I knew your voice but I never have seen you before. I'm surprised we have never met."

Why had he not known that Reverend Hamilton had such a beautiful daughter, Walker wondered. She had the most perfect lips he had ever seen. Her face was without blemish or wrinkle. Her blonde hair was parted on the right but extended to a point just below her ears. She was five feet ten inches tall and slim. How had he missed such a gorgeous woman when he was so close to her father?

"I've come into some very puzzling and shocking information concerning my father."

Walker became grim, recalling his meeting with Reverend Hamilton the previous week. He sat silent awaiting more information.

"The trust officer at Central Bank is an acquaintance of mine. He and I often meet at seminars and sometimes we have joint business matters for our banks. He called me the other day and told me that although he might be betraying a confidence he felt that I should know something. There is a $20,000,000 trust at his bank in the name of the 'Ecumenical Society of Fairfield' the card and the trust instrument for which bear the names of my father, Father Leahy and Ben Schwartz. He said the FBI was investigating the account. The FBI had asked that he not tell anybody about the investigation and he told me I must not let on to anybody that I know about the matter. He felt as a friend he had to tell me about it."

Walker was thunderstruck. Twenty million dollars! What were his friends up to? He did not think he could tell her that the three men had been in his office within the past week.

"Did your friend say anything about the actions of the FBI? What did they want in particular."

"All my friend thought he could tell me was that the FBI was investigating."

"And you learned nothing about this trust?"

"Nothing."

"Do you know anything about your father's connections outside the church? I already know about his associations with Father Leahy and Ben Schwartz."

"Both my parents are ordained ministers. My mother is assistant pastor. My father is still a missionary. He and mother were missionaries in Nigeria after seminary. Then they were in World War II and after that they settled here. My father has a wide acquaintance with prominent people and one of the reasons the church likes him so well is that he brings in many well-known speakers."

"What do you know about his work outside the local church?"

"Only that he does a lot of outside counseling. I know absolutely nothing about an 'Ecumenical Society' or about $20,000,000. That just shocks me."

Walker had no idea what he could do for this lady — much as he would like to. He wanted to know more about her.

"Can you tell me anything more about your family?"

God's Mafia

"There isn't much more. I'm the only daughter. I have two sons, ten and eight years old. My husband died in a plane crash three years ago. I've been at the Fairfield Bank for ten years. My father should be retired, but he doesn't want to retire."

"What about Father Leahy and Ben Schwartz — what do you know about them?"

"Only that they are friends of my father and of our family."

"Isn't that a strange trio? Is their relationship the reason for the word 'Ecumenical'?"

"Maybe. I just don't know anything about that. Quite frankly I don't know very much about my father's affairs. I am here only because of this twenty million dollar trust. There is absolutely no way my father would come by that much money in a hundred years. I understand Mr. Schwartz is a wealthy man, but even he would not have that much money in a trust here in Fairfield."

"And you have not seen fit to talk to your father about all this?"

"He has obviously kept me in the dark. I have no basis to talk to him except the information I have on a confidential basis. I don't have an entrée to open discussions. But I am concerned. I'm frightened. My father is not so naive as to be a party to something he knows nothing about. What has he gotten into?"

"You are talking about the best friends I have. I know they are not racketeers. I'm as distraught as you are. I haven't the least idea what this could be about."

Janet sat forward and put her hands on the desk. Walker was captivated by this woman — strange as it seemed, on the basis of a ten-minute acquaintance. "If I work with Uncle Ben and try to have him persuade them to come to see you maybe you could find out something."

Walker looked at her more closely. "They've already been here," he said.

Janet sat back, startled.

"I really could not tell you that," Walker said. "But since you make this suggestion I feel I must tell you. And there is nothing more I can tell you. Not because of any ethical problems but because they refused to tell me anything."

"What did they come in for?" she asked.

"To see if they could stop the FBI and Justice Department from bugging your father's and Father Leahy's homes."

"And they would not tell you what this is all about?"

"That's right. They said it was all a big secret and to reveal the secret would ruin 6,000 people!"

"Six thousand people!" she exclaimed.

"Six thousand people, $20,000,000, a long standing organization. In addition, there are three drug busts and the three people convicted have told the government everything that I have been told is a secret. Now, the government is after your father and Father Leahy and, I suppose, the so-called society, whatever that is!"

Janet sat upright in her chair, but she was in a daze. She could not speak.

"Janet," Walker finally managed, "I hope I can call you Janet — I'm in this as deeply as you are. These people are very important people in my life, too. I have nobody else — no wife, no brothers or sisters, no parents. Except for them I'm alone. I'm as desperate as you are."

She raised her head and looked at him. "What can we do?"

"I don't know," Walker replied. "Not until we get to the bottom of this. Your father, my friends, are not racketeers!"

She rose from her chair. "I don't know what arrangements I am to make with you. I'll be glad to pay you a retainer."

"You will do nothing of the kind. In the first place I don't know that I can do anything. In the second place, we must try to help our dearest friends." He held out his hand. She took it and smiled for the first time.

"May I call you from time to time?" she asked.

"We will call each other. We will keep each other informed. I'm so glad you came in. I don't know how I could have missed you all these years. Have you lived here all the while?"

"Yes. I've been with the bank the past ten years. I live on State Street here in town with my two children. They, my parents, Father Leahy and Ben Schwartz are my family." The conference ended with Janet still perplexed and worried, but somehow, she felt comfortable with this lawyer.

God's Mafia

Walker sat alone. He did not call in his secretary. He wanted to think about this intriguing case and this remarkable woman.

Frank Walker had been practicing in Fairfield for nearly seven years. After practicing in the state capital, Crystal City, for a year he had accepted a position as assistant district attorney in the DA's office there. He spent three years in that office and then decided to start his own practice. He did not want to join any of the large law firms. He wanted to be independent. He decided to become a country lawyer and practice alone. He had experienced pressure in the District Attorney's office — more pressure than he liked. He knew he would get the same degree of pressure in a big city firm. He was a sportsman. He loved to hunt. He played a good game of golf and in winter he loved to go north to the ski slopes. He had never had any ambition to make a lot of money, or even to acquire a huge law practice. He had rented a store front on the main street of Fairfield and had remodeled the building into a neat, well-appointed law office. He managed to acquire clients. He handled the cases a small town lawyer gets — torts, divorces, contracts, criminal cases. He was highly respected by the bar of his state — a reputation he had earned as a relatively young lawyer by beating older, established, lawyers in tough cases. He was not a "settling" lawyer. He enjoyed trial work. In the DA's office he had worked with the best criminal lawyer in the country, Paul Nagel. One of the reasons Walker had left the DA's office was because Nagel, the star, was difficult to work with. Nagel did only one thing: try law suits and win them. He was quite the celebrity, having beaten organized crime many times. His name was in the papers often. All in all, the DA's office did not suit Walker's laid-back lifestyle. In his own office he worked five days a week, except when he was preparing for a trial and then it was 12 hours every day, seven days a week. But he could choose when to work hard and when to play.

Frank Walker was a bachelor, but his apartment was not a typical bachelor's abode. He had a taste for art and he had furnished his attractive dwelling after consulting his many women friends. There were not many single women in Fairfield for a bachelor to choose from, but Walker had acquired quite a group while he was in Crystal City and that remained his "dating" place. He had many men friends, and played golf, hunted and skied with male company. On occasion, a girl friend would go skiing with him. He was a "solid" drinker, able to drink with the best but never to excess.

Walker had led a very interesting life. Plenty of company, no permanent ties, doing what he wanted to do, but he was now 36 years old and had done it all. Where to from here? He was at home in Fairfield. His family had moved away when he was five years old. He had come back after deciding not to go 'big time.' An only child, his parents were now dead. He had no near relatives and his friends in Fairfield had been acquired since his return. His principal place of camaraderie was the Fairfield Coffee Shop, the old restaurant a few blocks from his office. He always had breakfast there where the affairs of the town, the state and the nation were all debated. It was where he had befriended the Reverend Hamilton, Father Leahy and Ben Schwartz. Leahy, Hamilton and Schwartz had been friends for several years before he came onto the scene. Those three often appeared together for breakfast and sometimes even left together. They'd gone to ball games long before Walker made them a foursome.

It was strange that a Presbyterian minister and a Catholic priest should be personal friends, stranger still that the third part of the team was Jewish. The local scrap dealer lived in a large colonial house, a landmark that Schwartz had spent a lot of money restoring to its early American style. Although it was one of the larger homes in the city, Schwartz lived there alone. On holidays, he often had parties, not for the elite but for people receiving welfare and the homeless. Schwartz was an enigma. He was apparently wealthy but, except for his beautiful home, his lifestyle was simple.

Both Hamilton and Leahy had been with their respective congregations for a long time, Hamilton for nearly 35 years, Leahy for 25 years. It was rare for a pastor to remain with one congregation or one parish so long. Hamilton should have been retired and Leahy should have gone elsewhere. They were each permanent parts of their churches and of their community. As for Schwartz, he had come to Fairfield in 1960.

Frank Walker's deep loyalty to his friends was in juxtaposition with his instincts as a lawyer who had worked in a prosecutor's office. The Society's so-called "secret" was typical of a criminal operation. It could not be explained by the pastor/penitent relationship. If the organization was lawful there was no reason for secrecy. Obviously the government knew more about the organization than he did. This fact was particularly bothersome. His friends knew that three former members of the Society had already told the secret to the federal authorities, yet they expected him to be their counsel while refusing to tell him what the government obviously knew! His friends were not stupid. There was a reason for all this. Was it a valid reason? Or was it a disguised use of the fifth amendment?

One possible consolation occurred to Walker. If the government, whether in the local DA's office or in Washington was considering this a matter within RICO the ultimate decision would be made by his ex-colleague, Paul Nagel, the ultimate authority in the US Attorney's office on RICO cases. It would be a strong case if he approved it for prosecution. On the other hand, maybe nothing would come of the matter.

Two weeks later Janet made another appointment with Walker. "I'm sorry to bother you again," she began, "but I haven't been able to think of much else since I left your office. I just can't make any sense out of this whole thing. I can't even put together a crime which would come out of what we know to date. Three people who happened to be members of an association have pled guilty to the sale of drugs. How does that involve my father?"

"That depends on what the three told the prosecutors. Since the government is tapping your father's phone lines it means that they've been told that your father is involved."

"But how could my father be involved?"

"We have covered that before. The combination of drug sales, a long established organization and an accumulation of $20,000,000 is sufficient, under RICO to seek an indictment. That's not our problem, Janet. Our problem is that your father, Father Leahy and Ben refuse to explain matters to us. I cannot understand that. The FBI obviously knows the explanation, why shouldn't I know? Their claim of pastor/penitent privilege just doesn't make sense."

"All their lives my parents have tried to help others," Janet said in a pleading voice. "They have never wanted money or power or prestige. All they wanted was to be ministers of the Gospel. Father Leahy could have made millions playing professional football. Ben Schwartz has all the money he'll ever need. There's no motive."

Walker took Janet's hand. "The government doesn't have to prove your father made money in the project. All they have to do is show he had some connection to the operation. What about your mother? Would she know more than you do?"

"I'm sure she knows everything, but she won't say anything. They are like one person. They started going together as undergraduates at Alma College, a Presbyterian school in Michigan. They graduated together, went to seminary together and each became a minister. In 1940, they went to Africa as missionaries right after they were married. In 1943, my father went into the Army as a chaplain, my mother as a WAC. After their respective discharges they got jobs as chaplains in the state prison system. They came here in 1950. The Fairfield Presbyterian Church hired both of them. I'm their only child."

"And what about Father Leahy?" Walker asked.

"You know all about him. He is a wonderful person and a great friend of our family. He is younger than my father. They are great friends."

"Janet, your father and Father Leahy are very likely to go to prison if the three drug dealers give details of an organization which the government has concluded is criminal. Why will they go to prison? Certainly not for the so-called secret. The government knows that secret and its attorneys don't believe it to be a defense. At least it looks that way now. Their going to prison will not protect the 6,000 members of the Society. Something is missing Janet. And I can't guess what that might be."

"For me, the worst part of all is that my father has kept from me a secret of this proportion." She shook her head.

"Janet, don't be resentful of that. We all have secrets. As a lawyer, I have secrets. As a trust officer, you have secrets. You have information about people and their affairs which you do not tell to your most intimate friends."

The words struck Janet like a hammer blow. "Indeed," she thought, "I hold such a secret with Paul Nagel!" She was on the verge of tears as she left Walkers' office

Two weeks passed before Janet made a third appointment with Walker. By now she was despondent. Walker greeted her at the door and knew immediately something was wrong. "What is it?" he asked. She said nothing, merely handed him a piece of paper. After seating her, he sat down on his side of the desk and began reading.

Dear Malcolm:

Would you be good enough to take me back? I've tried it on my own. I can't make it. It's been rough. I'll be glad to pay the monthly 7.5%. You can write me at the address on this letter or you can call me at 1-616-555-9600.

As ever,

Harold Ritchie

"There's the big secret," Janet said choking back tears.

Walker searched his mind for ways to comfort her. "Janet, please don't despair. There is an answer to all this. We will find it."

"Why, why hasn't he told me about this?"

"We don't need to go through that again. I'm sure this is not what it seems."

In fact, this bit of evidence Janet had uncovered shocked Walker. Apparently, people were paying Hamilton for the privilege of working. That explained the $20,000,000. A state statute specifically prohibited a contribution to any organization as a condition of employment. That, however, was merely a misdemeanor, nothing to cause the FBI or the DA to investigate, unless extortion was involved. That was prohibited by at least two federal statutes, RICO and the Hobbs Act. Although the Hobbs Act was aimed at the bribing of public officials, court decisions had extended its application to private transactions. This was serious enough to interest the Attorney General. No wonder Paul Nagel was involved.

FOUR

Not long after Ben Schwartz arrived in Fairfield in 1960, he purchased the only scrap yard in town. He also purchased and restored one of the older homes in town, a place known as "the castle." He had no family and rambled in it alone except on holidays when he held a "holiday brunch," a party that ran for three days. Schwartz made it a point to invite the poor as well as the well-to-do. The meal would begin at eight in the morning each day and continue until noon. The food was catered by the Fairfield Coffee Shop and Schwartz completely financed it.

Everyone knew he was a wealthy man, but no one knew the source of his wealth. It was assumed that he had a fortune before he came to town. The scrap yard could not have maintained his beautiful home or financed the annual "brunches."

There was no Jewish Community in Fairfield. Although Schwartz spoke English without accent, he was an immigrant from Germany where his family had followed the Reform branch of Judaism. While maintaining their Jewish tradition and practices, they had tried to accommodate their practices and beliefs to the modern world. Ben Schwartz observed Jewish worship and traditions privately even without a synagogue. His knowledge of finance and world affairs were impressive, and he always participated in community activities.

Hamilton and Leahy had been struck with Schwartz' knowledge as well as his awareness of world problems. They soon discovered that he was well-read, a student of world affairs. The three friends made trips to cities to hear concerts, vocal recitals, plays and lectures. Vera Hamilton would frequently go with them and, on a few occasions, when she was a child, Janet had also gone. In fact, her social acumen and worldly consciousness had been learned in the company of these men and her mother. Sometimes she had even gone to baseball and football games with them.

Three weeks after the three had met in Walker's office, the county sheriff, Herb Dolan, came into the coffee shop. He approached the table where Walker, Leahy, Hamilton and Schwartz were conversing and sat down with them.

"I'm glad I caught you all at once," Dolan announced after he had seated himself.

"How are you sheriff?" inquired Walker. "Have you got one of my clients again?"

"No," Dolan responded curtly. "I've just received a call from the office of the Federal Marshall in Crystal. They have warrants for you, Mal, and for you, too, Father Leahy. A grand jury has indicted both of you under RICO. I told the Marshall that I did not want him coming to this town to arrest two of our most respected citizens. I told him you would meet him at the Federal Courthouse whenever he wanted you, and that I would see that you got there."

There was a stunned silence. Walker had expected some action by the DA but not this, not the arrest of these two! As soon as he recovered from his shock he said, "I'll call Nagel right away. I know he'll be handling the case. I'll find out how much bond he's requested. What are we going to do for a bond?"

"There will be no problem with the bond," said Schwartz. "That's the least of our problems. Find out about the bond and I'll arrange for it. Let me know how soon we must appear."

Sheriff Dolan interjected. "You must appear immediately. There isn't going to be an appointment. I had trouble stopping the Marshall from driving out here now."

"But we can't leave this very instant for Crystal. We've got matters to take care of first," Hamilton protested.

"Sorry, gentlemen, I agreed to get you there as soon as possible. Go to your respective offices and I'll pick you up in a half hour."

"Frank, call me about the bond," Schwartz said as he stood to leave. "Gentlemen, I must call the New York office to alert the organization. Newspaper headlines will create panic."

Everyone in the coffee shop was watching them and murmuring. "Ben, let's go to my office," Walker said. "We can make our calls from there."

Reverend Hamilton looked at Leahy. "Here we go Pat. I guess we'll find out what prison is like from the inside." He was smiling. Leahy shrugged his shoulders. "My problem is getting somebody to take over my parish."

"Quiet, gentlemen," Walker continued. "Our friends here are wondering what's going on. Father, you will be back in your parish house this afternoon." Walker put on his best lawyer front.

As the five men left the coffee shop, somebody cracked, "Sheriff, don't put them in with the drunk drivers."

Walker told his secretary to cancel all appointments and to put in a call to Crystal City for Paul Nagel. "Mr. Schwartz will then want you to put in a call for him."

On the phone Nagel's voice was friendly. "Hello, Frank. It's been a long time since I've heard from you. What can I do for you?"

"I'm representing Father Leahy and Reverend Hamilton. We are bringing them in immediately and we will want an immediate arraignment and bond set. I'd like to know how much bond you want so we can have it with us."

"One hundred thousand dollars for each," Nagel responded without further comment. Walker winced. Covering the mouth piece he looked at Schwartz. "They want $200,000. It will have to be cash."

"Tell him we will have it there."

"Paul," Walker said, "we will have a cash bond when we arrive."

Nagel laughed. "I should have made it $500,000. I know your clients have the money!"

"What's the charge, Paul?"

"Extortion and conspiracy to finance narcotics sales."

Walker's voice betrayed no emotion. "We'll meet you in the courtroom as soon as we get there. I suppose Judge Kowalski will be handling the case."

God's Mafia

"That's right," responded Nagel, then, "I assume that all this is by agreement with the Marshall."

"It is," Walker said. "Good-bye, Paul." His hand shook as he put down the telephone. $200,000! Where was that money coming from, Walker wondered. Obviously from Schwartz. Only he could raise that much money so fast.

Schwartz was talking to Nelson in New York. "Bob, Leahy and Hamilton have been arrested. The whole thing will be in all the papers this afternoon. You've got to reach everybody in the organization you can. They must not learn of this from the newspapers."

Surprisingly, Nelson was calm. "After our last board meeting we alerted everybody."

"But now Leahy and Hamilton are involved. That will be a shocker."

"I'm sure it will be. And we'll get that information out immediately."

Schwartz gave Nelson as many details as he could including the fact that the charges were extortion and conspiracy to aid and abet the sale of drugs.

The appearance was not before a magistrate. It was before Judge Ron Kowalski. That's the way Nagel had wanted it. All proceedings were to be before Kowalski unless the judge directed otherwise.

Walker entered a plea of not guilty and asked that the defendants be released on their personal recognizance. Nagel objected. "Your Honor," he said, "I appreciate that these men appear to be responsible and I'll concede neither has any record. But the charges are very serious and there must be no appearance of favoritism. I think the bonds should be $100,000 each."

The judge agreed. "Mr. Walker, these charges are very serious. I'm going to order bond in the amount of $100,000 for each of these defendants."

The bond of $200,000 was quickly posted. Nagel approached Walker. "You will let me know what preliminaries you want."

Walker nodded, then thanked the sheriff for his thoughtfulness and help. Then he addressed the others. "Please meet me in my office as soon as you get back to Fairfield."

Walker reached his office, before the others got there. Janet was waiting. The sheriff soon dropped off Leahy and Hamilton. When they were all assembled, Walker held up the indictments. "You are charged," he said, "with extortion. They claim that over a period of several years you have demanded, and gotten from the prosecution's witnesses, 7.5% of their net income in return for having extended loans; that the loans were paid back with interest, but the 7.5% was never returned. That 7.5% was used to start new businesses."

"The Ecumenical Society did that," said Leahy.

"You've mentioned that. Now tell me who, or what, is the Ecumenical Society?"

Father Leahy answered. "That's us, Frank. It's our idea and we are responsible for it, Mal and I."

"You are part of this Ecumenical Society?"

"Yes," Leahy answered.

"These are the people with whom you have a code of silence. Is that correct?"

"Yes," Hamilton answered.

"Do these people simply send you — or the Society — 7.5% of their income every week, month or year?"

There was silence. Janet was transfixed. The scene had virtually immobilized her.

Father Leahy finally spoke. "Frank, this is where we came in. We can't tell you any more."

Walker put down the paper he was holding. "Look," he said, "there isn't any secret anymore. It is now a matter of court record. I've got to know what this is all about."

Reverend Hamilton replied in a firm voice. "Frank, you will never learn from either of us what this is all about."

Janet was now in a state of shock. Walker pressed on. "There is no way to beat this rap unless you tell me all about it. We know you are not guilty, but we don't matter. What matters is what a jury will think, and they had better know it all, if in fact there is anything more than what appears right now. We know that some money was loaned to three ex-convicts. Are you saying this was not money from your Society?"

"We know that the FBI traced the money back to our fund in Central State Bank. But we are not saying any more," Hamilton responded.

Walker was getting angry. "Let's bring this absurdity to an end. I take it that you do not intend to testify."

"We will not testify to anything which we are pledged to keep secret," said Father Leahy.

"So you will plead guilty to the charge. Is that what you are telling me?" Walker's countenance was no longer pleasant.

"We are not guilty of extortion or selling drugs," Reverend Hamilton said and clasped his hands and brought them to his lap.

"Frank, this has been going on for 30 years. Why is it now criminal?" asked Father Leahy.

Walker was quick to answer: "It probably was criminal all the time, but under RICO, the *Racketeer Influenced and Corrupt Organization Act,* there has been an extra effort to stop it. The act gives the government extra leverage in fighting organized crime. The very act of taking somebody else's money illegally and putting it into legitimate business is a crime. And that appears to be what happened here."

Again silence. Janet was at her wits' end. "Father," she cried, "you are not making any sense. This is not like you. What is it? What have you gotten into?"

Hamilton did not look at his daughter. He said to Walker "Pat and I will go to prison before we betray a confidence. It doesn't make any difference what the government knows or doesn't know."

"That's right," Father Leahy confirmed.

"All right, gentlemen, just tell me what you want me to do."

"Just protect our secret," Father Leahy responded.

"Even though your secret is your only defense?"

"Correct." Leahy and Hamilton spoke simultaneously.

"You understand, don't you, that when the government's witnesses testify, I cannot stop them just because what they say is supposed to be secret." Again, Walker was trying to stop the absurdity.

"We understand that," Hamilton retorted. "When the witnesses have testified to the 7.5% withholding and the loans they repaid they still will have not revealed the secret! But if we testify, we may be compelled to reveal it. That's what we must avoid."

"In other words," Walker responded, "you think it is possible for the witnesses for the prosecution to testify that you took 7.5% of their income on the threat to put them out of business and that they borrowed money from you to finance drug purchases and sales and still your secret would be preserved — even though you might go to prison."

"That's right." Hamilton spoke and Leahy nodded.

"Gentlemen, I don't think you need me. There is nothing I can do for you. You really don't want to defend this case. The best way for you to preserve your secret is to plead guilty. That way it won't be necessary to have a trial."

"Wait a minute, Frank," Schwartz interrupted. "A plea of guilty will not do what we want. If they plead guilty, the secret will become irrelevant because the purpose of the secrecy will be gone. You see, if these two are guilty a lot of other people are guilty, including me. I think this case must be tried. Maybe it will be lost. So far as you are concerned, Frank, they are guilty unless they can explain what has been going on. Well, I happen to know what has been going on, and even though they may technically be guilty I know that they are not criminals."

Walker shook his head. "I'm sorry, Ben, but that's double talk. There is no such thing as technically guilty but still innocent. They are either innocent or guilty, period!"

Schwartz wasn't so sure. "I can recall cases in which everybody but the jury thought the defendant guilty. But the jury's opinion is the only one that counts. I know enough about these men and what they have done to believe that no jury will find them guilty."

"Then perhaps you can supply the necessary testimony," Walker suggested.

Schwartz smiled and looked at Janet. "When this lady asked me to tell her the secret I told her I could not tell her what her father would not tell her. And I can't tell anyone else either."

Janet could not restrain herself any longer. "Frank," she said, "wouldn't you represent them even if you suspect they are guilty?

Haven't you done that before? Particularly in appointment cases?"

"Not when I'm about to be clobbered by my old buddy, Nagel."

"Paul Nagel?" Janet said. "He's going to prosecute my father?"

"That's right. The best prosecutor I've ever seen. I'd as soon get in the ring with a professional boxer as fight that guy, especially with both hands tied behind my back. This is not a typical public defender case. These men tell me they are not guilty, and how can I go into court without a defense for people who tell me they are not guilty? I happen to know them well enough to believe them. I won't participate in such a sham."

It was clear to Janet that she was not going to change the minds of her father and Father Leahy. She had better try doing something about Walker. "Whom would you suggest as defense counsel?" she asked him.

"Frankly, Janet, I would have to think about that. I don't know anyone sufficiently capable who would see this any differently than I do. You can't defend against as strong a case as this appears to be when your clients tell you they are not guilty but refuse to defend themselves. That will be just as bizarre to any good lawyer as it is to me."

"Frank," Janet pleaded, "can you picture them going to court without counsel? The court is not going to appoint a public defender for a couple of people who have just put up $200,000 in cash as a bond."

"That will be up to Judge Kowalski. I'm sure it will be a first for him."

"From my personal knowledge in cases that had no real significance I've seen counsel represent people who are guilty or who had no defense. After all, counsel can get enough information from witnesses called by the prosecution to demonstrate that, although guilty, the defendants had no criminal intent. I think you could persuade a jury that these two men are entitled to consideration sufficient to free them. After all the jurors are laymen. Technicalities mean less than nothing to them. Some juries like to show the government that they can ignore witnesses who testify to reduce their own sentences. You know that happens, Frank," Janet pleaded.

Alfred J. Fortino

Walker noted how clever this woman was. She was not saying, "For God's sake, Frank, these are your friends. The least you can do is hold their hands as they go through this." She was not appealing to emotion. She was appealing to him in terms of the reality of a criminal case where the defendants are not thugs with criminal records. He tilted his head but made no answer.

Encouraged, Janet continued, "I think you could produce any number of character witnesses."

"If they don't take the witness stand I won't be able to do that."

What Janet had not said was now foremost in Walker's mind. These were his friends. He had no choice but to do exactly as Janet had suggested! At last he said, "You win, Janet. I'll stick with you. I don't know what we do next, but we will do something. For now, let's all go home and think about this some more."

Janet arose from her chair and thanked him. Leahy and Hamilton said nothing. Schwartz shook Walker's hand. "These men are innocent. Believe me, there's more to this than these men's lives. I'm sure we will manage to make a case, somehow."

The next day Walker received a letter in a blank envelope with no return address. Inside was a certified check from Central State Bank of Fairfield. It was for $25,000, payable to him. It was marked "Retainer," but it did not indicate who had supplied the money.

Twenty-five thousand dollars was more money than Walker had ever seen before, more than he'd ever been paid as a fee for services, much less as a retainer. He set the check down and thought, "Everything which happens in this case goes in one direction — the wrong direction." Next he observed, "Nagel is no fool." He knows much that I don't know. He recalled Nagel's laughing remark about the bond, how he should have made it a half million dollars. Walker thought about calling Schwartz. After all, it was Schwartz who raised $200,000 in cash for the bonds. Yes, he would call Schwartz, but not just now. Right now he was going to cancel the rest of his appointments, get out of town and have a good, stiff drink.

FIVE

When Janet arrived home from Walker's office, she found in her mail a personal letter from Paul Nagel. She quickly opened it:

Dear Janet:

I have written and rewritten this letter many times. As I write this final draft I am sure it will not achieve what I wish to achieve. For a year we have made a routine of dining together at the Conference on Poverty. I've enjoyed it very much and I've heard you say that you have also enjoyed it. I've always looked forward to the meeting of the Commission but it is time for me to tell you that I look forward more to being with you.

Of course I can and will tell you this when I am with you next week. Why, then, do I write such a letter? Frankly, because in writing I can better say what I wish than I can in talking to you. I must compose my letter to you carefully and not impetuously. It is easier and better for me to write that I am in love with you than it would be to profess my love for you over a dining table in a public restaurant.

Down deep inside I feel that I am preparing my pleading for my case in advance of submitting arguments at our meeting. Maybe that is why I write.

Anyway, my dear lady, I love you.

As ever,
Paul

Janet put down the letter. "My God," she exclaimed aloud, "he doesn't even know who I am?" She was struck by the irony. For nearly a year she had waited for this, for some expression of Paul's feelings for her. Then he does it after commencing the process of putting her father in prison. A word came to mind: *weird.* She remembered how she had admired this man. What was she to do now? What would he do when he learned who she was? For a moment she considered taking the letter to Walker, but that did not seem appropriate. In fact, she did not want to share the letter with anyone else. Somehow she could not be angry. She was much too rational a person to react like an offended child. It was obvious that his profession of love could no longer be entertained by her and certainly he would be terribly embarrassed when she identified herself.

Janet decided not to respond to the letter. She would dine with Paul Nagel as she had done in the past. She was interested in seeing what would unfold.

Meanwhile, Janet Wingate's world, as well as the world of her parents and Father Leahy, were changed by forces beyond their control. The headlines in newspapers around the country were typified by those which appeared in the Crystal City Press: "Priest and Minister Indicted As Racketeers." The subhead read: "Clerics accused of extorting huge sums from parishioners. Millions used to establish private businesses in violation of Federal Statute." Fairfield was in a collective state of shock. The patrons at the coffee shop were quick to defend their friends. The big question raised by the media was: "How could a poor priest and a Presbyterian minister come up with $200,000 in cash for their bonds?" The answer supplied by the friends of the coffee shop was that it was Ben Schwartz who came up with the cash! Certainly he could do it. As for this 6,000 member Ecumenical Society, was it really a cartel for extortion and the sale of drugs? Impossible, but then what was it? Although everybody in town was fiercely loyal to the two defendants few voiced their doubts in talking about $20,000,000 and a religious organization which seemed to have no purpose. The underlying question was: "How could our friends get mixed up in such a racket?" The national media emphasized the doubt because that was what was most notable about the whole thing.

The Presbyterian Church of Fairfield announced its support of their pastor and put him on paid leave to allow him to prepare his case and defend himself. The Catholic parish made a public announcement of support for their priest.

The most hurt were Janet's boys. Their peers were not very considerate. It pained Janet to see her sons slip into even minor depression. What bothered her even more was her suspicion that the attitude of the seven to ten year olds reflected the attitude of their parents. This correlation shocked her. It probably was a whisper which though unheard by her was uttered in many circles: "Can you believe it! Right here in our town. Dealing in drugs!"

Many people called Janet as well as her parents to report that they didn't believe one word of the horrible accusations. If there was anything they could do they would gladly do it. Most important, they must not let themselves be railroaded. The real blows came from calls from all over the United States excoriating, and denouncing them in language profane and foul. The only defense at both the Protestant manse and the Catholic parish house was to shut off the phone line.

Janet tried to be objective. Most of the local people had faith in her father. But that did nothing for her two sons. To them her father had long been a hero. She had tried hard to assure them their grandfather was innocent, but the voices of the boys in the playground and on the street rang in the boys' minds night and day.

On the day Janet was to go to the meeting of the Commission on Poverty her mother came down with a heavy cold. To her surprise, Walker offered to pick up the boys at school, keep them in his apartment overnight and take them to a big league baseball game on Saturday. He had called her at her office to volunteer.

"Frank, you don't have to do that. I can get a baby-sitter for the weekend."

"I think it would be good for this old bachelor to be with a couple of boys for a weekend."

This perplexed Janet. What bachelor in his thirties would want to spend a precious weekend with an eight and ten year old? However, she could hardly refuse. "That's very nice of you. I appreciate it very much. I hope they don't wear you out."

Janet saw Nagel as she entered the conference room at the state capital. He motioned to her as she took her seat at the oblong table. She waved back. Her seat was across the table and at the opposite end. A representative from the governor's office was speaking.

"I'm here," the lady began, "to convey the governor's thanks for your hard work for better than a year. A summary of your discussions has been submitted to the governor and he is pleased with your recommendations. We would like to prepare a bill within the next six months, and the governor would appreciate suggestions to amend the present statute. What should we keep, what change. Your input will be very helpful."

Nagel expressed surprise. "I thought we were to start from scratch and propose a whole new law. Our discussions have not been focused on amending but on completely restructuring. And that is what I have understood to be our function."

The lady smiled knowingly at Nagel. "Indeed you were expected to make your study as broad as you saw fit. But as we approach the legislature, we must obviously work from what we now have."

Janet surmised that there had been a change of heart in the governor's office. She thought it necessary to bring this out immediately. "I agree with Mr. Nagel. I sense that the governor now feels he must be satisfied with something less than a complete re-write."

"I don't think it was ever the intention of the governor to start a completely new program. We simply wanted to correct the present one." The lady was polite, but positive.

"Perhaps, then," Janet continued, "we might be given specifics to illustrate the changes the governor has in mind."

Nagel looked at Janet and smiled. The others around the table were perplexed. They, too, wondered what was going on as the lady from the governor's office said, "Neither the governor nor I ever believed this commission should question the operation of private charities. Yet it would appear from the transcript that you are attacking some private charities. This commission was to have concerned itself with the role of the state with regard to the poverty problem, not with the role of private charities."

God's Mafia

Nagel was not to be put off. "Some private charities are part of the overall problem. They are using the plight of the poor as a showpiece to create empires which really do good not for the poor but for the workers in the charitable organization. Some of us think that when 75% to 85% of donations goes to overhead with only 15% to 25% going to the poor, some sort of regulation should be imposed on those charities. Such an operation resembles a racket. They get money tax-free, and the donors deduct what they give from their income tax. Of course, the charity is a non-profit organization so it doesn't pay taxes."

"This commission was not intended to serve as an arm of the IRS, Mr. Nagel," the lady said. "We will simply raise issues unrelated to the function of this committee if we pursue such a course."

The governor's representative eventually left the conference and the commission went on talking, but neither Nagel nor Janet followed much of the discussion. Nagel only had in mind the evening meal, and Janet was busy thinking about Mr. Nagel's attitude toward charities which would explain his actions against her father.

They met at the same table they had used many times. Janet was tense, and Paul noticed it. "Please don't take these people too seriously," he said. "Ultimately, the governor will have to decide if he is going to do the job right or just make a show. I don't think he dares to do anything but try for a complete overhaul of the system."

Janet was in no mood to carry on such a conversation. She managed a weak smile. "I guess we'll just wait and see what happens."

Paul went on. "Janet, I'm an old bachelor. I'm forty six years old. All of my life I have tried to be effective, constructive, to do something worthwhile. I tried to steer clear of the spotlight. I'm simply trying to live up to the heritage of my family. All their lives they tried to help little people. I've tried to do it as my mother suggested. She told me not to try it by political activity, but to become a first rate lawyer and fight it out in the courts. That's my life."

"That's the most I've ever heard you talk about your goals." Janet was being polite, still waiting for the punch line.

"It was not until I met you that I began to realize how much of life I had missed. My work has been my life. I've never hunted or fished, or played golf or cards. I've never allowed women to be a part of my life. I realize now what I really wanted was someone to love, someone with whom to share life. Frankly, I have fought that feeling. I couldn't see myself as a married man. I've lost that fight. I cannot get you out of my mind. And now I don't want to try any more. I want very much to show you how I might bring happiness to you too; how we might make a life together."

Janet said nothing. She simply sat and looked at Paul. He tried to comprehend her mood. Was she angry? Disgusted? Disinterested? He fully expected her to tell him politely that she was not interested. If only she would say something!

Without emotion Janet said simply: "I am Reverend Malcolm Hamilton's daughter."

Nagel's mouth dropped open. Silently he drew back in his chair. He could find no words. Janet did not relish his embarrassment. In fact, she felt sorry for him. "All these months you have not once expressed any desire to get better acquainted. You seemed to enjoy my company, but not once did you express any fondness you might have had for me. Apparently, you had more than one secret, more than the secret involving your trust. I was not to share in that one, even though it involved me. How do you suggest we handle the situation now? Am I to stand by while you put my father in prison or do you think I could start a relationship with you while you diligently try to convict…" She caught herself, realized she was being cruel.

"I'm sorry, Paul. I'm sorry for both of us. I will be glad to excuse myself if that will relieve matters. Or I will stay here and we can have our meal as usual. I don't feel very talkative, though."

Finally, Paul Nagel pulled himself together, leaned across the table so that his face was close to Janet's and said: "When I wrote you to tell you I loved you I did not know you were Reverend Hamilton's daughter. Now I know. For your information, my dear lady, I still love you. You are not your father. You are the only woman I have ever loved. What you have told me does not change that. You may hate me and that is my loss. I'll never hate you or stop loving you."

Janet was surprised. She had wondered how he would react. She had not expected this. She spoke softly, without passion. "Paul, my problem is that I'm pretty sure that if you had known it would have made no difference to you. If it were your own father you would have prosecuted. You are a machine."

"Janet, you know me better than that."

Janet was stopped, speechless. He was right about not being a machine. One of the reasons she had been so fond of him was his compassion for others. Tears came to her eyes. She shook her head as though that might get rid of the nightmare.

Nagel struggled to find words to help her. A hundred thoughts flashed through his mind. He thought about how he had hesitated, how he had doubted the defendants could do this sort of thing, how Washington had pushed him. It was no use. None of that would help. He stared at Janet in her anguish, loving, admiring her more than ever, but helpless to say anything. He wanted to ask her what she wanted him to do. He must not ask that question! The implications of that question and any answer she might give could only result in complete disaster. There was nothing he could do. He was trapped!

Paul noticed they had caught the attention of other people in the dining room. He rose, went to her side and helped her to her feet. He whispered, "Please, Janet, people are staring. Let's go outside." She immediately composed herself, raised her head, took his arm and left the dining room and the hotel. The fresh air helped. He clung to her as they walked through a crowd. The roles were suddenly reversed. Janet was walking firmly, in complete control. Paul was clinging to her arm as if steadying himself. The irony struck him. On a cool evening on the grounds of the capital, would be the first and the last time he would ever be this close to her! It was both the beginning and the end of his only love affair. There was no way he could have this woman! But he would go on loving her. It would be consolation enough that at least she had once considered him a potential lover.

They returned to the hotel. He escorted her to the elevator. He didn't care who might see him now. He took her face in his hands, turned it up to him. "Remember always, I love you." With that, he walked away.

It was not quite eight o'clock when Janet reached her room. She did not want to stay there. She checked out and drove home. When she reached her house, she saw Walker's car. Entering, she saw Walker seated on the floor with her two boys. They hardly noticed her. As she approached, she saw that they were playing Monopoly. Brent, her youngest, was animated. Walker finally looked up and saw her. "Well, look who's here, boys. Weren't expecting you until morning."

"I decided to come home. What's that you're playing?"

Brent was happy to explain. "It's a new game, Mom. It's fun."

Walker got to his feet. "We had a great day. You have quite a pair here. They both beat me. How was your day?"

"The same. Nothing new."

"I brought some ice cream," he told her. "Won't you join us?"

"I think that's a great idea," Janet responded, grateful to put aside the day and the thoughts that plagued her.

Janet found the ice cream and served it on cake she had baked before leaving. As she surveyed the scene, she saw how happy her sons were. They apparently had forgotten for the moment the harassment they had suffered because of their grandfather.

"We went to the high school football game, mother," Jasper, the ten year old, told her. "I'd like to see more games."

"We can probably arrange that," Walker assured him.

Janet was impressed at what adult male companionship seemed to mean to her boys. It struck her again how very much her sons missed their father. And here was Frank Walker substituting for their dad and the boys seemed happy, happier than they had been for a long time.

Suddenly Brent now wanted to go back to the Monopoly game. Walker didn't object so they all went back to the living room and sat on the floor. Janet was intrigued. The old bachelor was actually enjoying it! Or he was doing an excellent imitation of happiness. She sat and watched without saying a word, just observing. She wondered why a man would do that? Men don't generally demonstrate a fatherly attitude toward strange children.

Janet announced bedtime, she managed to get her boys upstairs and came back down as Walker was gathering up the Monopoly paraphernalia. "It's late." Frank announced. "I should go."

She remonstrated. "How about spending a few minutes with the mother?" She was surprised at her forwardness.

God's Mafia

"OK," Walker responded, "I might as well entertain the mother too. She deserves some attention." He smiled as he spoke.

"That's very nice of you," said Janet, also smiling. "Why don't you have a wife and children?" she asked forthrightly.

"That's a very good question, as the man says who does not know what else to say. I guess my best answer is that I never found a girl with whom to have a family. That sounds a bit trite, but I think it's the only answer I have. You've been very quiet this evening, and you're home early. Things go badly in Crystal?"

"Somebody is putting pressure on the governor. He's backing off. The objective of the Commission now is to amend the present statute on welfare so that we can make it more efficient."

"Was the mission ever any more than that?"

"We thought we were to investigate and analyze the entire poverty and welfare scene, both public and private. Our minutes reflected some sharp criticism of charity in the private sector. We thought something should be done about the fact that sometimes only 20% of the donations get to the poor. It seems we're treading on some prestigious institutions."

"Not all private charities are rackets, Janet. Most of them do a good job and the bulk of the money gets to the poor. You will always have some bad apples in the barrel. Don't attack the whole industry to get at the few bad ones."

Janet was silent as she thought of the contrast between Nagel and Walker. She laughed. "Maybe it could be a defense for my father that, after all, his operation is a very insignificant part of all donations given to religious organizations?"

"There's a difference between proposed legislation and violation of a current statute."

"I suppose so," Janet replied as she continued to compare the two men with whom she had spent the evening.

"My guess is that it is not like you to quit when the agenda is changed."

"I haven't quit. I just had to get away from it for a day." She had no intention of stating the real reason she had left. That was personal.

Walker could tell that she was preoccupied. "It's time I headed home. It's been a pleasure to be with your boys."

"Frank, I hope you know how much I appreciate your help. The boys were alive and had a great time today."

It seemed like an excellent entree and Walker jumped at it. "I'd like very much to have the opportunity to pick up your spirits too."

Janet smiled brightly, "Are you asking me for a date or do you want to baby-sit me?"

"Given the choice, I'd prefer a date."

"I don't think I'd be very good company."

"Let me be the judge of that."

"Try me some time."

"I plan to," Walker said as he left.

Janet went back into the kitchen, poured herself a glass of orange juice and returned to the living room. She sat in an easy chair, leaned back, and with juice in hand pondered the day. Very quickly her mind focused on the two men courting her. Walker was considerate, kind, down to earth. Nagel was considerate, kind and down to earth as well. But what a difference! One was concerned about the world, the masses. The other was concerned about a person, a child. She wondered if Nagel would even notice her children. Nagel would be forever looking at the forest. Walker would look at a tree! And yet it was Nagel who sought out a paralyzed child to help. Janet smiled. Walker was not so complex. His love would be direct and simple!

SIX

Six months passed before any action was taken on the case. Meanwhile there was much activity on both sides, The day after his terrible day with Janet, Nagel searched through the file. Was there something he had missed? He re-read the statements by Murray, Fitzgerald and Martino. Their testimony certainly made for a case of extortion. They also proved that each had borrowed money from the society to buy cocaine for resale. None would testify that the defendants knew about the drug sales. All they would say was that when the money was loaned the defendants knew that two of the ex-cons had previously sold drugs. Each would testify that Leahy had approved the loan to Martino and Hamilton the loans to Murray and Fitzgerald. There was also the tape which the FBI had made of conversations in the Hamilton home. There would be the testimony of Sutherland as to the investigation. There was a statement from an agent of the IRS. That was it. Was it enough? Should an effort be made to obtain more evidence? Could these three men have lied for the purpose of obtaining a reduced sentence?

Nagel went to the crucial question. It was quite possible that a jury would not convict if the prosecution's witnesses testified that the defendants were not aware that the money was used to finance the sale of drugs. These sales were the so-called predicate acts which had to be shown to make a case under RICO. Would it be enough that the witnesses would testify that the defendants knew the purchasers had dealt in drugs in the past?

Whatever the weakness of the drug case, Nagel thought, there was no defense against the charge of extortion. There were cases in which the court had held that the fear of economic loss was sufficient to make a demand for money extortion. The threat of violence was not necessary. Why would two apparently respectable clergymen do such a thing? That question, Nagel concluded, was of no significance in the case, though it was significant to him personally at this point. If only there was something to give purpose to this scheme!

He had to convince a jury that the purpose was obviously to extort money from helpless people and put it into legitimate business — precisely what RICO was intended to stop — to the tune of over $20,000,000! What other purpose could there be?

Then there was his personal problem: To succeed meant losing the woman he loved. If he lost the case he would still lose her and, in addition, he would be pilloried as an evil prosecutor who tried to imprison two decent, respectable members of society!

If Janet is right, what evidence is there to show it? Every member of the Board of Directors had a prison record; every one of them has become a millionaire by this scheme. Just what philanthropy did the Ecumenical Society espouse and support? Where were its worship services, its charities? The organization had but one purpose — to extort from the helpless and to use the money to operate legitimate business! This was the cleverest scheme he had ever encountered. Janet Wingate just didn't know what was going on like so many wives and daughters of mobsters!

After three weeks of waiting, watching and worrying, Janet called Walker. "Why is there such a delay?" She asked.

"This is not unusual," Walker told her. "There is always a heavy criminal docket. It may be some time yet before we are heard."

"It's like waiting for the ax to fall. I'm afraid I'm not coping too well."

Walker saw an opportunity. "You should get out," he suggested. "All you do is work all day in your office, take care of your kids and then fret the rest of the time. Why don't you join me for dinner out tonight. Maybe there is a good movie we might see. How about it?"

"I just don't feel like doing anything."

"Why don't you try? There is nothing for you to lose. I'll drop by

God's Mafia

at 6:30 and take you out to dinner. Maybe I can help you put the case our of your mind for a couple of hours."

"Thanks, Frank. Maybe you have a good idea. I'll be ready at 6:30."

"What about your boys? Shouldn't they have a meal out of the house?"

"I can leave them with my parents."

"How often have you gone out with your sons?"

"Now that you mention it, not very often."

"I'll pick you all up at 6:30."

Janet was surprised. Why would a bachelor want to go on a date with two pre-teens and their mother? Interesting!

The evening proved very pleasant thanks to Frank Walker. He engaged the boys in a lively conversation, mostly about sports. Janet had a hard time keeping up with it, but she was delighted with her sons' response to Walker's observations about life and baseball. He also talked to them about hunting and fishing, something they had never done. He told them he would take them hunting and fishing, but the boys while not interested in becoming hunters and fishermen, found that, for the first time since their father's death, they were talking guy stuff with an adult male. They were old enough to appreciate this was a very nice "elderly" gentleman who was actually interested in them.

Walker's rapport with her sons made Janet's day. Relieved of a heavy burden for a few moments at least, she felt grateful to this kind and considerate man. Most men would not even have thought of the boys; Frank had made them the stars of the evening.

In the course of the evening, Janet told Walker that she had to be in Crystal City the following Saturday for a sub-committee meeting of the Governor's Commission on Poverty.

At noon that Friday Walker called Janet to ask if he could take her boys to the high school football game the next day. "You'll be out of town. I can take them out for breakfast, drive to the football game, and get them home about the same time you return from Crystal City."

Janet didn't know what to say. This was too much. "Frank," she said finally, "you don't have to do that. I have a routine with my parents. It's a second home for the boys. I'm sure you can do something better than spend the day with a couple of kids."

"You might be surprised to know, Ms. Wingate, that I would prefer to spend the day with Brent and Jap."

"That's very nice of you, but…"

He interrupted her. "Janet, please."

Janet did not feel she could acquiesce. She simply did not understand, but she could think of no reason to say 'no.' In fact, 'no' would be rather insulting and she was sure she did not want to insult him, not because he was her lawyer, but because she valued his friendship. The admission surprised her.

"OK, Frank," she said. "I really appreciate this very much. The boys need a father image. I mean they need adult male companionship." She fretted for a moment about what he might think she meant to imply.

Walker in fact was pleased with the word, *father*. "This old bachelor needs the companionship of sons, he said proudly." After he'd hung up, Walker reflected on his motives. Why was he doing this? He barely knew this family! He knew the answer. He was doing it to please her! He was doing it to say that the boys would not be a hindrance to any relationship between them. What a calculating person he had become, he smiled to himself.

Janet kept her hand on the phone after she'd hung up. What just happened? she asked herself. Here was a guy who didn't mind associating with a middle-aged woman with two sons who were almost teenagers. This was something she dared not think about.

At the meeting in Crystal City Janet found herself in an awkward situation. One of the female members insisted on a conference that included her and Nagel. She maneuvered the two of them into a corner.

"I think," the woman said, "that it should be decided whether we are talking about a new state program separate and apart from a federal program or a restructure of the current Federal/State program. I'd appreciate your thoughts."

Nagel said nothing but Janet spoke immediately and decisively, gesturing with her hands as she spoke. "I don't think we've even considered the possibility that this state or any state can handle the welfare problem without Federal help. It's my impression that the Governor simply wants suggestions as to how the present system can be improved. He wants Washington to get an analysis from the point of view of the states. It would be counter-productive to eliminate Federal funding. After all, the biggest problem is that there is not enough money to do an adequate job. It seems to me that, the trick is to come up with efficiencies which will result in more money going to the poor. I don't think anybody can rationally claim that money can be saved. The problem is getting more of it to the people who really need it. One of the things this committee must do is find out how much of every dollar allocated goes for overhead and how much to the poor. I'll bet that in some instances it's ten to one with one going to the poor. That's what has to be changed. But first this committee must prove that supposition."

Nagel admired her vehemence and her eloquence. Before he could say anything, she turned to him for confirmation. "I think I've heard you express those very thoughts from time to time." Nagel simply smiled and nodded.

At this point, the woman who had brought them together departed. It appeared that Janet's response was not what the lady had expected. Janet said to Nagel, "I wonder if anything worthwhile is going to come out of all this."

Nagel could speak to that. "It's better than doing nothing. The Governor is using this committee to lay the groundwork for some new legislation, but just as you say, it will be tough. It will be necessary to write a whole new program, but now we know that's not going to happen."

The conversation ended, but neither made a move. Janet felt ripped apart. Figuratively, this man was doing it to her. How could he destroy her father while declaring his love for her? Her frustration gave voice to the thought. "How can you destroy my father at the same time you tell me you love me? How can you do that?"

In an almost pleading voice, Nagel said "Please remember I fell in love with you before I ever heard of your father. And when I found myself in a position of prosecuting your father, I didn't know he was your father. My love for you is real. It is not something which changes because a relative of yours has been arrested. Perhaps if my feeling for you was something less than it is, I might decide not to care for you. I might be able simply to turn off my affections. I know I cannot do that. I will not do that. I don't expect anything from you. I understand. But that does not mean I can stop loving you, because I can not."

The answer disarmed Janet. She could not hate this man. She could not love him either. To ask him to dismiss the case against her father would look like a bribe! It would be like threatening to deny him what he most wanted if he did not do as she asked, an act similar to the act he thought her father had committed. Instead, she said, "I love my father dearly. He is innocent and you will learn that the hard way." With that she turned on her heel and walked away.

Janet was home by five o'clock but it was almost 7:30 before Walker pulled up in front of her house with the boys. She opened the door and let them into the house. "Did you have a good time?" Janet asked as she reached for Jap's hand. Neither he nor Brent responded, but it was obvious they'd had a full day. They both seemed quite tired.

"They're exhausted," Walker said, "and they have had plenty to eat. They should go directly to bed."

"Come in and tell me all about it," Janet said. "Are you all right?" she asked the boys. They just nodded and Walker answered for them. "They slept most of the way home. They're wiped out."

"OK, boys," Janet said, "run along to your rooms. I'll see each of you in a few minutes." The boys slowly headed up the stairs.

"Wow," exclaimed Walker, "I didn't realize what a job it is to handle a couple of boys. I know they had a good time but they're tired. I'm beat, too."

"May I get you a cup of coffee or a cold drink?"

"A cold drink sounds like a good idea."

Janet was soon back with a glass of lemonade for each of them.

"How was your day?" Walker asked.

"Usual stuff."

After an uncomfortable pause, Walker remarked that he should run along.

God's Mafia

"I hope the boys were not too much trouble."

"Oh no! But I found out that I can't act their age! Usually an old bachelor can act like a kid when he's with grown-ups. Not so when you're with a couple of kids. I've never felt so old!"

Janet laughed. "That's what's been aging me. I don't mind since they are mine."

"Yes, I know. I'll tell you a secret. I'm jealous of you. They are fine young men."

"Thank you." Janet smiled and instinctively reached over and took Walker's hand.

"I'd like all of us, you, the boys and myself to have a picnic tomorrow in the park," Walker said as he put his other hand on hers.

"Haven't you had enough for this week?"

"No."

"Let me see how the boys are in the morning." Janet patted Walker's hand. "I'll call you after church."

At 11:30 the following day, Janet called him. "I have a picnic lunch ready. We'll pick you up in 20 minutes."

"I'll run down to the supermarket and get a cold watermelon," Walker replied.

The picnic at the park provided Walker the opportunity to be alone with Janet. Although his interest had started at an office conference less than six months earlier, it now occupied him.

After most of the hamburgers and half the watermelon had been consumed and the boys were at the playground, Walker addressed Janet across the picnic table. "I like this. How about you?"

"I like it too."

"If we do this often enough it will help relieve your worries about the case."

Janet was pensive. "Frank, the case will be in my mind until it's over, but I'm in favor of this sort of thing. I love those two little guys; they are my life."

"Do you suppose," Walker asked, "that you might make room for me?"

Janet blinked. What a fast operator! Then she smiled. "Frank, you are old enough to know the answer to that question. You know perfectly well that a woman in her middle thirties with two soon-to-be teenage boys and no husband wants a man. And it's not just to help with the children. It's to have a man, period! I'm not one to pussy-foot, Frank. I want a man to sleep with, to eat with, to go out with. I want a husband! The problem is finding the right one. I trust that I am clear."

"Loud and clear." He almost saluted. Janet had shocked him with her candor. What a woman! "Please put me on your list of admirers and suitors and I'll try my best to compete."

"There is no list, Frank. Let's just keep company for our mutual benefit and see what develops."

Frank wanted to take her hand across the table, or better, walk around the table and take her in his arms. He felt sure that neither would be appropriate at that moment.

Called from the table to settle a dispute between her sons, when she came back she asked Walker: "How am I to judge a guy who talks the way you do after only a few weeks' acquaintance?"

"Be very careful," Walker smiled. "Be wary! You just never know about men. I suggest you give such a guy plenty of time to prove himself. It would not be fair to push him off right away. He might be quite serious and with honorable intentions. After all, a guy has to make his move sometime and let me assure you this guy has enough interest in you to get an early start."

"Not bad," Janet said when he'd finished. "Not bad at all."

The boys came back and finished eating everything in sight. Frank and Janet spoke to acquaintances who came by and got to know one another better.

Upon arriving at Janet's house after the picnic, the boys dashed towards the house. As Janet opened the car door she remarked, "It's not like the first time." Frank grabbed her arm to hold her back. "This is my first time," he said.

"You told me you were once engaged to be married."

"Yes, but this time I'm pursuing a whole family, not just a mate."

Janet let go of the door handle and turned to face Walker. "That I find very hard to understand."

"My dear lady, you are not in my situation. I'm 35 years old. I have absolutely nobody: no father, no mother, no brothers or sisters. Believe me, it is a lonely life no matter how many friends I can muster. If you don't mind, and if you will give me the chance, I'd like to prove myself worthy of you, your children, your father and your mother. And then I'll be lonely no more."

Janet laughed. "Frank, you are a very good lawyer. And a good negotiator. You know your needs and you know mine. You are speaking words I want to hear, and now that we have opened negotiations let's both try to make a deal." She extended her right hand. Walker took it and shook it. But he also put his lips to hers as well. To his amazement tears came to her eyes. He could not guess the emotions bottled up inside this woman. The loneliness of a widow, the care of two children, the threat to her father and now, all a sudden, an offer to share her burden. But could she love him? It seemed like a matter of mutual convenience. Was that enough?

That night Janet Wingate slept very little.

In the midst of a horrible tragedy she had been propositioned by opposing lawyers in the case! "This must be a dream," she said to herself. But it was not a dream. She shook her head as she lay awake. First she rebuffed Nagel and then she virtually surrendered to Walker. She should not have encouraged Walker. How could she pour out her heart to a man she hardly knew? She had spoken her innermost thoughts, her most intimate desires. Why?

As if in answer to that question, pictures flooded into her mind, pictures of her sons playing Monopoly on the floor, pictures of the picnic. Frank was kind; he was considerate; perhaps he could be loving. He was certainly far different from Nagel who was, indeed, filled with love for the world.

She thought about the kiss at the end of the evening. Could she start again? Could she get it all back? Why should he take on a family? Because he loved her? "No, that's just not possible. I don't know him and he doesn't know me. There hasn't been enough time!"

She could not do this time what she had done so often — throw up her hands, decide to think about her problems another day and go to bed. Tonight she had to think it through, because time was now pressing. She felt she was losing in her struggle to raise her two sons.

They were so confused! She didn't know how to help them. If ever she needed a man, she needed one now, but what was driving her: the welfare of her sons or her desire for a man? If it was the latter, she was ashamed to think that under her present circumstances, at the ripe old age of 35, she would give a second thought to love. As she pondered further, she reconciled both urges; why shouldn't she have both? In fact, for his sake, must she not be a lover as well as a mother? And then she wondered, could she be a "young bride"?

With that question, Janet began reminiscing. An only child, her life had consisted of home, church and school. She had gone to church camp as a child and to a girl's camp as a teenager. She dated when she was in high school, attended school parties and was very active in school affairs. She was a member of the Debate Team, the Drama Club and the International Relations Club. She was a good student, graduating in the top 10% of her class. Popular with both students and teachers, she was her parents' pride. As the Presbyterian Minister's daughter, she was also prim and proper. All boys held themselves at a distance, avoiding at all times the appearance of familiarity, to say nothing of sexuality. A kiss was rare and always "appropriate."

College, however, was different. Away from home, no longer known as the minister's daughter, an attractive woman who possessed charm, grace and intelligence, Janet was much sought after on campus. Some very handsome young men noticed her. Both in class and in her extra-curricular activities she made the acquaintance of desirable males.

Her roommates were more worldly than she. They educated her in the ways of young collegiates on a modern campus. Initially, she was shocked and somewhat frightened. Her roommates were surprised at her naiveté until they learned of her background. Their counsel was tailored to her condition: gentle but real, almost statistical. They told her that perhaps 75% of men expected intercourse in the course of any relationship, while less than 30% of women expected it. She must be tolerant of both views while choosing her own way.

Attentive to the counsel she had received from her peers, she observed with great interest what occurred all about her. She dated, albeit rather infrequently. She received many invitations to various functions and she went to movies, concerts, picnics, and other events, sometimes with mixed company, sometimes with only female company. She had witnessed the conduct of some men as described by her roommates. She had survived all her encounters some of which had become rather "heated," without compromising herself. All the men in those situations had been gentlemen. They had respected her.

What puzzled Janet back then were her own feelings. She concluded that she was frustrated, but what really bothered her was that she thought she really wanted to go "all out." Only the vision of her parents compelled her not to experience what she called "the ultimate." Her feelings were exacerbated by the literature she was now reading. Alone in her bed, fully awake, she thought, "My life has not been real. I've been in a cocoon. Why shouldn't I become 'fulfilled' like the women in novels?" She had experienced enough to know that the "supreme joy" must indeed be wonderful. What shocked her was that she longed for this much-publicized ecstasy. Would she forever deny herself this pleasure? Must she wait until she married? And could she ever get a man if she remained a prude or an icicle as she had heard in bedroom discussions with her roommates.

There came a time when Janet thought she no longer loved her parents. Her trips home grew infrequent, even though she was still only a freshman.

Instinctively, however, she was still sufficiently bound by her family ties to persuade her to obtain counsel, much as she dreaded to pour out her innermost conflicts. She made an appointment with the school counselor, a Ms. Schroder, who was in her fifties, much to Janet's disappointment. What would an old lady know about a young woman's problems?

The session opened with talk about everything but "the problem": Janet's home, her studies, her roommates, the state of the world. Then the lady asked: "How can I help you?"

Janet had prepared herself for that question. "Ms. Schroder," she said, "my problem is personal, very personal. I'm having trouble with my relations with men. I want what I can't have. Sometimes I think I'm not normal."

"You want to sleep with a boyfriend?"

Alfred J. Fortino

"That's the problem. One part of me wants to very badly and the other part would never forgive me if I did."

Ms. Schroder smiled. "Let me assure you, you are a very normal young lady. The question is: How does one handle the situation? That's why you came here, isn't it?"

"Yes," Janet replied expectantly.

"How old are you?"

"Nineteen."

"Young lady," the older woman began, "I hope you will not be offended if I approach this matter in the most simple terms. I do that not in deference to your ignorance but because we have lost our perspective in the relationship between men and women. I shall call it the 'sex act' only because that is the current colloquialism. It is also called coition, copulation, fornication, coitus, coupling, as well as some vulgar names which need not be mentioned.

"Bear in mind that the act itself is simple, quite uncomplicated, and instinctive. It is not exclusive to human beings. The entire animal world engages in it. You know all this, of course, but I would guess that you have never reduced it to that level. I do it today because it is so important to understand that life, not simple physical life but all civilization, starts at the common point of creation — not only of physical being but of social, ethical, moral, psychological, cultural, and spiritual being. And it is precisely at that point that the paradox of life becomes apparent. The act of love can be a most base act or it can be most sublime. It can be an animal act or a sacred consummation of love.

"The irony in all this is that in the formative years of life, before one has had a chance to learn much about anything, the physical urge prevails without any understanding of the dimensions of the process. We may live in a home in which there may be love and harmony between our parents but we are not in a position to know that this bit of tranquillity originates in the bed. For the most part, as we seek to understand this powerful, almost overwhelming urge, we see and hear only the base aspects of it. It is 'sex' and it is always devoid of connotations of higher, nobler aspirations. It is always forbidden fruit stolen in the night or hidden from the light of day. Until there comes a time when it becomes such a casual thing as to be indulged in anytime, almost anyplace. There is nothing sacred, nothing really intimate in the act anymore. It is not the consummation of a strictly personal relationship. It is something like a sneeze, to be covered with one's hand, the noise muffled."

Janet had winced when she heard those words 15 years ago. But now, on this night when she was thinking of once more becoming a wife, her thoughts turned to her first marriage. She recalled her first night with David Wingate. She smiled as she thought back. How awkward it had been that first night! She had really been quite disappointed. Her problem had been that she had to instruct her man in the act of sex while trying not to give him the impression that she was really experienced, which she was not. Obviously David Wingate had never counseled with anyone like Ms. Schroder.

Janet recalled the early days and nights of her marriage. Now it all seemed funny. But she had followed up on Ms. Schroder's counseling. She had read enough to instruct a man in the act of love with marvelous results. She recalled the supreme gratification of the embrace of a man and a woman in nudity and in ecstasy, the shower of kisses all over each other's body. What a joy!

Then she had lost it all. She remembered the despondency, the horrible loneliness, the great weight of her obligations as a parent, the struggle to structure a new life. Could she have it all back again? She reached a decision: she would try to get it back! With that decision she felt a sense of relief, of hope. She firmed her jaw and raised a clenched fist. She would take charge of her life. She would not turn away from problems, or from love! Let the future challenge her!

SEVEN

Whatever sophistication Father Leahy might have acquired over the years in his ministry, he was completely unprepared for the media blitz that descended upon him. Newspapers, radios, television and scandal sheets had a field day reporting that a minister and a Catholic priest had been arrested as drug dealers!

"EX-CONS PROMISED JOBS IN RETURN FOR KICK-BACKS."

"MOB OPERATION HIDES IN THE ROBES OF THE CHURCH!"

"PAUPER PRIEST AND POOR PRESBYTERIAN MINISTER PUT UP $100,000 BONDS!"

The stories recounted how people became millionaires with the use of money forced from people unable to help themselves! Even the media that sought to be objective only reported that there had to be something more to the story; the accused men could not possibly be criminals! However, as is often true in a highly publicized case, the accused never got the benefit of the doubt.

Patrick Leahy was the third child born in a close family in an Irish neighborhood in Boston. His father had worked for the City of Boston since graduating from high school. His mother married at 20, two years after finishing high school. She was a clerk in a downtown department store at the time. The local church was the center of family life and Patrick had been an altar boy. After graduating from high school, instead of going to work for the City as his father and two older brothers had done, he prepared for the priesthood. While he was still in grade school, a Catholic grade school, there had come to his parish

God's Mafia

Father James O'Neal, a man in his late fifties. Father O'Neal was too old to take on a metropolitan parish, and some of his congregation had wondered why, at his age, he was still nothing more than a parish priest. As far as Patrick Leahy was concerned, however, he was very grateful and happy to have Father O'Neal in his parish. Although Patrick Leahy was only ten years old when Father O'Neal came into his life, he matured quickly as he saw in Father O'Neal veritable personification of his Lord. Patrick was an extremely sensitive child. At home, the discussion always turned on the trials and tribulations of a municipal worker, of how tough it was simply to live, about how unfair it all was: a continuous stream of pessimism, frustration and bitterness.

Patrick's life was no easier on the streets or in the playground. He had seen, from a distance, the operation of the gangs. He had also seen the degradation brought on by poverty among those who were not as well off as he. Unlike other children, he stood apart, and from the time he was able to think about people's conditions, he tried to relate what he saw to what he had been taught to believe. He had heard platitudes at home (when he was not hearing cynicism), but until he met Father O'Neal he was unable to link his perceptions to his beliefs.

One day while he was in Father O'Neal's office receiving instructions as to his duties as altar boy, the telephone rang. The priest answered, listened for what seemed a long time, then asked, "Where are you?" His next words were, "I'll be right there." Father O'Neal hung up the telephone, turned to Pat and the other boys and said, "I am sorry but I have an emergency." Patrick watched Father O'Neal rush out of the office, dash to his car, and drive away. He learned later that Father O'Neal had gone to the precinct police station, where he signed a bond for release of a teen-ager. Patrick never saw the boy, but Father O'Neal took the time to talk to Patrick about what had been done.

"That boy is all alone in the world. Yes, he has a father and a mother but they have decided he isn't any good. They have six other children and after having tried for many years to correct this boy they have given up and were going to let him shift for himself while in the grasp of the law." Father O'Neal explained that for the past six months he had worked with this boy, together with several other boys and girls who likewise had no guidance at home and were adrift on the streets. Father O'Neal was not only a priest but virtually a parent as well.

"The boy's real problem," Father O'Neal told his altar boys, "is that he is somewhat retarded. He is not as smart as his brothers and sisters, and he is easily misled. He needs someone to persuade him that he is worthwhile, that he has potential and that he must try. I know that I can help that boy; he is God's child just like everybody else. He trusts me because I am the only person who has paid any attention to him. I love him, and I think he will do what I ask him to do. If I can just get him into the right channels, he will be saved."

Pat Leahy had seen Father O'Neal do similar things, not just with children but with grown men and women. In high school he had seen the results of Father O'Neal's efforts. He marveled at it and saw these people, young as well as old, as the precious products of Father O'Neal's love.

Patrick Leahy was a serious student, but his size also made him a serious athlete. He was a sophomore in high school and still growing at six-foot-three and 200 pounds, all of which was muscle. He quickly won the starting position at fullback and also won the adulation of his family, his school, his buddies and the newspapers. His closest friend was still Father O'Neal when a tragic accident took the priest's life. Through the efforts of many people, but particularly Father O'Neal, Patrick Leahy had won admission to Notre Dame University. He had both the grades and the athletic ability for admission, but as in almost every case he needed help and he got it. Father O'Neal was the first to inform him, and it was clear to Patrick that Father O'Neal was overjoyed.

A week later, Patrick picked up the local paper and read about the death of Father O'Neal. The Priest, now in his 60's, had come upon an automobile accident in which a child was pinned beneath the car. Before anybody else arrived, Father O'Neal tried to lift the car off the child. In so doing he had a heart attack and died. The boy was saved.

Patrick Leahy was crushed. His dearest friend had died. At the funeral many people paid tribute to Father O'Neal, described the love they received from him, and shared anecdotes of how he had dedicated himself to the service of the Lord and his people. Then and there Patrick Leahy determined that he would become a priest.

At Notre Dame, Patrick Leahy was converted into a tackle. Now at six-foot-four and 280 pounds, he played with a vengeance, as though he had to prove that a man with compassion and love could outperform those who had come from the streets. He was considered for All-American teams, made some and attended numerous banquets and TV shows. He received offers to become a professional football player, but he could never escape Father O'Neal's influence. Now, he too was a parish priest. Or was he a criminal?

Sometimes Pat Leahy felt that the Reverend Hamilton was a present day Father O'Neal. Reverend Malcolm Hamilton had done many of the things that Father O'Neal had done, and he had done them in many parts of the world. In Malcolm Hamilton, Patrick Leahy had found a kindred spirit. They were both mavericks. In their discussions, they had agreed that there had to be some more effective way to do the Lord's work. Neither the state nor the church had come to understand God's word, they thought. In their many talks, sometimes over a cup of coffee at the Fairfield Coffee Shop, sometimes in their respective offices and sometimes on hikes through the woods, they pondered what was wrong. They continued to ponder as they read newspapers, magazine articles and recent books. Things simply weren't working. The world was going the wrong way.

The priest first met Reverend Hamilton at one of the bingo parties his parish held once each month. He was pleased that the Presbyterian minister had come to his bingo party. Hamilton introduced himself and sat next to the priest. "I wish I could use gambling to raise a little money in my congregation," he said, with a smile. "You put on pancake brunches and pot luck dinners." Father Leahy responded. "Your rich parishioners don't need the gambling come-on. My poor people always hope to win a buck with their charity."

The "Ecumenical Society" procedures outlined in the indictment against them were, indeed, their handiwork! For years they used them as a means of helping people who needed help and who could get no help elsewhere. To think, these procedures now constituted crimes!

Perhaps they had always been criminal. How was it that he, a Catholic priest, was also a "racketeer?" He shook his head. How could they have been so wrong? Yet, there it was. Even their lawyer had concluded they were guilty! He thought of his relatives in Boston, of his Bishop who had consented to the entire operation. What shame he had brought upon everyone!

It was all coming apart, crushing both Hamilton and himself and wreaking havoc on many other people! He could take whatever might come, but Vera Hamilton deserved no part of it. Nor did Janet Wingate or her two sons. If he could shoulder the penalty alone, leaving his friend out of it, he surely would. Perhaps the government might accept a guilty plea from him and let Hamilton go. But a plea of guilty would be catastrophic for so many other people!

He could have been a simple parish priest. One day he might have become a Monsignor. He could have looked forward to peaceful retirement. His friend Hamilton would be retired now. And what about Ben Schwartz? Sooner or later he would be indicted. He had become a co-conspirator. He had worked with them to sponsor, promote and manage the Ecumenical Society! What would happen to him? And the Board of Directors. Were they not equally vulnerable? What a horrible mess! How could he have gone so far astray? He and Hamilton had indeed forced people to pay 7.5% of their income in order to keep their jobs! They and the board had indeed played God with people's lives. By what right? By what mandate? Whose mandate? And what about all that money — $20,000,000 in cash, receivable, bonds, stocks. How could he dare join with others to control or manage that? Was this the result of love of money? That was it, love of money. And that was evil!

❖❖❖

Two months after the arraignment Father Leahy called Reverend Hamilton. "I need you," he said. And Hamilton had replied, "And I need you."

And so the huge Father Leahy and the diminutive minister met each other at their favorite woods which were not a public park and whose ownership they really never knew. They started walking together. Neither spoke until Father Leahy asked "Except for Ben Schwartz who else knows our secret?"

"My wife," answered Hamilton.

"And my Bishop," said Leahy.

They continued to walk, staring down, saying nothing.

After a long silence the priest looked up and asked, "How can we keep this from blowing up in our faces?"

Hamilton shrugged. "Murray, Fitzgerald and Martino will provide enough testimony to convict us. Their testimony may be discredited, but how many others are ready to testify?"

Leahy stopped and turned to Hamilton. "Why should they testify? They've never had it so good! They were nothing! Now they're respectable, have good jobs. Some are millionaires!"

"Let's not forget, Pat, all these people have criminal backgrounds. Questioned, they may panic. Who knows what they might say?"

"It's been 30 years. For 30 years some of them have lived normal lives. They have all lived well. Why would they talk? They can lose everything."

"So what? They might be willing to pay that price to avoid prison. They are aware or soon will be that the three men charged with drug-running cut a deal. They may be led to believe that if they volunteer, they'll get immunity."

Once again both men walked silently, their heads partially bowed. Without raising his eyes, Father Leahy said, "So much for loyalty. There seems to be a price on that too. When the price becomes too high, loyalty is abandoned."

"Tell me, Pat," Hamilton said, "should we maintain secrecy even if others are ready to bail out?"

Leahy turned to face his friend. "You know we've got to take the rap, even if those we have helped turn against us."

"Yes, of course. We have no choice. But why are we so anxious to protect the others? Never mind. The answer may be a variation on the theme, 'honor among thieves'." His tone of voice was strange to Leahy, who could not determine whether Hamilton was disgusted or resigned or both.

Hamilton stopped short. "Let's stop this commiserating. Let's get out of here. Let's go to my house."

Soon after they climbed into their respective cars and drove off, another car left the parking lot.

"Vera," Hamilton said to his wife as they entered the den, "Pat and I have been walking, talking and thinking. We're afraid it's all over."

"Does that come as a surprise to you?" she asked. "What did you expect?"

The two men looked at each other without a word but with a common thought: *indeed, what did they expect?*

"You are locked in," Vera continued. "That's the way you have arranged it. It's been all your own making. Let's hope the jury doesn't believe the three ex-cons and that nobody else testifies. You are not the first to learn you have broken the law."

"This is the first time I've heard you say we might lose the case," Hamilton said, surprised.

"I didn't say we were going to lose. I said the only apparent evidence against us is what you have arranged. It's your own rules which may beat you. You can't vow to keep the operation a secret, refuse to testify and expect to win. Your lawyer has told you that."

"But you know we cannot talk," the minister stated.

"Oh yes, I know that," his wife replied, "and I know why you can't talk. But even if you talked, what could you say that would save you? You insisted people had to pay 7.5% of their income to your society if they wanted financing or work That's a fact. You can't deny it. That happens to be in violation of the law. Frankly I don't think the jury will believe three drug peddlers who plea bargained, and I don't think a jury will convict a couple of clergymen who cannot be shown to have taken one cent and who have placed the money in a trust to be used in providing other jobs.

Father Leahy smiled. "My dear lady," he said, "I appreciate you reminding me that we should have faith in people who sit as jurors even to the point of ignoring the law."

"Father," Vera Hamilton answered, "it happens all the time."

EIGHT

Frank Walker felt obliged to make some effort at preparing a defense, virtually impossible since he had no witnesses and the case seemed complete against his clients. Being nice was no defense. His clients could not testify! What could he do about that? Could he make an appeal to the court that because of a statutory prohibition against it the defendants could not defend themselves? Of course he had no authority which permitted relief on that account. Among 6,000 people, would there not be somebody with knowledge of the case who would be willing to testify? Apparently he would get no help from his clients in this quest. They didn't want anybody to testify. Perhaps he might talk to Schwartz. Schwartz knew the secret. If he didn't feel he could divulge it, perhaps he might know somebody who would. Then again, was it possible that his clients were just fronts, innocent of whatever illegal business was being conducted? Walker's speculations with that theory did not last long. He knew his clients too well to believe they would be a front for anybody. They were not dupes.

All this was getting Walker nowhere. He put down his pen and called Schwartz. "Ben, I'd like to talk to you. Can you spare a half hour? I'd be glad to come to your office."

Schwartz said he would prefer to go to Walker's office, and he was there in ten minutes. "I came immediately," he declared, "because I assume that something has happened."

"Nothing new," Walker assured him. "That's my problem. I'm at a standstill. I don't have any way to move. I have no way to prepare a defense. I'm beginning to think I don't have a defense."

"What do you want of me?"

"There must be some answer to this riddle, Ben. How much of a secret can you have among 6,000 people? What kind of a secret is worth the lives of two very fine people?"

"That valuation of the secrecy is not mine. The sanctity of the secret is solely the judgment of Pat and Mal. They have decided they would rather go to prison than tell that secret. What I can tell you is that the lives of many people would be ruined by its disclosure. How do you think it's been possible to maintain the secret for all these years among all these people if it were not a matter of people's lives? Think about it for a moment, Frank. Is the duty of a priest or minister or a rabbi less than that of a newspaper man who is willing to go to jail before he will reveal his source?"

"But a newspaper man is not faced with two or three felonies which might put him in prison for life."

"So, it is a matter of degree. Believe me, the secret these men hold is of far greater significance than the secret a newspaper reporter holds."

"Entrusted as I am with the lives of these two people, shouldn't I be permitted to judge the relevance and seriousness of the secret?"

"No."

"Oh." Walker could not respond to the emphatic negative. What more was there to say?

Schwartz felt sorry for Walker. "Frank, you must understand, your clients are aware of your plight. You are not expected to do the impossible."

"Doesn't it occur to anybody, that I might have some of my own doubts when I know $20,000,000 has been accumulated from all these people and that when a bond is set at $200,000 it is produced in cash in no time at all? What's that money for? Is there some reason other than to make a few people millionaires?"

"Frank, if I rob from Peter is it a defense that I give to Paul? You tell me that the crime of extortion is committed when money is demanded on the threat of loss of a job or a business. That's exactly the situation here. That's admitted. What point is there in going any further, in divulging secrets?"

"Ben, I cannot tell you that it is a defense if you give to Paul. But

I can tell you that what is done with what you take from Peter may have a bearing on the circumstances of the original taking of the money. There are all sorts of organizations which require payment of dues, assessments, fees, charges, etc.… And if you don't pay you lose your membership and you will lose what you have paid in the past. Just because the government calls this extortion does not mean that we cannot show it is something else. As for the drug charge, our defense is that we never sanctioned such sales and they were made without our knowledge. But on the deduction of 7.5% we have no defense unless we tell more about the organization."

"The question, then," said Schwartz, "is whether the organization can survive without secrecy. Obviously, that is what has concerned Father Leahy and Reverend Hamilton all these years. It is hard to imagine what would be the impact if everything would be made public. For 30 years all these people have maintained the secret. If it were not a vital part of the operation, do you think it would have been maintained?"

"Ben, the operation appears to be criminal. The fact that clergymen run it, that there is no violence and no criminal intent to harm anyone makes no difference. What do you know that will change that perception?"

"Believe me, something has not been voiced, but to do so would be a disaster. For Pat and Mal it is a matter of trust."

"Their integrity will put them in prison!" Walker shook his head in resignation.

"And, I'll be there with them," said Ben as he arose and left the office.

❖❖❖

Janet's life was now in complete turmoil. Her attitude towards her father was no longer so certain. She was afraid to talk to him, or to her mother. The realities as she perceived them brought her pangs of doubt. She was beginning to believe what she dared not believe. The bottom was falling out of her life. Her foundations had been shaken. If she doubted her father, she'd doubt the world. Paul Nagel, Frank Walker, were either of them real? There was her world, and then there was the real world. Her world, it seemed, was a fairy tale, a Shangri-La. She'd better start living in the real world. There was too much heartbreak in fantasy-land. Really, all she had was her sons. She'd best make sure they didn't stay in their fantasy world. They must be taught life's cold realities.

NINE

Two weeks after the lawyers on each side of her father's case had come on to her, Janet sat in her office reading the local paper. A headline caught her attention: "Handicapped boy receives self-propelled wheel chair." She read on. "The appeal for donations to purchase an electric, self-propelled wheel chair for Bryan Dibble has finally brought success. The drive for $11,000 had bogged down at $6,000. Today an anonymous gift of $5,000 made possible the purchase of the chair which will permit the boy crippled by a football injury to move about by himself."

Janet stopped. She knew Paul Nagel was the anonymous donor, but why hadn't he talked to her about it. Was he terminating his trust? What was going on? Without further thought, she called Nagel.

"Paul, I see you've given money to buy a chair for the Dibble boy."

"What makes you think I did that?"

"Because I'm beginning to understand you. It's been hard, but I'm beginning to catch on."

"I suppose I should have told you, Janet. I really did not want to take the money out of the trust because all that will be needed for college. I thought I could keep my secret even from you. I was wrong."

"You're a very secretive guy, Paul Nagel. I'll not expose you, of course, because I respect people who do not shout their beneficence from the housetops but you might have guessed that perhaps the trustee should have knowledge of this added feature. We could at least keep the chair in repair, replace batteries, etc.… Did you intend to take care of all that and still remain anonymous?"

Of course she was right, Nagel thought. "That would be diverting funds in the trust from its intended purpose. Believe it or not, Janet, the people who publicly raised this money got enough to provide for repairs and new batteries."

Janet was stumped. She thought she should end the conversation. Somehow, she didn't want to. "Are you sure," she asked, "that you still want me to handle this trust?"

"Yes, I'm sure. I trust you just as much as ever. You are the same person I originally trusted. The fact that I must prosecute your father does not change that. Nor does it change the fact that I love you."

Again, Janet was startled. "What kind of man are you?"

"I don't suppose I can answer that question. I don't know what kind of man I am. I know that, in spite of everything, I love you and, late though it may be, I'm telling you. Janet, I'm sorry about everything but I can't be something I'm not, strange though I may be. I'm telling you exactly how I feel, and I don't expect anything from you."

Janet didn't know what to say. At least Paul knew how he felt. She didn't know what she felt or why! She was angry about the situation, but she could not be angry with him. It was not his fault, really. He was trapped! What a mess!

There was now an embarrassing silence. Nagel expected her to say something, give something. Janet didn't know what to give. "Paul," she said finally, "I love my father. He is the most wonderful man I have ever known. Good bye." And she put down the telephone. She had not been truthful with Paul. She was not so sure about her father as she had represented!

No sooner had Janet put down the telephone than it rang. It was Walker. "It is my recollection," he began, "that you said, 'Try me sometime.' Is this an appropriate time?"

Janet laughed at the word "appropriate." If only he knew how appropriate it was! "This happens to be quite an appropriate time to call. Whether there is an appropriate time for a date is yet to be discussed."

"How about tonight?"

"That's rather forward of you," she said. "Let me see what I can do with my boys."

God's Mafia

"I understand. When might I hear from you?"

"In about 20 minutes."

"Great."

Walker was determined to make an impression on Janet. Trouble was he didn't have any idea about her likes and dislikes. He made dinner reservations in Crystal and reserved tickets at the University Auditorium where the University Symphony Orchestra was in concert. Had Janet told him she could not make it he would invite a friend. However, Janet called in 15 minutes to tell him all systems were "go."

"I've made dinner reservations in Crystal and obtained tickets for the symphony concert," he then informed her.

Surprised, Janet hesitated. How could he have done all that in 15 minutes? He must have made reservations earlier. Maybe he had season tickets. She told him she would arrange for her children to spend the night with her parents.

The drive to Crystal usually took 40 minutes. Walker was determined to fill the time with plenty of conversation. He picked up Janet at her home at five o'clock.

"I hope you like symphonic music," he said as they seated themselves.

"It happens that I prefer it, but I'll take music in any style. I love it."

"Do you get a chance to take in many concerts?"

"On occasion when I am in Crystal."

"With Paul Nagel?" Then, before she had a chance to respond, he asked, "How is your acquaintance with Nagel playing out these days?"

"Not very well. He didn't make a connection between me and my father. He learned it only after the arrest."

Walker wondered whether he should continue with this line of inquiry. There was no way to cut it off without demonstrating jealousy or unease. It seemed natural, so he asked, "How is he handling the situation?"

"Very simply," Janet answered. "He tells me he is sorry the situation has developed as it has. He seems to think that he can prosecute my father or that he must prosecute my father, without disturbing his relationship with me. He recognized that I might take exception to that, but he assures me that he still thinks highly of me."

Walker drove in silence. Finally he asked the question foremost on his mind. "How close is your relationship with Nagel?"

Janet gave a short, almost inaudible laugh. "There never has been any relationship. Dinners have always been casual, always in the same place, always Dutch treat. In almost a year, that has been the extent of it." She did not consider it necessary, or wise, to tell Walker about Nagel's recent change of attitude.

That's just like Nagel, Walker thought. Such a woman, and he does nothing about it. That's not the Walker way!

It was hard to avoid thinking about the case en route to Crystal. There's a full evening after we get there, Walker thought. He must make the trip interesting, at least not dull. "How do you manage this proxy business on the Governor's Commission? You are a permanent substitute. How do you manage that?"

"It's an ad hoc committee without status in any law or regulation. The governor just decided he wanted some input on an informal basis. He wanted my boss on the committee, but right after he was named my boss got into merger talks, so he asked me to sit in for him."

"Why you?"

"That's a good question. I came up with Smith in the ranks of the bank. He's been there longer than I have, but not that much longer. We got to know each other pretty well. I know his wife and daughters and I'm probably as close to him as anybody." She paused, then changed the subject. "Frank, what kind of a guy is Nagel, really?"

"I can't say much more than I've already told you. Nobody really knows him very well. He's a loner. He's obsessed with his work. He is an ideologue but he is not loud about his convictions. He's the man in the local DA's office when it comes to organized crime. He calls the shots. In fact, Washington often confers with him in cases in other districts. He's no shrinking violet. He simply lives in a world of his own."

"Is he honest in his belief, or does ambition overrule common sense?"

"The reason for his success is his judgment of cases. He is sure of his ground before he goes into court."

"So he must feel pretty sure about our case." Janet was prodding. She could not absolutely set aside her father's case.

"Janet, if your father had come clean with the FBI, I don't think we would be in court. Paul Nagel is not an overzealous, self-promoting guy. He is quite naive, really."

"You're describing a nice guy," Janet said looking straight ahead.

"Nobody ever said he was anything else. But he is determined to finish first. Of that you can be sure."

Janet fell silent and so did Frank, both with thoughts about Paul Nagel. By sheer happenstance, Frank and Janet went to the same dining room in the same hotel where Janet always dined with Paul Nagel. The waiter recognized her and seated them at the same table. She felt embarrassed, though there really was no reason for it.

After they ordered, Walker spoke, "How do you manage to raise two fine boys and still work full time?"

"I manage because I have two very nice young men for sons and two loving parents who help. That is, until this nightmare hit us. I admit I'm having a difficult time right now. It's hardest on my sons. Their peers are either very supportive or very malicious; there seems to be no in-between. It's hard for eight and ten year olds to hear their grandfather called a racketeer. Jap is having a real bad time. Brent takes it a little better but not much. I had to go to the school last week because for the first time in his life Jap got into a fight. Worst of all is the depression. Believe me, kids can get very depressed. I fight that all the time and get no help from the teachers. They are strictly 'hands off.' It's disgusting."

Walker leaned across the table as if to give some strong advice. "You need a man to help you."

Janet smiled. "You were just wonderful with my boys. They think you are quite a guy. They took the Monopoly set to their grandparents tonight. All four of them will play. Thank you very much for your help."

Walker continued his move. "I'd like to make a deal with you. You have a couple of boys who need an adult male. I'm an adult male who is just plain lonely. Could we plan some outings for the four of us? Believe me, I'm being selfish. I need you and maybe you can use an old bachelor."

"Come on, Frank," Janet teased, "you don't need a couple of boys. You can be footloose and fancy free. The last thing you need is a couple of rambunctious boys."

"Maybe, but can I assure you that I could use the companionship of two boys and their mother. I'll confess the mother really intrigues me."

Janet laughed, thinking, "This guy is something else. He knows all the angles and how to play them." Out loud she asked, "Are you sure you know what you are doing?"

"No," he replied. "I've never tried to make a four-sided deal before, but I really like what I see and I'm willing to take a chance. You, my dear lady, have nothing to lose. I may be helpful, but if I'm not, all you have to say is 'good bye, so long'. I'm hopeful, of course, that from time to time I can have you to myself. Like tonight. Generally, I'm pretty well behaved." When Janet said nothing, Walker pressed on, "You can't deny that right now you can use me."

"Frank Walker, you seem to have made this date for the sole purpose of entering into a deal. That doesn't sound very romantic to me."

"Oh, but I don't play my best hand on opening. I save that for a more appropriate time, in a more appropriate place. Rest assured, however, that I can be quite romantic."

"I take it that you have had a lot of experience," Janet said, playing along.

"I do not come to you untutored and inexperienced. I'm not an old veteran of many wars, but I have had several light skirmishes, none of them of serious portent. I should warn you, however, that I do not plan to skirmish with you. This is no flirtation. I mean business."

"You have determined all this after meeting my two sons?"

"In part, but also because I've seen you in action in my office."

Janet had enough of the game. She said warmly "I warn you; tread carefully in these parts. This woman has some very strong desires, and you may start something you can't walk away from. I'm 35 years old, a widow with two boys to raise and educate. I don't expect a man to do that for me, but I sure expect him to be a devoted, dedicated mate who will be at my side all the time. You may not be interested in that, but when you tell me you are serious I want you to know what 'serious' means to me. Let me warn you, also, that I've been looking for such a man. You might get netted like a salmon."

Walker had heard such candor from her before. He guessed he had opened himself up for it, however. He was careful with the next few words.

"You have described your problem. Please listen to mine. It is short and brief. I'm alone. I have nobody. No matter how hard I try to be, as you say, 'footloose and fancy free,' I am still lonely. No matter how many friends one may have on the outside, he is lonely without someone to love."

Janet was pleased with those words; more, she was happy. She would give the relationship a chance, for Frank had the right intentions. She would try him. "I guess we need each other," she said, "Let's give ourselves time to explore the matter."

"Spoken like a trust officer." Walker smiled and held out his hand. She took it and they shook hands on the deal.

"Not very romantic," Janet said to herself. "Just as well. He has been very good each time we have been together. My sons like him. I like him." She would settle for this — for the time being.

The rest of the evening went well. The concert was delightful and Janet was able to forget her problems for the moment. Frank was happy because Janet seemed happy. On the ride home they talked about the concert. However, Paul Nagel still lurked in Janet's mind. She had learned a little more about him, but she was not sure he was 'real.' Frank was a man who seemed to be quite real. How quickly, she thought, he had hit upon her deepest desires. And how readily she had responded! What was happening to her? She thought of her children and her parents. This guy actually wanted to fit into her life. No wonder she had been so silly, sharing her most heartfelt emotions to someone who was little more than a stranger. Would she have done that with Nagel? No, but Nagel still remained in her thoughts.

TEN

"An Angela Burgé is here to see you," Phyllis Keating, announced over the intercom.

"Does she have an appointment?" Walker asked.

"No. It's about the Leahy/Hamilton case."

Walker sat up. "Send her in."

A tall, beautiful black woman walked into Walker's office. She was better than six feet tall. Her hair was tinged white but, face was youthful as well as beautiful. She could have been anything from 35 to 50 years of age. Well dressed and with obvious good taste, she was a lady of some means, Walker thought.

"Please have a chair, Ms. ...I'm sorry, I didn't get the name."

"Angela Burgé," the woman responded, and spelled it out for him.

"My secretary tells me you are here about the Leahy/Hamilton case. Are you a reporter?"

"I am not a reporter, but I do have some questions I would like to ask. I am personally involved in the case; I'm not a nosy intruder."

"How are you personally involved?"

"I am a member of the Ecumenical Society."

"I understand there are 6,000 of you. You are the first to come forward to ask about the case."

"I know. That's because we have all been sworn to secrecy and nobody wants to break the vow. Nobody wants to disobey Father Leahy or Reverend Hamilton. I'm not here to disobey the wishes of those men but to see what can be done to keep them out of prison."

"How do I know you're not a newspaper reporter?"

God's Mafia

"Call Mr. Schwartz. You know him. He will identify me."

Walker called Schwartz immediately. "I have a lady here who claims she is a member of the Ecumenical Society. Her name is Angela Burgé. Do you know her?"

There was a pause. "I'll be right there," Schwartz said. In less than five minutes Schwartz walked in. "Hello, Ben," said Ms. Burgé as she stood to greet Schwartz.

"What are you doing here?" Schwartz asked.

"You didn't think I would let this get completely out of hand, without coming forward did you, Ben?"

"What makes you think it is 'out of hand'?"

"Let's say, then, that I came here to make sure it is not out of hand. Mr. Walker was reluctant to tell me the current status until he was sure of who I was. Why don't both of you tell me all about it?"

Schwartz felt he should remind Angela of her oath of silence. "Angela, you of all people know why we must keep our secret."

"I sure do and I have been quiet. But I'm not so sure we can keep quiet much longer. Do you expect me to keep my mouth shut while Reverend Hamilton and Father Leahy go to prison?"

"That's the way they want it." Schwartz spoke the words as though he did not necessarily agree with the idea of continued silence.

"But is that the way 6,000 people want it?" Angela looked at Walker; Still puzzled, he had nothing to say.

"Angela," Schwartz went on, "your people are the ones who will be the worst hit if the secret is out."

"Ben, the question is not who will be hurt but will we save everybody even if we all keep our mouths shut? To put it another way, what will happen if we don't talk?"

Walker still said nothing. He was anxious to hear the rest of this story, but at that moment Miss Keating announced over the intercom that Janet Wingate was here for her appointment. "Have her come in," Walker told his secretary.

Janet walked in, greeted both Walker and Schwartz and was introduced to Ms. Burgé "This lady came to talk about the case. We are in the process now. Please sit over on the couch, Janet. Listen in."

Schwartz turned to Janet. "I've known Angela Burgé for a long time. She is a member of the Ecumenical Society. She came to ask our lawyer how things were going, and Walker called me to identify her."

Angela Burgé repeated her question. "What are our chances of winning this case if we say nothing?"

"Right now we have no witnesses." Walker admitted. "We have no way to counter attack. We have to hope the jury will not believe the prosecution's witnesses."

"And what will they say?"

"According to the indictment, they will testify that the defendants recruited them out of prison and promised them a job if they would pay 7.5% of their income to the Society. The Society used the money to establish and operate various businesses for some of its members, all contrary to law."

"Ben, isn't that what we are doing?" the lady asked.

"Yes," Schwartz replied, "but for the benefit of those who gave the money."

"And how are we going to tell them the true story if nobody is talking?" Angela Burgé asked sarcastically.

"That's the question I'd like answered," Walker interjected. "Ben, you deny there's been any extortion. What do you call it, and how are you going to explain the difference?"

"Extortion is stealing by misrepresentation or threats of violence. We have done none of that."

"Extortion's also taking money on threat of loss of employment, property or money. And if these 6,000 people don't pay, they lose their jobs or their properties," Walker retorted. "And if the person giving the money doesn't consider it for his benefit, it doesn't matter what the recipient says the money is for."

Ben was silent. Then he asked, "Is it extortion when one must pay union dues in order to work?"

"Union dues are paid for specific services provided by a union. Can one who gives 7.5% be sure he will get anything?"

"If he needs it he will get what he needs," said Schwartz.

"How do we get that before a jury?" Walker asked.

"By the testimony of the Prosecution's witnesses," Schwartz responded.

God's Mafia

"And you will count on that and nothing more?" Walker was looking at Angela Burgé as he spoke.

"I begin to get the picture," Angela Burgé said. "It's a tough situation. Make no mistake; if we tell everything the damage will be horrible. If we don't, it will be just as bad. I don't see how you can count on the likes of Murray, Fitzgerald and Martino. They've made a deal. They're going to keep it. They will try to convict us."

Janet was fascinated as well as frightened. "For God's sake," she blurted, "will somebody please tell us what this is all about?"

Angela Burgé spoke slowly. "I am here because I wanted to be sure that I understand our predicament. It appears that the real 'Catch 22' is that if we don't talk we lose and if we do talk we ruin ourselves. Nelson paints the same picture I see here today. I see no point in going on this way. I hesitate because I dearly love Malcolm and Patrick whom you know but not nearly as well as I do. I do not want to disappoint them, but they are in the center of this catch 22.

"Let me tell you a little about myself. I am presently the president and sole owner of American Standard Service Company. We provide services, temporary and permanent, from domestic services in the home to janitorial services in offices and small business. We provide LPN's, stenographic services. We are headquartered in Indianapolis but we also operate throughout the midwest. I have 3,000 employees, nearly all women. I've been in operation over 25 years. I have a family, a husband and two daughters. One is a junior in college, the other a freshman. My employees have families too. I am on the board of directors of a bank! I'm chairman of the Indiana Association of Professional and Business Women; I am active in my Altar Society. I've been regarded as a highly respected business woman. I have a beautiful home and my income is over $400,000 per year. I am part of the secret these two defendants have tried to protect."

"Which is?" The words come out before Janet could stop them.

"I am a former prostitute! Many of my employees, both men and women, are former prostitutes. None of my friends and business associates know this. Nobody, except my husband, knows my secret. My two daughters know me as highly successful, highly respected woman. The last thing I want is for them to know my history. The same is true in the case of my employees. In fact, many of their husbands or wives know nothing of their past.

"Perhaps that will help you to understand our problem. Mr. Walker, can I take the witness stand and tell a jury that I owe everything I am and everything I have to the men who took me out of prison and gave me a chance no one else would give me?"

Stunned, Walker and Janet were unable to respond. Schwartz lowered his head and closed his eyes.

"But, really," Angela said after satisfying herself that no one could answer, "The secret is more than my past, more than my employees' past, more than the past of the other members of the society, all of whom are ex-convicts. The secret also includes a moral commitment which is ours and ours alone. This moral commitment is now a part of our lives. Secrecy is essential to its preservation. To publicize it is to make it a spectacle, a public show and exhibition which would destroy its moral content. Can you imagine what the media would do with this?"

There was a moment of silence. Schwartz spoke up. "Angela, you must now finish your story. You cannot leave matters as they are. They must know your story."

"From the age of 12 until I was 17, I was a prostitute. My mother was a prostitute before me. I never knew my father. My mother was murdered when I was 12 years old and I was left to fend for myself. I was in and out of jail and finally I was sent to prison for a year. While I was there, Father Leahy came to see me. He sat opposite me in the conference room and told me that my time in jail would soon be over and he had come to help me. He'd arrange for me to start a new life if I wanted. Those were his exact words.

"I laughed at him. 'Those robes don't fool me. I know what men want,' I said, and I was sure that this man wanted the same thing. I said, 'You don't need to talk to me like that. My services will be available to you when I am out of here. As long as you are willing to pay the going rate you can have me.'

"He said, 'Young lady I am not interested in what you have been doing. Believe me, I am interested in you as a person and I am here

God's Mafia

in God's name to take you out of that life and into something better.'

"I laughed again. 'I haven't seen this act before,' I said. 'And I've heard a lot of messages from a lot of men.' I hadn't believed any of them and I wasn't about to believe this man.

"Finally, the priest said to me, 'You think about it. I will come back to see you again.'

"Two weeks later, he was back again in the same conference room and he said, 'Have you thought over what I told you?'

"I was quick to tell him that there wasn't anything to think about. 'I already told you how I felt. You don't need to make special arrangements to take care of me, because I'm not about to become your exclusive mistress. You got to do business with me the same way I do business with everybody else.'

"He smiled and said, 'Young lady, I know how you feel; I know the life you have led, and I know how men have treated you. I am going to keep coming back here until you believe me and are ready to give me a straight answer.'

"I looked after him as he left the room and began to wonder, 'Is this man for real?'

"Sure enough, within a week he was back again. Meanwhile I had done a little thinking. What did I have to lose if I said to him that I was willing to cooperate? If he was like the others, I could handle it; and if he was for real, who knows what might happen?

"When my mother was murdered I was absolutely alone in the world. There was nobody who even knew me, and I didn't know of a single relative. My mother always kept me in a world apart from hers. She put me in a high-priced private school as soon as I was ready for kindergarten. She could do that because she had a very good income. My mother was illiterate, a non-person, really. She had no birth certificate and she never did anything that would identify her. She had no bank account. She never wrote or received any letters, and she only dealt in cash. All her life she experienced nothing but abuse, physical and financial exploitation and outright cruelty. She was smart enough to rise above all that. As a prostitute, she started in the streets. She always had a boss, a pimp who held her a virtual slave, but she was really enslaved by more than one person. It was the whole system. She could never hold on to any money. She had to pay others, or they'd turn her in to the police. Her pimp beat her. Finally she did something about it. The manager of a rundown office building was one of her regular patrons. She made a deal with him to rent her 'vacant' office space which she used as a bordello. The space was vacant so far as the owners knew, but she paid a handsome rent to the manager who pocketed the money.

"My mother obtained an entirely new clientele in her new 'office.' She was safe, because nobody suspected that she was operating out of an office. The rent she paid was nothing compared to what she used to pay her bosses. So far as they were concerned she was gone, probably dead. She developed a 'high class' clientele, which is how she kept me in a very nice private school. I saw my mother in an apartment which she rented from the manager of the office building. I was with her almost every weekend. Her office hours were always during the daytime. She never ventured out of her apartment at night.

"My mother was very proud of me. I was the best student in my class. She told me all about herself, about the world she lived in, about her work, and about men. She kept money in tin cans hidden in her office and apartment. She insisted that I have money hidden away in my room at school. She made sure I wasn't a non-person. I had a birth certificate and I was registered at school. She paid for my schooling in cash by the week so that the cash payments did not raise suspicions in the minds of the school authorities.

"When my mother died, her identity was unknown. She was found dead in her 'office' by the building manager. He reported that she was a trespasser in a vacant office, and her death by asphyxiation aroused no more suspicion than the death of any vagrant. Who ever murdered her did it carefully. There were no wounds, no blood, but all the hidden money was gone! Her old bosses had finally caught up with her, probably through one of her clients.

"I was devastated. My only contacts with the world were through the school and the office building where my mother operated. I loved my school, but, of course, I could not stay there. To work I needed a work permit, but I was not old enough to apply for a permit. I did not inform the authorities at school the circumstances of my mother's death, only that she had died. I told them I would have to leave school and I simply walked out. Had I told them the real story they would have turned me over to the police and I didn't want any part of them.

"I asked the manager of the office building to make the same deal with me that my mother had made, but he'd have nothing to do with a minor. It would have meant a prison term for him if I'd been caught.

"I decided that the only way I could finish my education was to earn a lot of money like my mother had. I didn't fully realize what that meant. When I could not close a deal for the office, I turned to the streets! Dressed as a streetwalker I looked a lot older than 12. I was no skinny 12-year old child. I was tall and could talk the talk.

"It was horrible! Many men were kind, considerate, appreciative, but some were animals. I could not always tell what I was getting into I was often raped; of course, it was rape under the law but since I was asking for it I couldn't report it. Pretty soon you adapt yourself. You learn to take care of your customers, lest you lost them. After a while it's all mechanical, a mockery of affection. Sometimes I'd almost throw up in disgust. But, there were times when the process was pleasant and the affection genuine.

"I was determined to get an education and become somebody. I was willing to work the streets to get my education, but I could not avoid the syndicate. They came after me and I paid them. I had no way to hide from them.

"I thought I could pay them and keep them off my back, but the more I paid them the more they wanted. It finally dawned on me that their program was designed to keep me in poverty. That way they could control me. So I started to keep my money to myself. I didn't report all my earnings. They had a remedy for that. They didn't beat me up; they just put the police on my trail, I'd serve 30, 60 or 90 days in county jail and then be released. I finally was put in prison for a year. I was almost through when Father Leahy came to see me.

"When my term was completed, Father Leahy came to the jail and took me with him to a convent where he left me in the care of some wonderful nuns.

"I was not in the convent for more than two weeks when Father

Leahy took me to a dormitory which was part of a school. He told me that I could study and complete my high school training and then he would see where we would go from there. Those were his words. By this time I believed him. I didn't know what I was getting into, but I was satisfied that I would be better off than I had been before. I really studied. After all, it was what I had wanted more than anything. It was what I had prostituted myself for. I had no difficulty making 'A' grades and the school administrators and Father Leahy were all very pleased with me. While I was in this school I met Reverend Hamilton.

"When I was a senior and about to graduate, Father Leahy brought Reverend Hamilton with him and he told me that they would be at my graduation, would provide me with the proper clothes, including the robe which had to be purchased, and they would be my sponsors for any occasions which took place at graduation. At this time, my world was changing fast. I was valedictorian of my class and I was proud of myself for the first time in my life. I also realized that I owed it all to this one man.

"Father Leahy told me that they had arranged a scholarship for me at Northwestern University and that they would supply the rest of the money I'd need to go to school. They also told me that they expected me to do nothing but study and study hard, because they expected me to make the same kind of record in college that I had made in high school. They said it would be necessary for me to prepare myself for my future. What future, I began to wonder. Where was I going? All I knew was that I was going in the right direction.

"I graduated from Northwestern then went on and obtained an MBA. After that, Pat and Malcolm told me that they had a plan for me. They wanted me to organize a company that would employ many people. They told me to give some thought to a practical company whose services would be in great demand. 'That takes capital,' I reminded them. 'Where is that coming from?'

"Reverend Hamilton said, 'We will provide it, but of course we have limitations. Nevertheless we think that we can provide enough capital for you to start a small business and we hope that you can make it grow.' I was to give some thought to the type of business we could start.

"Hamilton said, 'There is one other thing. We would like you to employ women who have been prostitutes, who have served time in jail.' At last the light went on in my head! I could see a glimmer of what these men wanted to do. They had helped me, they wanted to help others, and now they wanted me to work with them. Lots of women would give their right arm for that kind of opportunity. I was ecstatic. I threw my arms around them both and unable to speak, nodded my head up and down, up and down, like a yo-yo.

"It may sound trite but at that moment I was reborn. At that moment I became a new person. I was going to do something worthwhile. I told them that I would do whatever they wanted. I think it was Malcolm who then said: 'We believe that God loves everyone and we also believe that the reason so many people find themselves in the position you found yourself is because man has failed, not God.' I began to cry. I can't remember when I had last cried. I thought of all the hookers in that nasty little world of the streets. How wonderful it would be to embrace them and give them the kind of opportunity that I'd had and know they would turn their lives around just as surely as I was about to turn mine around. I began to believe for the first time in my life, that maybe there is a God after all."

"I started to do what Father Leahy had done with me. I went out to the jails and talked to streetwalkers. It wasn't hard to find them. I gave them virtually the same talk that Pat had given me. Slowly we built up the company until we brought it to where it is today. I pay 7.5% of my net income to the Ecumenical Society; every one of my employees also pays 7.5%. We all do it willingly. We all appreciate what has been done for us and we all want to help do it for others."

When Angela had finished, Janet was on the verge of tears. She could not hold back. "I knew it! I knew it! That's my father. Oh my God! Why didn't he tell me?"

The others waited for Janet to compose herself. Finally Schwartz spoke up. "Who is to make this decision? Who has the right? I trust you now know why the defendants would never violate this trust. As you can see, it involves even more than the sanctity of the confessional. It involves the lives of hundreds, thousands of people."

Angela said, "You can be sure that I have thought and prayed about this. I was once a pagan, now I am a Christian. I am Catholic; I think God has sent me here. At least, this is where I find myself after my prayers."

Walker rose to his feet and looked out the window behind him. Outside, was a nicely kept lawn which provided a quiet, peaceful, attractive scene. Whenever imponderables arose his active mind found the grassy scene. After several minutes, he turned back and said, "Of course this is not a legal question. One might think that there might be a legal responsibility to the 5,997 other members of the Society to remain silent. And, insofar as the defendants are concerned, there may be. They have been persuaded by the moral mandate, however, not the legal promise of protection. We can't persuade them to testify, and I guess we shouldn't. Nor can I, as a lawyer, subpoena any member of the Society, not even you, Ms. Burgé.

"Let's suppose, for a moment, that somehow we got into the record all that Angela Burgé has told us. Would that constitute a defense? Three people will testify that they paid 7.5% of their net income to this Society for the sole purpose of obtaining money and with the fear that they would not be able to do business if they didn't contribute. That, legally, is extortion! Now somebody else comes along and says, 'I was subjected to the same conditions and I paid gladly because it saved me.' One person says, 'I gave because I had to.' The other says, 'I gave gladly because I was helped.' Does that mean the first person does not have a legitimate complaint under RICO?

"Ordinarily it would be my opinion that whatever Ms. Burgé's testimony as to her situation, it would not be a sufficient defense against the charge brought on behalf of others.

"Unfortunately, the prosecution does not have to show a pattern of racketeering if the charge is extortion. One act of extortion is enough to convict. However, ironically, in this case it is entirely possible that the pattern might be a defense against extortion. If 5,997 people similarly treated don't consider it extortion, it may not be extortion. It is interesting that prior cases concerning extortion hold that it is the impression of the alleged victim and not the intention of the accused which determines whether a crime is committed!"

"What does all that mean?" Schwartz asked.

"It means that we might persuade a court to consider such testimony if we care to produce it."

All eyes turned to Angela Burgé. She smiled. "How am I different from the defendants? That is my problem. That is why I have prayed for help, why I have not spoken up sooner. I have decided that if I do not speak up I will have done a greater harm to the others than if I tell it all. I don't know how much they will be hurt if I speak, but if I don't speak our two saints will go to prison and the Ecumenical Society will die. Of course, if there is any possibility of winning this case without my testimony, it would save the lives of many men and women who have not told their wives and husbands, their children and their friends that they were once prostitutes, pimps, burglars, murderers and rapists!"

"You said that 'ordinarily' Angela's testimony would not be a sufficient defense. What did you mean by that?" Janet asked.

"There is one eccentricity in RICO. In order to prevail under RICO, the prosecution must show a *pattern* of racketeering. Maybe Ms. Burgé's testimony might prove that although there is a pattern, that pattern is not one of criminal racketeering but a pattern which provides benevolence and charity."

Angela smiled wistfully. "My husband knows everything. My children know nothing! I know that I am a new person, that the old person is no more, but will anyone else believe that? And will it matter? That is why, my friends, nearly 50% of all persons released from prison are back in prison within months of their release. The public does not believe criminals can rehabilitate themselves. In fact, it is a matter of public policy that they should not believe. Public records are kept to be sure that the society will not forget! That's why ex-convicts have had to band together in the Ecumenical Society, to help keep secret our past while we help each other cope. That policy has been the genius of these two men. It has been their compassion and most of all their determination, their love, which has given us our lives back. If the law now convicts them, all they have done is lost! Whatever price I must pay, whatever price all of us must pay, we will pay it! But these men are not going to be crucified, not so long as there is a breath of air in my body!"

Angela Burgé was now standing alongside the desk, pounding her fist on the desk top. Janet, tears streaming down her face, dashed across the room, threw her arms about Angela's and clung to her. She didn't say a word. She simply clung, it seemed, for dear life.

Schwartz looked on without show of emotion. He had long known this story. Walker was moved as much by Angela's eloquence as by the story she told, but his mind was fogged by Janet's emotions which permeated the room. He rose to his feet but said nothing. He stared out the window and breathed slowly and heavily.

Soon they were seated once again, with all eyes on Walker. He had a good witness. But he now knew the reason for the secret, and it was a good one. He looked at Janet. "Now that we know, Janet, we must preserve the secret if at all possible."

Janet snapped to attention. "Oh no," she blurted. "We must tell the secret. We must tell it to the world. The world must know this secret. Don't you see, this is the greatest thing to happen in a hundred years. These people we are so concerned about — we must not pity them. They are as much heroes as my father and Father Leahy. They have sacrificed all these years to undo a terrible wrong which the state and the people have imposed on ex-convicts. They are all heroes!"

Angela looked at Janet. "We are not heroes, Ms. Wingate. We are all repentant. We are saved by the grace of God. We have done what we have done, not because we are great people but because we must. We would never call ourselves saviors. We are the saved. We must not aggrandize ourselves. We must forever be meek."

"She sounds just like Paul Nagel!" Janet thought.

ELEVEN

The meeting at Walker's office broke up without having reached a consensus. Walker was not yet ready for conclusions. He was anxious to talk to Janet alone. He asked Angela Burgé and Ben Schwartz if they would come back if necessary. Both said they would make themselves available at any time. To Janet he said, "I'd like to talk to you for a few minutes."

After the others had gone, Walker approached Janet. "I want to make sure we're on the same wavelength. Shall we use Angela Burgé's testimony? If we do, how should we handle your father and Father Leahy?"

"The answer to the first question is simple: we use it. The answer to the second question is more difficult. I really don't have an answer to that question. I'll need to think about it."

Walker surprised Janet by saying, "I'm afraid that I disagree with you on the first question and my answer to that would take care of the second question. Angela Burgé loves your father and Father Leahy. She'd do anything for them, even commit perjury. However, today I have learned not only the secret, but the importance of the secret. The lives of other people are really dependent upon it. Before today I could not fathom the importance of the secret. Before today I could not fathom how lives of other people could be dependent upon the secret. I don't think we, or Ms. Burgé, have the right to play loose with other peoples' lives."

Janet kept calm. "And so my father and Father Leahy become sacrificial lambs."

"That's what they want to do."

"No, Frank, what they want to do is to save the Society. Maybe Angela is right. Maybe the way to save it is by speaking out. We'll surely lose it if we remain silent. She's convinced me of that. Tell me, Frank, what do you think will happen if she tells her story in court? True, some people will be terribly embarrassed. Is that worse than losing it all? Let's put aside this matter of trust. That's what's really at the bottom of my father's anxiety: betraying a confidence. He won't have to do that. Angela Burgé takes the rap for that. She has more to lose than my father. And I still believe that when this story is told, the country will regard the whole bunch of ex-cons as heroes, as people who have 'overcome adversity'.

"We have to betray my father and Father Leahy. We cannot tell them about Angela Burgé's testimony. In the end, I think they will agree with us. Frank, this is war and in war somebody always gets hurt. The only objective here is to win the war. We can't pussy-foot around and worry about somebody getting hurt or somebody being embarrassed."

Walker looked at Janet admiringly. This was one tough lady. This was one wonderful woman. He came from behind the desk and took her in his arms. She did not object. "We will do it your way," he said, "and we will win!" Janet buried her face in his chest and cried. He held her tightly.

"I'm not going to leave you alone," he said. "It is past five o'clock; my secretary has gone home. Let's go to your house and talk to the boys. Let's tell them that everything is going to be fine. Then let's all go out for dinner."

Janet still clung to him but she said nothing. He held her until she was ready to leave. Without another word, they left the office together, got into Walker's car and drove off, leaving Janet's car behind.

By the time they reached the house, Janet had calmed down. Jap was watching TV; Brent was reading. When they saw Walker, they jumped up to greet him.

"Sit down, boys," Walker said. "Your mother and I want to talk to you about your grandfather. He is going to be all right. Today we found what we have been looking for, and it will prove your grandpa is a hero, not a criminal. He and Father Leahy have been doing some wonderful things for people. The police misunderstood it, but now we have somebody who will tell all about it from the witness stand."

The boys did not fully understand what Walker was saying, but the message that grandpa would not go to prison got through. When Walker told them that there would still have to be a trial, they were disappointed, but at least they could look their tormentors in the eye, sure that their grandpa was innocent.

Janet felt drained and was happy that Walker was explaining things to the boys. "Now, let's all go out to dinner," Walker suggested. Again, Janet was grateful. She was in no condition to prepare a meal, no matter how skimpy.

Throughout the meal, the boys carried on a constant chatter with Walker. They asked questions about the trial. They asked questions about grandpa. Walker fielded all the questions, while Janet did little more than nod her head from time to time. When it was time to leave, Walker drove back to the office. Janet drove her car home, and Walker took the boys home.

It was now eight o'clock. A little too early for the boys to go to bed. Walker accompanied Janet and her sons into the house and turned to leave. "Please don't go," Janet pleaded. Walker was happy to oblige. Brent soon had the monopoly set out, and the three started a game. Janet did not feel like participating. She went into the kitchen and puttered. At nine o'clock she told the boys it was bed time. Reluctantly the game was brought to a halt and the boys went upstairs.

When the two were alone, Janet asked Walker, "Can I help with the trial preparation? I've done it before when the trust department got involved in a lawsuit. In fact, I did all the preparations. The lawyer simply tried the case in court."

"I know it will be difficult to wait for the trial," Walker replied, "but how will you find the time to do that?"

"I'll take a leave of absence. I only need to check into my office in the morning. Mr. Smith will understand."

"I hope working together will not destroy our budding friendship."

"I cannot thank you enough for all you've done for us so far. You've been more than just a friend."

"I've been more than a friend because I want to be more than a friend. That may sound coy, and it may sound childish, but it says what I mean. And now I'd better get out of here." With that, Frank Walker departed.

The next day Janet called him to say she would be in his office the following morning. At nine o'clock, she entered Walker's suite, and his receptionist steered her to the library after letting her know that Walker was in conference. In the library, Janet found the file. There was very little in it. In a yellow legal pad she began writing what she and Walker had to do. First, would there be other witnesses? Second, if there were none, should some be sought? If so, how many? In about ten minutes, Walker joined her. She showed him the pad.

"Our first order of business," Walker said, "is to get Angela Burgé back here. When we question her we'll know what to do next." He called Burgé who agreed to return immediately. Walker suggested that Janet write a complete history of her father and as much as she could about Father Leahy. He also asked her to call Father Leahy and request his presence as soon as possible because Walker had a few questions for him.

Father Leahy visited Walker's office the next day at one o'clock. "Father," Walker asked, "do you know whether the DA has talked to any members of the Society except these three? After all, there are 6,000 members. It would seem that the prosecution would want more testimony."

The priest shook his head. "I haven't heard of anybody else talking to the FBI. But remember, we're a secret organization. A membership list isn't available to the public."

"But Martino, Fitzgerald and Murray would know others. The FBI could have gotten names from them."

"I don't believe those people know other members. They didn't come to our conventions, and they've never served as directors."

"But they had employees. They knew them."

"Yes, they knew their employees, and their employees donated 7.5%. The FBI probably questioned them, and they refused to talk."

God's Mafia

The FBI would consider such refusal to talk as *omerta*, Walker thought, the Mafia's code of silence. They'd conclude there'd be no point in continuing the questioning. Anyway, the government didn't need any more witnesses. They had three; they only needed two predicate acts under RICO. And, as for the charge of extortion, they needed only one, and they had three! Walker addressed Leahy. "Father, do you admit there is such a thing as the 'Ecumenical Society'?"

"I do."

"Do you admit there are 6,000 members?"

"There are many members, but please don't try to cross-examine me further." The priest spoke in a calm but firm, voice.

Walker had no intention of pressing Father Leahy further. He would build a defense for him without his help. "Father, I don't want to bother you. Is there anything more you would like to tell me with regard to the upcoming trial?"

"No." The priest's voice and demeanor were resigned, as if to say, "Let's get it over."

The following day, Angela Burgé came in. "Ms. Burgé," Walker asked, "supposedly there are 6,000 members in the Society, supposedly all with a history similar to yours. How many of those are likely to testify for the prosecution, and how many for us?"

"None of the members want to testify. Next to prison, the last place any of them ever want to see again is the courtroom. What's more, no one wants to break the code of silence. I don't know whether the government has contacted anyone, but I have talked with a few and I think I can convince them to testify. Joseph Carl for one. Arnold Rothstein is another. I am sure we could get several others. There are many who think as I do. We won't let Father Leahy or Reverend Hamilton go to prison."

While Walker was questioning Burgé, Janet came in and she joined the discussion. "Angela says she can get other members to testify," Walker told her.

"How many?" Janet asked.

"Conceivably we could produce a hundred witnesses. I don't know whether the other side has been able to get some members to testify. I hope to have a better idea about that after the pre-trial hearing, but by way of preparation we should prepare several possible witnesses."

Angela said, "It seems to me that the number of witnesses matters less than explaining what the Society really is, what it tries to do."

"Exactly," Janet exclaimed. "We need witnesses other than Angela to testify about the purpose of the Society and how it operates."

"The best man for that is Bob Nelson," Angela offered. "He is the guy who knows the concept and how it works. And Ben Schwartz, the financial brains."

Walker was already planning the pre-trial hearing, anxious to see how the court would handle the proceedings. If he was able to obtain hundreds of Society members to testify, Nagel would surely seek out others to testify in support of his present witnesses. Among 6,000 people surely there were some who would agree with Murray, Fitzpatrick and Martino! "How many defectors are there among the 6,000?" he asked Angela.

"People have dropped out of the Society from time to time. Our records indicate that 15% have left the Society. Of that 15% we can trace 5% back to prison. The other 10% we cannot account for. They may be leading lawful, constructive lives, or they may have returned to crime. We simply do not know. That's still a lot better than the 40% to 50% recidivists who go back to prison within 18 months of their release. That's the national average in the correctional systems throughout the country."

Those were figures Walker had not heard before. It was information which had to get into the record! These figures described not only what the defendants were doing, but proved that they were highly successful!

"Who has these figures?"

"Robert Nelson, our executive director."

"Where is he?"

"He's in the New York office."

"The New York office? Can you tell me more about that?" Angela Burgé told Walker about the operational headquarters of the Society. Walker wanted to know more, but she had to catch a plane back to Indianapolis, so the conference ended.

God's Mafia

As she left, she said to Janet, "Your father is a great man."

"Janet," Walker exclaimed after Angela had departed, "you were right. This case has national implications. Your father and his buddies, Leahy and Schwartz, have been helping to solve the crime problem in this country! They are reducing recidivism by almost 40%!"

"They are also saving souls," Janet added. "I'm telling you, Frank, I'm going to see to it that my father and his colleagues are recognized for what they are. They are pragmatic, down-to-earth evangelists — and they are ecumenical!"

Ben Schwartz called at Walker's office at three o'clock in the afternoon the following day. He was greeted by Walker and Wingate. "You wanted to see me?"

"Yes," Walker said, "It seem we have lots to learn about the Ecumenical Society. We must know all there is to know. Tell us about the office in New York."

"New York is the operational headquarters. That's where the business is managed."

"Why New York?"

"Because you can't hide that large an operation in Fairfield. Ours is a secret society. The office in New York is not one of those flashy Fifth Avenue palaces; it's in an old six story building. We occupy a small office on the fourth floor; there's no name on the door or foot traffic to the office. All transactions are by telephone or mail, except for the monthly board meetings. Each employer in the Society forwards to New York the money collected or owed by the usual banking procedures. All disbursements are made the same way."

"Why then are the trust funds in the Central Bank here in Fairfield?"

"That's where the trust was started, and that's where it has remained. The trust is managed by the bank and the money goes into the trust fund from the New York office. We make disbursements of large sums on loans or purchases directly from the trust fund but all operational expenses are paid out of the New York office."

"How did you manage to start this operation?"

"Father Leahy and Reverend Hamilton started it on a shoestring about five years before I arrived. It was little more than an idea when

I came along. I gave them the money to move it along."

"How much did you give them?"

"Over a period of three years between $500,000 and $600,000."

"Are you still giving them money?"

"No. They're independent."

"How much do you take in each year?"

"Around $11,000,000 from employees plus 7.5% from employers. That amount varies."

"Do you pay income tax on that?"

"No sir."

"Why not?"

"Because it is not earned income."

"Is a gift tax paid?"

"We structure the transfers so that there is no gift tax. We make no transfers greater than $10,000 each tax year for any one person or entity."

"So you take in $11,000,000 per year tax free?"

"That's right. We really take in more than that. The employers obviously pay 7.5% of much more than $25,000 or $30,000 per year."

"Have you ever been audited?"

"Yes. We pay income taxes on all earned income from investments, royalties, rents, etc."

"You passed IRS audits then?"

"So far. The IRS is not through with us."

"Have you ever been penalized or found to be owing taxes?"

"No sir."

Frank and Janet were startled by Schwartz' answers. "We have not always had this much income. Our growth has occurred in recent years. The operation is one that feeds on itself. The more members we take in the more money we get."

"You mean you have applicants?"

"I know only of one applicant. That is Joe Carl, one of our more successful members. All the others were recruited."

"Who does the recruiting?"

God's Mafia

"In the beginning Father Leahy and Reverend Hamilton did it all. Now we have employers who recruit for their staff."

"How do you determine whom to recruit?"

"That's one of our most difficult tasks. You see, this is not a reform movement in the sense usually associated with reform. Father Leahy and Reverend Hamilton discovered many people in prison who should not be there not because they weren't guilty of a crime, but because they were salvageable people, people who could be rehabilitated and made productive. The program has signed these people up and given them the chance to make as much of themselves as they wished in return for 7.5% of their net income This payment is not for dues; it is not an assessment or a fee. Because there is no promise of what will actually be done for the giver, there is no quid pro quo. You pay the money; you may be helped, or somebody else may be helped."

"How in the world do you manage to keep 85% of your people with that kind of set-up?"

"Well, they're not forced, you can be sure of that. Don't ask me to explain that to you. Ask those who have signed up and stayed on. Angela gave you a pretty good idea. Everything in the Society consider this 7.5% a moral obligation. It's what you would call a religious experience. This is not a cooperative! You give because you must; It's a moral imperative. But you receive only what you need! The genius is that this imperative comes in the context of repentance, of atonement and of redemption. If ever there was a case of moral rebirth this is it. The gift is not to the Society. It is to God! Talk to Bob Nelson about this. The 7.5% is analogous to Social Security. With Social Security, however, you are supposedly assured that in the future, in 30 years maybe, you will receive some benefits which will be helpful. With this 7.5%, if you have a need, help is offered now, not 30 years from now! Do you need a home, do you need a car, do you need help with drugs, do your children need an education? The Society helps now! And, remember, these people can't get help any place else. They have a criminal record. No bank will loan them money; no employer will give them a job. There are five, six, seven million unemployed people who have never been to prison. How does an ex-convict get a job? He doesn't.

He goes back to crime, then back to prison, in about 50% of the cases within 18 months of his release from prison. The Society even provided capital to start a business!"

Walker and Janet listened, spell bound. "This is impossible!" Janet said "You cannot provide everything. From ending drug addiction to capital to start a business. No institution can do that!"

"Exactly," Schwartz said, "it just doesn't seem possible. It is unbelievable. But it's working and, when you think about it there is a good economic basis for its working. It operates the same way ordinary insurance operates. Not everybody who pays a premium gets anything back on his insurance policy. People will insure their homes against fire and other losses for a lifetime and never collect a dime! Nobody complains about that. People buy term life insurance and after 20 years stop paying and get nothing. Nobody complains about that. Think of the millions of dollars paid in insurance premiums for which the payer gets nothing.

"In the Ecumenical Society, nobody is assured that he or she will ever get anything for their money. Then again they may get much more than they have paid, just as with insurance. It all depends on individual needs.

"However, there is also a vast difference between the Ecumenical Society and the regular society. The payment has no explanation or description in our legal system. Why does one pay? Because one must! One must because one is alive and has the blessings of God! The Society operates in a milieu which you cannot explain within our current social system. Again, Bob Nelson, our executive director and our in-house philosopher, can explain it better than I. But I must tell you that there is a marvelous fellowship among the members. They sustain each other and everyone takes personal pride when they see somebody succeed. Each has contributed to that person's success!"

"This is a huge anomaly," Walker observed. "It just doesn't seem possible that people who have committed crimes punishable by prison sentences would or could participate in such a highly religious operation and stay with it for years."

"There are incorrigible people in prison," Schwartz replied, "who cannot function in the world with other people. There is no hope for them. There are others who cannot cope although they are not necessarily incorrigible. And then there are people who are in prison more by circumstance than by their own pre-disposition. The kinds of people in prison are not much different from the kinds outside. We try to find who are, as we say, salvageable. They will need help, but we think they can make it. Certainly, no public program will help these people. Things like parole, probation, half-way houses, etc., are not enough. That's why so many who leave prison are back within two years. What's more, the public cannot afford a program like ours. It's extremely expensive. But the ex-convicts who pay for it feel a tremendous sense of achievement in this program. People who'd abandoned life or been abandoned feel they have achieved the impossible. Since it was done jointly, it makes for fellowship and great pride, which is what was needed all along."

Janet could hardly contain herself. She was joyful yet resentful. "Uncle Ben, how could you go on for so many years and keep all this a secret from me? My God, this is the greatest thing to happen this century, yet you and Father Leahy and my father have kept it such a secret. How could you?"

"Don't think the secret has been incidental to the program. The secret has been its foundation. Not only the lives of the members but the life of the Ecumenical Society was at stake. We could not become a public institution with the announced purpose of helping ex-convicts. We could not afford the responsibility any more than the Federal government or the states could afford it. Besides, the genius of the program is that it is self-help. It is not charity; it is not welfare. We believe that the program can exist only so long as it is private, belongs to the participants and is not considered charity sponsored by public or private funds. Think for a moment what it would be like if everyone knew there was a free rehab program for ex-prisoners. We couldn't cope with it financially; it would become just another half-way house, just an extension of a prison sentence."

Frank and Janet wanted to ask other questions but they were now so filled with wonderment that they had to take time out to gain a proper perspective of what was obviously more than a criminal case. It was a phenomenal movement which could change at least one aspect of life. Still, there was one more question Janet had to ask "Ben, do you think the Society can survive a trial, even if we win?"

Schwartz looked at both Walker and Janet and hesitated for a moment. "I don't think so. If we are completely successful, if we are totally vindicated, if we are lauded and praised, it will be the worst thing which could happen to us. Our program will become a public program. It will become a part of the 'correctional' system with all its flaws."

No one spoke for several moments. Finally, Walker said, "Catch-22."

Janet thought, "Paul Nagel." As she thought of how what Ben Schwartz verbalized coincided with Nagel's beliefs, she wondered if Nagel might be convinced to simply drop the case. "Why don't we go to Nagel, show him what we have and ask him to just drop the case?"

Walker shook his head. "There's no way the government can drop this case. Not only has there been a lot of publicity, the secret we expose will have no effect on Washington. Factually, our clients are guilty! They have forced people to give them money which they have put into private businesses. The moral considerations, the statistical benefit vis-à-vis recidivism are no defense. But a jury will consider those factors and be persuaded in spite of the legalisms. More than that, for Nagel to drop this case in its present status would indicate a deal which would be panned royally by the media."

"The media is not the trier of this case," Janet shot back.

"Of course not. But it makes a judgment anyway and under the circumstances known to the public, it would be outraged if the case were dismissed. The Department of Justice must consider public reaction. The people determine what it can do."

TWELVE

"We've got to alert the membership without causing panic." Janet said to Walker the next day. The membership had been alerted that Leahy and Hamilton had been indicted. Janet now felt they should be told that their secret was going to be revealed in court.

"How do you tell almost 6,000 people without making public what Ben calls the foundation of the Society?" asked Walker.

"It's not possible," Janet said. "There is no time to speak to each person; you cannot send a letter that says your secret will be revealed in court so you'd better tell your spouse about your past. Can you imagine a woman telling to her husband, 'I work for a company that hires only ex-prostitutes. I was once a prostitute!'" Janet shook her head as she spoke. "Father was right. There is no way this secret can be told."

"Angela must testify that all her employees were prostitutes," Walker argued. "That fact exemplifies the purpose and the philosophy of the entire operation. We will try to get the prosecution's case dismissed so that it will not be necessary for her to testify. If we don't prevail in that motion we'll put into evidence everything we can get and hope for the best.

"Your father was right, Janet, when he said it would be possible to try this case and not reveal the secret. If neither the prosecution nor the defense knew the secret it would not come out in the trial, but then the verdict would be 'guilty,' which is all right with the defendants!"

"I must stay away from my father." Janet was on the verge of tears again. "I won't be able to restrain myself. I'll either blurt out the secret or I'll hold him tight and have an awful cry."

Walker could say nothing to that. It struck him that Leahy and Hamilton were saints. Without further discussion they continued with their respective tasks: Janet writing "hoped for" testimony and the story of her father as best she could; Walker thinking through and writing the legal rationale of their defense.

It was after five o'clock when Walker put down his pen. Janet was still writing. "Isn't it time to feed your family?" he asked.

"Oh my gosh!" Janet exclaimed and reached for the phone. There was no answer at her home. She called her parents.

"The boys are with us," her mother said. "I picked them up and brought them over. I'm about to feed them."

"I'm sorry, mother. I was running late but got no answer when I called to tell them."

"Why don't you come here, too?" This had been happening for years. Grandma would pick up the boys and take them to her house and Janet would join them later.

Not this time. "If you don't mind, mother, Mr. Walker and I are working on the case and we should stick with it for a while longer."

"I know you have been busy. The boys can stay here tonight. But you should go home and get some sleep."

"I will probably be here another hour, maybe two. I'll see you tomorrow." After hanging up, Janet looked at Walker. "Frank, I feel terrible. I feel like I'm double-crossing my father. I'm lying."

The attorney rose from his chair, walked over to Janet and lifted her out of her chair and into his arms. He held her tightly and she clung to him. "I don't want to compound your lie," he said several minutes later, "but we are not working any more tonight." He picked up the telephone and ordered dinner delivered to his office. Then he took Janet by the hand and led her into the reception room. He sat beside her on a full-sized couch and held both her hands in his. The room was dimly lit by the setting sun which shone through the window. It was so still they could hear each other breathe.

"Don't let this get you down," he said. "We've found a way out; we can't let our emotions beat us."

"I know," she whispered, "but I'm just beginning to understand my father. We cannot let him go to prison, but what is important to him are the lives of 6,000 people, not his own life. Mother must have been in on this scheme all along. She knows that my father is ready to sacrifice himself, and she is not about to cross him as I am preparing to do."

"Janet, you know that your father will be saved if we tell it all, even if he is found technically guilty."

She smiled wryly. "In the end I hope he will understand why we did what we did."

She got to her feet just as the meals were delivered to the front door. Walker greeted the caterer, paid him and carried the food to the library. He quickly cleared the library table and spread a table cloth over it. He placed napkins and silverware delivered by the caterer on the table, he then walked over to where Janet waited and escorted her into the library. "My dear lady," he announced, "I offer you herewith the best dinner in the most private dining room in Fairfield."

"You are very sweet, Frank, but I'm just not with it tonight. I'm very sorry."

He helped her to a seat and then seated himself opposite her. She sat stock still. Walker waited for a moment, then said, "I thought you were a fighter. You talked a great fight earlier today. Are you surrendering already?"

Janet looked up. "Oh, I'll fight. I'll fight our enemy. It just breaks my heart that I have to fight my father too."

"You are not fighting your father. You are saving everything he's given his life to build. Let's not get sentimental and blow it."

Janet picked up a fork and placed it on her plate. "You really care, don't you, Frank?"

"I care more about this case, about you, about your family than I've ever cared about anything in my life."

"Why? Why should you take this so personally?"

"You know, you are about the most cynical person I've ever known. You don't trust anybody, least of all me."

"It is not that I don't trust you, Frank. It's that there seems to be no place in life for the things my father and Father Leahy believe. You are kind but I'm sure this is all strange and silly to you."

Walker slammed his fork on the table. "How can any man love

you? You just won't believe somebody who has tried to tell you he cares. What in the world do you expect?"

"I'm sorry, Frank. I'm afraid to expect anything; I'm afraid to love. When a man like my father is accused of being a criminal, a racketeer, an exploiter, then the whole world has changed and everybody is an alien."

"Janet, please. Don't panic. You did so well when we had nothing; now that we can win, you're losing it. Come on, snap out of it! If you don't believe I love you now, eventually you will know better."

"Frank, I want to go home."

"You are not going home. I will not let you stay home alone, and I won't let your sons see you in your present state. You'll stay here with me until you shape up. This is not like you, Janet. What is it? Is it something I have done?"

She stared at him. For a moment she was her old self. "Yes, Frank, it is what you have done. In the midst of this horrible mess you have been too wonderful to be true. I haven't dared take you seriously. Believe me, I've wanted to but I don't even trust myself."

Rising, he walked over to Janet and took her in his arms. This time the kiss was real. He showered her with kisses without saying a word, and she went limp. He could do as he pleased. Finally, an arm encircled him. Then she returned the kisses. She ran her hand through his hair and talked over his shoulder. "Frank, I warned you to be careful, said you might start something you couldn't get out of. I think you've done it."

Frank pulled her back. "That's more like it. You and I are one. We'll live with this together, and after this we'll stay that way."

Janet reached for him, pulled him to her. "I'm human, Frank. Maybe I'm weak, but I need you."

"You are human, thank God, but you aren't weak. I need you just as much as you need me."

Exhausted Janet lay down on the couch and was very quickly asleep. Walker cleared the table. Most of the food was still on the plates. He put it all together in a bowl, gathered up the table setting and then returned to the reception room and sat on the floor beside Janet. He watched as she slept and was soon asleep leaning against the couch.

God's Mafia

It was nearly three in the morning when Janet awoke. For a moment she was startled. She saw Walker, now awake, gazing at her. "I must get home," she exclaimed.

"You can go now," Walker said.

She tried to straighten her dress and her hair. Frank took her in his arms again and kissed her, but she was anxious to get home. She dashed out to her car, leaving him at the door. Walker wondered if anybody had noticed. He decided he didn't care.

Janet's trip home was brief, but she was awake. She recalled the tender moments of the embrace, how she felt so secure in his arms, how she had finally embraced him. There had been room on the couch for him, but he had slept on the floor. Why hadn't he lain beside her? Why hadn't he tried to seduce her? Yes, this guy was for real.

"He really loves me," she realized. "I'm not just a sex object." And then Paul Nagel popped into her head. "Are you in for a surprise Paul! It won't be long before you learn the truth about my father and his co-conspirator. You think you're God? You are going to learn all about God!"

Thinking deeper, she decided she was really sorry for Paul Nagel. He was no fake. He was real, too. But he was wrong. She would show him he was wrong. She shook her head. How could she show him? She wasn't trying the lawsuit. It didn't matter who was trying the lawsuit. It was her fight. She was orchestrating it, directing it. "Help me, God," she moaned as she squeezed the steering wheel.

Janet was back in Walker's office at eleven o'clock the following morning after stopping at her office. Walker was in court, but when he returned he joined her in the library. He approached from behind, put a hand on each shoulder and kissed her neck, saying nothing.

Janet took his hand and turned to greet him. "Now that we aren't worried about the secret, should we have Schwartz testify? And Nelson, who seems to be the resident thinker?"

"I'm going to raise the question of witnesses at the pre-trial conference," Walker told her.

"But we can't wait for that hearing," Janet responded. "We've got to line up these witnesses as soon as possible. According to Angela we should also have Rothstein and Carl, whoever they are."

"We'll interview them as soon as possible, but remember, we may have a hundred witnesses. We don't know how many Nagel will have."

At the pre-trial hearing, Judge Ron Kowalski made it clear that he did not intend for the trial to become a media showpiece. "This case now has national attention," he announced. "We will be watched every moment for any little piece of the unusual. Let's make it short and sweet. How long will the trial take?"

Nagel said, "It can be very brief, as far as I am concerned. I will have fewer than ten witnesses."

"How about you, Walker?"

"I'll settle for that number."

Judge Kowalski said, "If there are going to be more witnesses by either side, I want to know as soon as possible."

"We are trying a case in which we are concerned about patterns, patterns of racketeering, and so forth. What constitutes a pattern?" Walker asked. "How many incidents demonstrate a pattern? Two or three, five or a hundred?"

"A pattern isn't necessarily proven by the number of witnesses. It can be demonstrated by one witness," Nagel said with authority.

"How do you do that?" Walker asked.

The judge interrupted with a smile. "With some judicially approved hearsay!"

"Hearsay?" Walker was astonished.

"The court is telling you, Frank, that under RICO the courts have taken some liberties with the rules of evidence." Nagel was terse. "I don't need a pattern for the count on extortion, and I only need two acts on a liquor charge, and I have three. The transportation of liquor is a predicate act under RICO."

Walker was skeptical. "Your basic charge is the placing of ill-gotten money with legitimate businesses. Don't you need a pattern for that?"

"The statute specifically requires that we prove two acts of racketeering as defined in the Act. An extortionate credit transaction is specially defined as racketeering and we consider 7.5% of one's income plus bank rate interest on each loan extortionate. We need prove only two acts. We have three." Nagel was his usual didactic self in expounding on the law.

"Your Honor," Walker continued, "we will offer testimony which will show that other people willingly paid the interest charged as well as the 7.5%. We contend that there are many more who have done so. If we are talking about racketeering and we have only three out of a hundred or several hundred, is it still racketeering?"

"The test," Nagel answered, "is whether the victim could reasonably believe, under the circumstances, that he was being extorted. If only one person has the perception the jury must determine in the light of the surrounding circumstances whether that is a reasonable perception. It is not the intent of the person who got the money or the number of people who gave the money."

Judge Kowalski looked at the indictment. "I see three counts here. One is for extortion, one is sale of drugs and the third is conspiracy. Don't you have to show a pattern somewhere? Why does the statute speak of a pattern of racketeering?"

"We must show either a pattern of racketeering or the collection of an unlawful debt," Nagel said.

"If it is your claim that your case is only for collection of an unlawful debt I must reserve the right to make a motion to dismiss, because there is no way you can make a case for an unlawful debt." Walker offered.

"I don't need to prove an unlawful debt to prove extortion. I don't need a pattern to make out a case of extortion."

Walker turned to face the judge. "Well, Your Honor, I can produce 5,997 people, all those in the Ecumenical Society, except for Nagel's witnesses, who will testify that they were not extorted."

"It is not how other people feel," Nagel objected. "It is how these three witnesses feel. None of the others can testify. If ten people are hoodwinked out of their money and only one complains, is it a defense that the others don't complain?"

"Let's not forget the purpose, the reason for RICO, is to stop racketeering and organized crime. For that matter, if Mr. Nagel wants to enforce only the Hobbs Act, we must still consider whether the Act is to be enforced to punish people who are doing nothing to help organized crime and which will not necessarily affect organized crime."

Nagel raised his voice. "I don't have to connect organized crime or demonstrate that organized crime has anything to do with this case. Anybody, even priests and ministers, yes, even churches, can be liable."

"Will somebody please tell me how all this relates to this lawsuit?" Judge Kowalski asked.

"We are talking about whether the testimony of other members of the Society is admissible to prove a defense in this case," Nagel offered.

"I'm glad you have raised this question here," the judge said. I would not like to face this in the midst of a trial. I'm going to give you my present opinion on this question, and if the other side wants to argue it before trial I'll be glad to listen.

"Two men are charged with a very serious crime. The case arises in a context which cannot be ignored. I don't think I can prevent the defense from producing whatever evidence they can offer to prove the absence of criminal intent. It may be, and probably is, their only defense. I cannot preclude them from introducing such evidence as they wish to prove their innocence. But 6,000 people? I'll tell you it won't be 6,000 people! I'll listen to any testimony from any knowledgeable person as to the membership and operations of any groups which claimed to be a part of this general operation."

Walker was able to report to Janet that they would be able to use the testimony of their witnesses.

Nagel called in Wicker and Draefus as soon as he returned to his office from the pre-trial hearing. "Did we ever consider trying to find other members of the Ecumenical Society?" he asked.

"No," Draefus replied, "why would we?"

"Judge Kowalski is going to permit other members to testify that they paid their 7.5% and were only too happy to do so."

"And that is a possible defense?" Wicker asked rhetorically.

"The judge feels that because of the religious background of the case, testimony should be allowed describing the operations that might bear on the intent of the organization."

"But that is self-serving," Wicker argued. "The complainants don't want to belong to any society, or pay any 7.5%. It's no defense that somebody else pays willingly. Do we have to take a vote to see whether the majority pay only because they must to keep their jobs?"

"So, Judge Kowalski would send to the jury the question of whether this whole operation was a plot to extort or a charity of some kind," Draefus thought as he talked.

"That doesn't make any sense and I know that's not what the judge is thinking," Wicker interjected. "He just doesn't want to leave any door open for an appeal. He is going to let them tell whatever story they want. At least, then, there can be no appeal on a question of evidence."

"Unless we should appeal on precisely that question," Draefus remarked rather casually.

"That will never happen. If we lose there will be no appeal. You know that." Nagel headed for the coffee pot as he spoke. "Nor will we make a motion to reconsider. I know Kowalski. He won't change his mind."

As he sat alone in his apartment that night Paul Nagel was in distress. As Janet anguished about her father, he anguished about her. What had this crusade of his cost him? Was it worth it? He was right, so what? Crime was still rampant, evil had taken on a holy form, and the court was going to aid that cause. What was it to him? For the first time in his life he had found someone he could love. And it was not to happen. He must sacrifice it for his crusade. Crusade! Whose crusade? Only his! Everyone else would stay on the sidelines and cheer — or boo. It occurred to him that his crusade had been his whole life. Nothing else had mattered. He had given away almost everything he had to Bryan Dibble and a host of others. He had never done anything else. What were his hobbies? There were none. When had he traveled? Never. He didn't know how to play golf, how to hunt or fish. He recalled his childhood, his parents. How angry he had been, how determined and now look at him! He was a freak. Even in the eyes of the woman he now wanted more than anything else, he was a freak!

Where were his school companions? His law school classmates? Working hard? Yes, but also enjoying life. Damn!

A small, quiet voice within seemed to speak to him. "Remember, you never wanted adulation. All your good deeds must always remain secret and without reward. Nothing you did was to be attributed to you, for if it was it would cheapen what you did. You have paid a high price for your way of life. Only now, when you have lost the only thing you have ever really wanted, have you realized the price you've paid. For what?"

Where to go from here? There was no choice. If he did not win this case — worse, if he dropped this case, the horrible price he'd paid would be for nothing! It suddenly came to him that he was about to fight his last battle!

THIRTEEN

Walker and Janet took statements from fifteen members of the Ecumenical Society and all agreed to testify if called. Among them were Joseph Carl and Arnold Rothstein. In addition, it was agreed that Schwartz and Nelson would testify. With their testimony the nature of the Ecumenical Society would be shown.

At last, everything was coming to a head! Jury selection went rapidly. Fourteen persons were sworn, two of whom would be eliminated after the trial.

The opening statement for the prosecution was made by Paul Nagel. "Ladies and gentlemen of the jury, the case for the prosecution is very simple. It is brought under the federal *Racketeer Influenced and Corrupt Organization Act,* Sections 1961 to 1968, Title 18 of the United States code. It is better known as RICO. This is a law passed by Congress in 1970 for the purpose of stopping money derived from crime from going into legitimate business and thus supporting crime syndicates. What you are about to hear is the cleverest scheme yet devised to do exactly what the Act was intended to prevent. These Defendants concocted a scheme to hide their operation in the cloak of the church. Mr. Hamilton, one of these defendants, is a Presbyterian Minister. The other, Father Patrick Leahy, is a Roman Catholic priest. They organized what they call the 'Ecumenical Society' as a religious organization, recruited persons about to leave prison and enrolled them in this so-called religious society and promised them a job in return for 7.5% of their wages. This 7.5% is deducted from the employees' paycheck and forwarded to the Ecumenical Society which then makes the money available for the financing and operations of private businesses owned by insiders in the Society, some of them Directors of the Society. And they have done very well indeed. They have accumulated over $20,000,000 in addition to money which they have loaned to these various private businesses. The Directors are now all multi-millionaires, all are ex-convicts with records. And this has been going on for 30 years! We caught up with this racket only because three of the members got caught selling drugs and they have agreed to testify here in this case.

"The recruiting is done very carefully. Only those with potential are chosen and they are actually trained and rehabilitated before they are put to work. The prisoners are desperate. They need work and they know they will not be able to get it elsewhere. And so they agree to this extortion 7.5% of their pay forever, or as long as they work. If they quit paying they lose their jobs. This is the best, or worst, 'protection' racket I have ever encountered.

"How did the defendants benefit from this operation? Frankly, we don't know. It is not always possible to show how anybody benefits from crime, but that does not change matters. We don't have to show how they benefited. We don't have to show they had a connection with organized crime. We will show that these two men organized the scheme and are still the over-all guides of the operation.

"You are going to hear a lot about God in this trial. Listen carefully, because God has long been used as an excellent cover for scams. We claim that this is what the defendants have concocted here. Don't be fooled by the pious pronouncements. Listen for the facts. All you need to decide is whether the complainants in this case have been forced to pay money just to keep their jobs or their businesses."

Walker noted that in his last exhortation Nagel said nothing about the sale of drugs. When the court asked if he wanted to make his opening statement, Walker thought it best to wait until he'd heard Nagel's case. "No, Your Honor," he said, rising halfway from his chair.

The first witness called by Nagel was James Murray, a short, red-faced, balding man, nattily dressed. "Please give us your full name and address, Mr. Murray," Nagel said.

"James Murray, Federal Penitentiary, Milan, Michigan."

"Will you please tell the jury the nature of your work, if any, and how long you have been engaged in it."

"I was the owner of Apex Drug Company, a distributor of prescription drugs, patented medicines and non-prescription drugs. I bought at jobber prices and sold wholesale to various drug stores throughout my area. I warehoused merchandise and distributed it. I had my own trucks and I also did some business by mail. I employed warehousemen and truck drivers and office personnel, a total of perhaps 50 people. I was in business for 15 years."

"Mr. Murray, you were a defendant, were you not, in the case of People vs. Murray which was tried in the Federal District Court?"

"Yes."

"And you were convicted of selling something other than what you just described?"

"Yes."

"Can you tell us what that was?"

"Cocaine."

"Did you receive a sentence for that?"

"Yes, ten years."

"Are you currently serving that term, that sentence?"

"Yes."

"Witness, do you know either one of the defendants?"

"Yes, I know both of them."

"What has been your relation with them?"

"I had a previous conviction for mail fraud, and I was serving time in prison when Mr. Hamilton visited me while I was still in prison and told me he wanted to help me."

"When was that?"

"About 15 years ago."

"What happened after that first conference?"

"He told me that he had been a prison chaplain and that he knew what it was like to be a prisoner. He also knew what it was like to be an ex-convict, because he had followed up on several of the men he had met in prison. He told me that he thought he could help me if I would cooperate."

"And what happened after that?"

"He and Father Leahy and some other people helped me start my business. They were able to help me borrow the money necessary to establish the business and for several years they provided me with operating capital. I borrowed from them extensively and I always paid the loans."

"And what were you to do in return for that?"

"I was to pay 7.5% of my net income into what they call their Ecumenical Fund. Each of my employees was to pay a similar amount. My employees were also to be ex-convicts."

"And what were you to get for that?"

"I was loaned the money to start my business. I borrowed $50,000 at 10% interest payable in 5 years. I used the money to lease trucks and to buy product. I catered to small independent drug stores and I competed with large wholesalers by working 16 hours a day, doing all my own driving and employing only one other person and a bookkeeper. As agreed, I hired ex-convicts. In fact, Reverend Hamilton got them for me. I did pretty well by working hard but as I got bigger my expenses got bigger and the competition got tougher. I thought I could make it by dealing hard drugs. Well, I got caught."

"Were you able to pay the 7.5%?"

"As long as I was making money I could do it. When the going got tough I was able to pay only at the cost of something else. But my employees always paid. I deducted it from their pay and sent it to the Ecumenical Society."

"Did you ever fail to pay the 7.5%?"

"No sir."

"Did you ever ask for relief from paying?"

"No sir."

"Why not."

The witness smiled. "Nobody failed to pay. Everybody paid, even when the going got tough. We were tied to them. We owed them a great deal of money and we had to have money to operate. We could not borrow at a bank or anyplace else. Remember, we all had criminal records. We were a captive market for the Society."

"After your original association with these defendants, but before this last conviction, did you have some other trouble with the law?"

"Yes I was arrested for running drugs. The case was dropped because of insufficient evidence."

"Was your money cut off?"

"No. They threatened to cut me off, but I told them I made a mistake and it wouldn't happen again, so they continued to finance me."

"As a matter of fact, you got in trouble with the law after that and this time you were convicted were you not?"

"Yes I received a light sentence. I promised Reverend Hamilton that it would never happen again and so they put me on their books again and loaned me money and helped me reestablish my business."

"So, both defendants knew that from time to time you had been selling drugs and they still helped you. Is that correct?"

"Yes."

"Mr. Martino and Mr. Fitzpatrick have also recently been convicted for peddling drugs, is that correct?"

"Yes. We're all a part of the organization of Father Leahy and Mr. Hamilton We've all contributed to them and we've borrowed money from them and we've always exchanged information."

"You mean the Ecumenical Society?"

"Yes."

"Didn't your employees sign an authorization card authorizing you to deduct 7.5% from their pay checks?"

"Yes sir. But if they didn't sign they wouldn't get the job. We had to furnish the Society the names and addresses of all our employees and copies of the authorization cards. If they did not sign we could lose our financing too. We also had to furnish copies of the discharges or paroles from prison. The only way for the employer to protect himself was to fire the employee who refused to pay the 7.5%."

"Did you ever figure what you paid for your loans when you add the 7.5% of your net income and the interest you paid on your loan?"

"Well, if we did not show a profit we were audited. If no profit was shown after two years we had to pay 7.5% of the cash flow."

"On average, what did you owe the Ecumenical Society?"

"I would average $100,000 annually."

"And what interest did you pay?"

"I paid anywhere from 8% to 14%, depending on the rate charged by banks, usually 12%."

"When you had an average year what might your net income be?"

"$150,000."

"So, if you paid 7.5% of $150,000, plus 10% on your loan. You would pay annually $11,250 plus $12,000 or $23,250 for the use of $100,000?"

"I guess that's right."

"That's about 23% per annum. Isn't that right?"

"I guess so."

"Mr. Murray, was it not possible for you to borrow $100,000 at 10% from somebody else?"

"No sir."

"Did you try?"

"Yes sir."

"Did you deduct the 7.5% from your income tax payment as a donation?"

"No sir."

"Why not?"

"I was told by the Society that I was not to deduct it and I was told by my accountant that the Society was not recognized as a 'charitable organization'."

"So what else did you get for this 7.5%?"

"Nothing."

"You got no training, no education, no rehabilitation?"

"No sir."

"Were you ever to be repaid the 7.5%?"

"No sir."

"Did you acquire any interest in anything with any part of that money?"

"No sir."

"For how many years have you been paying?"

"Almost 15 years."

"At an average of $11,000 per year?"

"Not quite. More like $9,000."

"A total of $135,000?"

"I guess so."

"I have no further questions."

As Murray's testimony concluded, Janet winced. Instinctively, her shoulders raised and her head lowered. It all sounded so devastating.

Walker began his cross-examination. "Mr. Murray, how long had you been in prison when Reverend Hamilton came to see you?"

"Five years."

"And this was your second or third time?"

"Second."

"What did you intend to do now that you were about to leave prison?"

"I was going to look for a job."

"Is that what you did when you got out of prison the first time?"

"Yes."

"Did you find a job?"

"No."

"So, what did you do?"

"I tried to do some business on my own."

"Did you succeed?"

"No."

"And so you were soon back in prison, right?"

"Yes."

"When Reverend Hamilton offered you a job, you didn't have to take it, did you?"

"No."

"In fact, he offered you more than a job. He offered to start you in business."

"That's right."

"And you took him up on it, and you operated a business for 15 years."

"That's right."

"And that was the only time you ever owned anything of your own, isn't that right?"

"Right."

"You didn't mind paying that 7.5% then did you? You were glad to pay it and you paid for many years. Isn't that so?"

"I don't know that I did it gladly, but I did it. I had no choice. Nobody else would even give me a job."

"But you didn't try to get a job elsewhere once Reverend Hamilton talked to you. If the deal seemed such a bad one, why didn't you try something else?"

"I knew it would be almost impossible for me to get a job."

"As a matter of fact, you were really shocked to think that somebody like you, somebody nobody else would even hire, would be offered capital to start a business, were you not? For 15 years it never occurred to you, however, that you were being robbed of your money, did it? During those 15 years surely you could have found money elsewhere. You were now a well-established businessman. But you never even tried."

"I told you I didn't try. Even after that 15 year period I could not have gotten money someplace else."

Walker approached the witness. "And you knew from experience that if you were a two-time loser nobody would give you work or money."

"I've already told you that I had no choice but to take up his offer. I didn't want to do that. I had to!"

"This money you got by way of capital and for operations, was that not a part of the money others paid just as you had?"

"I don't know where the money came from."

"Do you have any evidence or any reason to conclude the money came from any other source?"

"No sir."

"Did not other members of the Ecumenical Society pay the same 7.5% and borrow money on the same terms you did?"

"I suppose they did."

"You are now serving ten years in prison, are you not?"

"Yes."

"And that is a reduced sentence because you agreed to come here to give this testimony, is that right?"

"Yes."

Walker announced he was through with his cross-examination.

Nagel was brief with re-direct. "You testified you entered into a plea bargain as a result of which you gave the testimony which you have just given. Is what you have testified to true of your own knowledge and belief?"

"It is."

"Were there not times when you paid more than 12% interest on loans?"

"I have paid as much as 23% on loans."

"And that was in addition to the 7.5%?"

"Yes sir."

"You testified that the defendants did not supervise your liquor business. Is it not a fact that they never supervised any aspect of your business. Was it not true that you operated your business without any direction from the Ecumenical Society?"

"That's right."

"But after you were convicted of drug running didn't they know about it?"

"Yes."

"And did they loan you money when they knew you had dealt in drugs?"

"Yes."

"I have no further questions," Nagel said.

"I have no questions," Walker echoed.

FOURTEEN

The next witness was Joseph Martino. His story was almost exactly the same as Murray's. He testified that he was recruited by Father Leahy. Convicted of larceny, when he had about six months to go before his release, Father Leahy came to the prison where he was incarcerated and told him the same story that Reverend Hamilton had told Murray. He too, was loaned money to start up a business on the same terms and conditions which had been offered to Murray. He testified that shortly after he had started a home repair business he met Murray at one of the semi-annual meetings of the Ecumenical Society. Their businesses had nothing in common except that they were financed by the same source and they were both members of the same society. Martino also paid 7.5% of his net income, as did his employees. He had about 25 employees comprised of eight work crews who worked as teams.

Next to testify was Fitzgerald. He too was in the drug distributing business through which he had become acquainted with Murray. They did business with each other, and they exchanged information. Fitzgerald was also approached in prison by Reverend Hamilton and was made the same proposition on the same terms. He worked with the society until he returned to the narcotics business, a step which he now regretted and called a mistake.

All three witnesses testified that they had participated in the sale of drugs but without the knowledge of either of the defendants. They were nevertheless sure that the defendants had known about their drug dealings and had made loans and advanced funds with that knowledge. Each acknowledged that they had paid the 7.5% because it was the only way they could start and continue in business and that they would have preferred not to pay but had no choice. They continued to pay for fear they would be put out of business.

Each of the three principal witnesses for the prosecution testified that he was aware that there was a Board of Directors which guided the destiny of the so-called Society. They admitted that the employers chose this board but none of them had ever participated in choosing the board or in serving on the board. Although there were meetings of the Society twice a year, none had attended more than one or two meetings throughout their association with the Society. Murray had been with the Society 15 years, Fitzgerald ten years and Martino three. Each had made a plea bargain and had pled guilty to various charges and got reduced sentences in exchange for their testimony in this case.

The cross-examinations of Martino and Fitzgerald were similar to that of Murray.

The next morning, promptly at nine o'clock, the Judge rapped the gavel and asked Mr. Nagel for his next witness. Roger Morton was called to the witness stand. He identified himself as an examiner employed by the United States Internal Revenue Service. Asked if he had ever examined the income tax returns of the Ecumenical Society or conducted an audit, the witness testified: "I have examined several income tax returns by the Ecumenical Society and I have conducted audits. Our attention was called to this particular tax payer because it was not incorporated and it was never formally identified as an association, a joint-venture or any other of the usual business associations. We were also impressed by its rapid growth in recent years. We have gone over their returns from year to year and we have also conducted audits as best we could, although we are never satisfied that we had conducted a thorough audit."

"Will you please tell the jury what you learned by examining the returns and also by your audits, if anything?"

"We found that all taxes were always paid. We found no trace of any evasion of taxes or even any deficiencies which could be argued about. They paid taxes on all income received from all sources which they claim to be mainly dividends and interest and sometimes rents.

We find the association to be operating for over 30 years and in the last five years it has grown more than it had in the entire 25 years previously. Its income has increased rapidly and its cash reserves have increased as well."

Nagel arose from his chair and walked to the witness stand. "In the course of your examinations and your audit were you able to determine if this tax payer had a net worth?"

The witness responded: "Oh yes, it has a net worth of at least $20,000,000."

"And were you able to determine the source of that money? Do you know where it came from?"

"A great deal came from excellent investment practices."

Nagel pushed on. "From your examination of the tax returns and the income that appeared thereon and your review of their operations over a period of years could you justify their net worth on the basis of the income they had received over a period of years?"

"It is quite evident that although their income was excellent the assets of the company could not be said to have grown exclusively out of income."

"Why didn't you make an assessment of taxes due on the basis of net worth if the income seemed insufficient to explain the accumulation?"

"Sir, we are still trying to determine the source of the so-called donations. As to that question, the Society has refused to cooperate. They claim these are private donations, that they are sworn to secrecy, and they refused to tell us anything more."

"Well, surely the IRS doesn't quit just because somebody refuses to answer questions."

"No. We will be proceeding with our investigation. As you know, Mr. Nagel, the Attorney General is also investigating."

"What are you looking for?"

"Well, we have a right to question where all the money came from. We're told that, in part, it comes from donations. In our examinations of the tax returns of Murray, Martino and Fitzpatrick we found that no deductions were taken for those donations. So, we're having a little difficulty justifying our investigations. We cannot claim that we

God's Mafia

have lost revenue because of improper deductions, and we are hard pressed to show that the money claimed to be donations were in fact income to the recipients. There does not appear to be any consideration for the transfer of funds to the Society. That is, there is no apparent service or goods given to the donor. After all, if somebody wants to give money to somebody else and not deduct the gift from his income he can do it."

"What about gift taxes?"

"The transfers of funds which we checked were for less than the annual exclusion of $10,000."

"So, this so-called Society amasses millions of dollars and you can't find any legitimate source for the money except donations and you do not pursue the accumulation of the $20,000,000 any further. That's quite a deal for somebody, isn't it? Twenty million dollars and no income tax!"

"Taxes were paid on what we could determine to have been received as interest or dividends or rents or other legitimate sources of income. but that income was not enough to account for $20,000,000."

"Mr. Morton, can you tell this jury how the $20,000,000 was accumulated?"

"No sir."

"Then, why don't you make an assessment based on net worth?"

"We may do that. I guess we are waiting to see how you make out."

Nagel paused, looked at some notes on his desk. "I have no further questions of this witness."

Walker was on his feet immediately. "Witness, how long have you been with the IRS?"

"Fifteen years."

"Have you been conducting audits during most of that time?"

"About half that time."

"During your examination, did you receive cooperation from the Society's representatives?"

"Yes. Except when we tried to learn more about the donations and they refused to talk about them."

"Did they tell you why they refused to talk about the donations?"

"They simply said it was secret and confidential and they could not talk about it."

"On all other matters did they cooperate?"

"Yes sir."

"And did you find anything wrong with their records?"

"No sir."

"Was any assessment made for taxes due or any fine imposed?"

"No sir."

"Except for the claimed secrecy on donations did you have an idea, impression or suspicion that any attempt had been made to hide income or otherwise evade taxes?"

"No sir."

"Did you ask why the subject matter of donations was secret and not to be discussed?"

"Well, yes. We were surprised. And we asked a very simple question: 'Why the secrecy?' We understand those donations were not claimed as deductions. What was there to hide?"

"And the answer?"

"They said they were not hiding anything. They simply were abiding by an agreement among all givers that the donations would be secret."

Walker approached the witness. "Is there anything illegal about a gift?"

"I'm not a lawyer," the witness responded. "I'm an accountant."

"From the standpoint of the IRS, is there any violation of the tax code if one simply gives something away?"

"There may be. The gift might be subject to tax."

"To be paid by whom?"

"By the giver."

"But the Ecumenical Society would not be subject to such a tax, would it?"

"No."

"So, Mr. Morton, when you say that you are continuing your investigation of the donations, if you find that any tax might be due, it would not be the liability of the Society or of these defendants, would it?"

"It would not. But we are still faced with the large accumulation of money. We are satisfied it was not all earned."

Walker now turned to the jury while questioning the witness. "But the accumulation resulted from gifts plus income, isn't that correct?"

"Obviously. But when these people refuse to explain the accumulation we must try to find out how the accumulation was achieved. We are sure that the Society has the names of those who made donations but they refuse to show them to us."

Walker turned and looked directly at the witness. "As I understand it, you could, at this point, without further information, make an assessment simply on the basis of the accumulation. Why haven't you done so?"

"As I indicated, because we want to see how this case comes out. It may answer the question of whether we should proceed further. In any event what happens in this case will be very helpful to us."

"That's all the questions I have of this witness," Walker announced, and he sat down.

Nagel rose. "Call Harold Sutherland."

A man, in his thirties walked to the witness stand with a briefcase in his hand. He was well over six feet tall, very well dressed and self-composed.

Nagel started the questioning. "Will you please give us your full name, address and your occupation."

The witness responded by saying, "I am Harold Sutherland. I am an FBI agent and I reside in Washington."

"Were you asked to conduct a surveillance of the defendants in this case?"

"Yes I was directed by the department to go to Fairfield to conduct a general surveillance of the defendants, including electronic wiretap."

"Was that wiretap authorized by a court?"

"Yes, and I have with me a copy of the court's order." Sutherland took out a document and handed it to Nagel, and Nagel gave it to Walker for his review.

Walker handed it back to Nagel, who now addressed the witness.

"Did you make a recording of any conversations among these defendants?"

"Yes."

"Can you tell us when, where and how it was made? Pursuant to that court order what arrangements did you make for the tap?"

"We inserted a live microphone in a telephone and asked the telephone company to replace the phones in the Hamilton home and in the Catholic Parish house. We also placed devices in the rooms."

Walker expected this and knew he couldn't keep the jury from hearing the recording. It would be better to be nonchalant and give the jury the impression the tape was inconsequential.

Nagel then asked the witness to play the recording, which prompted Sutherland to reach into his briefcase and pull out a cassette player. At a volume loud enough for everyone in the courtroom to hear, the voices of Father Leahy, Reverend Hamilton, and an unidentified voice resounded.

Hamilton's voice was heard first: "We're in trouble."

"What now?" someone asked. Janet recognized Schwartz' voice.

"Murray, Fitzgerald and Martino have all pled guilty to selling cocaine. Apparently they worked together. I don't know whether they peddled it in the street or sold it wholesale to others. In Murray's case, this is his third offense. Fitzgerald has also been arrested once before. It is the first time for Martino. It was plea bargained for Murray and Fitzgerald. They were facing steep sentences. So, I think they talked to get reduced sentences."

Father Leahy said, "Murray could have gotten life. We can be pretty sure he and Fitzgerald made a deal."

"How did you learn this?" Schwartz asked.

Hamilton answered "There was a very brief note in one of the New York papers and the office in New York made some discreet inquiries through friends who are reporters."

"How many times have I warned you about Murray? You trust anybody and everybody. How much do they know?"

"They know the organization and they know some of the directors," Father Leahy responded. "They probably don't know many members, no more than five or six. They never really participated in

God's Mafia

the organization. Murray was with us for 15 years; Fitzgerald, ten; and Martino, three. However, they never were directors or attended any conventions."

Hamilton spoke. "It is not so much what these three can tell. It is more what the membership generally will feel about the break. All these years they have lived very well. They may think this disclosure will ruin them and they may panic. That's what's worrying me."

"So, what do we do about it?" Schwartz asked.

"I don't see that we can do anything about it."

"That's not an answer. We can't let $20,000,000 and years of work go down the drain. We must fight."

"And what good will that do?" Hamilton asked. "There will simply be more publicity and that will certainly bring us to the end. It's best to do nothing. Maybe the three will simply serve their time and nothing more will happen."

The tape ended and Nagel resumed his examination. "Did you verify that the persons who were speaking were the defendants in this case? And if so, how?"

"Yes. I was in a car parked across the road from the Hamilton home and saw the defendants go into the house. They did not emerge for some time. They were there between 2:00 and 3:30 and we timed these recordings at that same time."

"That is all, witness," Nagel said and looked at Walker.

Walker was tempted to ask Sutherland to interpret the conversation, but decided that testimony from his witnesses would be more likely to cast the recording in a positive light. The conversation could be construed as an innocent exchange, once the defense negated the prosecution's criminal conspiracy theory. In any event, he did not want to cross-examine an expert witness at this time. He didn't know what might come of it, and he felt more comfortable leaving the record the way it was. "No questions," he said curtly.

The judge turned to Nagel. "Call your next witness, please."

"The prosecution rests," Nagel said.

Walker was shocked! He could not believe that in a case of this magnitude, the prosecution would have no more evidence than had been presented. He rose and spoke to the court. "May it please the court, I would like to have the jury excused, since I would like to make a motion."

The judge beckoned the bailiff. "Very well. Bailiff, please take the jury to the jury room." To the jurors, he said, "You will be called as soon as the motion is argued." Then he turned to counsel and said, "We will take a ten minute break at this time."

Walker nodded and turned to Janet and the defendants. They conferred for a few minutes. All were grim.

As the judge left the bench, Angela Burgé came into the courtroom and walked over to the table where Walker, Janet, Father Leahy and Reverend Hamilton were standing. Her appeareance surprised the defendants and Walker and Janet as well. She was staying in a hotel room in the city and was supposed to wait for their call. All eyes turned to her, Leahy and Hamilton wondering what she was doing there and the others wondering what she was going to say. They did not have to wait long. "Father Leahy," she announced, "this case has gone on long enough without me. You haven't written or called. You are about to go to prison, and you expect me to simply read about it in the newspapers! You don't think much of me or of the many others who are just like me. You seem to think that there is nothing at all between us. This is all your business, your problem. Well, there are a lot of us who think this is our business, too, and we are not going to stand by and watch you blow it! I'm here to tell this court how it is. We can't afford to have you go to prison!"

The conversation was in hushed tones, but they all got the message very clearly. Leahy and Hamilton were speechless. Before either could say anything, Angela announced, "I'm not the only one who wants to tell the whole story. There are a lot of us who feel the way I do."

Father Leahy finally managed to speak. "Angela, do you know what you are doing?"

"I know what I am doing and pretty soon you are going to understand it."

Janet and Walker were frozen. At that moment Schwartz entered the circle. "Pat, Mal, there is no way you can stop her. She is the one who will lose. You have nothing to lose."

"That's not quite right, Ben," Angela interjected. "I've decided we will lose everything if we don't tell the story." She pointed a finger at Leahy and Hamilton. "I, the rest of us, have a right to defend our organization. That's what we are doing."

Janet noted that both her father and Father Leahy were nonplused. They had not counted on this. Angela Burgé was determined to carry them all! She had just removed from Janet's shoulders the greatest problem: how to handle the defendants. She had been masterful! With Angela around, Janet thought, this case could be won!

At the end of ten minutes the Judge entered. The bailiff rapped his gavel and called the proceedings to order. Walker addressed the court. "Your Honor, at this time I wish to make a motion to dismiss the indictment and to release the prisoners. The prosecution has rested its case and looking at the record it is clear that if we take all the testimony there is more than a reasonable doubt that these defendants are guilty of the charges made. I respectfully submit that there has been no substantive proof that these two defendants had any part in the sale of the drugs, that there has been any conspiracy, that there has been any evasion of taxes, or extortion.

"The prosecutions' chief witnesses have testified clearly that the defendants were never parties to the sale of illegal drugs. The witness from the office of the Internal Revenue Service testified that it had been determined that only donations were made and that those donations did not appear to be income. Those proofs which were intended to demonstrate extortion are nothing more than contributions which were voluntarily made. Moreover, the violations referred to by the prosecution are merely misdemeanors, not felonies. RICO does not apply to misdemeanors. Certainly that is not extortion. Nor does it appear by this record that there has been any conspiracy. There is testimony that there is an organization; there is testimony that there is interaction between the organization and the companies which were in fact convicted of the sale of drugs. But those don't add up to a conspiracy. Certainly if somebody goes to a bank and borrows money and uses that money to engage in drug trafficking that doesn't make for conspiracy between the bank and the drug dealer. Therefore, Your

Honor, I move the court to dismiss these charges and release the defendants."

The court turned to Nagel, who had already risen to his feet. "Your Honor the prosecution has demonstrated beyond any question of a doubt that there have been 'predicate' acts under the statute. It is only required that we show two such acts and in this case we have three. We have proof of a continuing organization and the defendants had knowledge that the convicted drug dealers had engaged in drug trafficking and continued to provide money for them. To be sure, the dealers testified that these defendants knew nothing about their drug trafficking. I respectfully submit that it is for the jury to determine from all the surrounding circumstances, the testimony of the drug dealers to the contrary notwithstanding, whether these defendants were actually engaged in financing the drug traffic. We do not have to demonstrate that either of these defendants actually participated in the sale. It is sufficient if the defendants participated in the enterprise, and if they had knowledge of unlawful acts previously committed. There is also testimony in this record that the defendants actually knew of the three predicate acts. The defendants and the three convicted drug dealers were members of the so-called Ecumenical Society. It is a proven fact that the Society financed the drug sales. Surely your Honor, neither this court nor this jury is going to be confined to the testimony that these defendants knew nothing about the drug dealing. Surely it is obvious under the Act that we have to look at the entire scenario and for the trier of the facts to determine whether in fact there was racketeering going on. We have an accumulation of funds, which is admitted. It is admitted, further, that it is obtained by donations. Donations for what? Donations for protection, of course! Remember, these drug dealers were to hire only ex-convicts! People whose jobs are on the line are easier to get money from and easier to control. This pattern is familiar to everyone. 'Protection money' is a term everybody understands. The word 'donation' as used in this context is a euphemism. As for the extortion, look at the circumstances. The three witnesses each testified that they were approached by the defendants to enter into their 'enterprise.' They were told that the conditions would be that they would have to make contributions. I respectfully submit that it is for the jury to accept or ignore the testimony of the three drug dealers as to the knowledge of the defendants. Certainly it is not the basis upon which this court can dismiss this case. These defendants are guilty of extortion. At least three men paid tribute in the form of so-called donations out of fear that their businesses would be lost. The so-called Society has literally stolen millions of dollars from people who could not help themselves."

The judge had been listening and writing notes. He now dropped his pencil and began speaking. "I am going to deny your motion, Mr. Walker. I do this because of the nature of this case and the full implications of it. I must say that your clients are either innocent saints who are being persecuted in the course of their ministries or they are the cleverest crooks ever to enter my court! At this point I must say that I don't know the answer. You may call in the jury, bailiff."

FIFTEEN

"Ladies and gentlemen of the jury," Walker said in his opening statement, "the defendants in this case are innocent! They are two devoted, dedicated men of God! All they have done has been to better a situation which has become the very worst problem our society faces today, the problem of crime. And here they are, about to be made criminals themselves! The law under which these defendants are being prosecuted, RICO, is a desperate effort by Congress to fight organized crime. In their anxiety to achieve that end, Congress constructed a net which traps innocent people. And that is what has happened here.

"Father Leahy and Reverend Hamilton have had vast experience with our criminal system. They have been chaplains in prisons and have counseled prisoners. They decided 30 years ago that the present system of crime and punishment simply does not work; in fact, it makes the problem worse. Almost 50% of all prisoners released from prison are back in custody within 18 months! We say this proves how hardened our criminals have become and is due mostly to the breakdown of the family and to prisons which simply punish and don't rehabilitate!

"What these two men have found is that there is another dimension to this problem, a factor not recognized by the government: the factor of society itself. For the fact is that when convicts leave prison they are branded. They might as well wear a scarlet letter on their clothing identifying them as criminals who are not to be trusted. Their criminal records are available to anyone who would employ them. So when ex-cons compete with five or six million unemployed people for jobs, who gets the job? Not only that, ex-convicts have usually had bad lives before prison and never really learned how to work, so they can't match others on this score either. What do we expect ex-convicts to do? They go back where they fit, into crime, hoping they won't be caught. It's the only way they can feed or clothe themselves. It's the only place they are comfortable.

"Society has no recourse but to identify and isolate ex-convicts. We cannot expect society to embrace those who have cheated and stolen, maimed or killed people, and say, 'Here, have my job.' We cannot accept that.

"Liberals say, 'It's those prisons. They don't rehabilitate prisoners.' Experience has shown that you cannot punish and educate at the same time, not because prisoners cannot learn, but because you either have a prison or a school. You either have prison guards or teachers. You can't have both.' And it's true. We have not succeeded in turning prison into a high school or college.

"Father Leahy and Reverend Hamilton saw this problem in the context of their work. They saw the crime problem as a part of the nation's loss of faith. They considered the role of the church in dealing with this particular segment of society. Conversely, they saw a real test of their own faith in bringing it to bear on this awful problem. They asked, 'Can the love of God be brought into this part of society and save souls?' They gave a great deal of thought to this question. They decided that in the past God's love was presented only in talks, in platitudes, never in real, concrete, workable terms. They decided that what was lacking in religion's approach to crime was a lack of resources. God's love must be shown by deed, by providing what is actually needed. Today we are all interdependent. To survive, men and women function within a society. Since the general society would not accept convicts, with their help, ex-cons would form their own society, an Ecumenical Society.

"I'm going to let the story of that society come to you from the witness stand. Today there are almost 6,000 ex-convicts in the Ecumenical Society who are gainfully employed, who are working members of our society. Only 15% of that number have left the Ecumenical Society and of those, less than 5% have gone back to prison. Contrast that with 50% of other ex-convicts. Whereas taxpayers are now spending over 400 billion dollars per year on the so-called crime problem, the program of these defendants has not cost you one cent!

"I ask you to listen closely to the witnesses, and you will see that these two defendants are not criminals. They are heroes. We need more like them."

Walker turned, and was about to call his first witness when Nagel rose to his feet. "At this time I'd like to make a motion, Your Honor."

The court asked the bailiff to take the jury out of the courtroom, after which Nagel said, "Your Honor, if this were a civil case I would make a motion for a judgment on the basis of counsel's opening statement. Since this is a criminal case, I must put on record that the opening statement of the defense to the jury fails to present a defense. I request that the jury be instructed that the only issue before them is whether the defendants have been parties to, have conspired or have aided and abetted in a violation of RICO. A grandiose scheme for the solution of the crime problem in this country is not a defense. We deem it a clever cover-up. In any event, it is completely extraneous to these proceedings."

Nagel sat down and Walker was about to rise when the judge rapped his gavel. "To save time," Judge Kowalski said, "I herewith deny your motion, Mr. Nagel. You have asked this court and this jury to take into account all the surrounding circumstances in this matter in determining the guilt or innocence of these defendants. They are charged with very serious crimes. Their intentions and their purposes in what they did are an integral part of the basic issue in this case. As I said in denying the defense motion to dismiss, these men may be horrendous criminals or saints. At least they should be given an opportunity to show their intentions."

Soon after the judge recalled the jury, Angela Burgé came through the rail. She went directly to Hamilton and Leahy who were seated together at counsel's table. She put one hand on the shoulders of each as she stood behind them. Walker now turned to the defendants and announced, "The defense calls Angela Burgé."

The witness was directed by the court to approach the clerk who administered the oath. The tall, beautiful, well-groomed Black woman stated her name. "I live in Indianapolis, Indiana. I am President and Chief Executive Officer of the American Standard Service Organization, with offices in Indianapolis."

Angela proceeded to tell the jury what she had said in Walker's office. The jurors, the judge, the courtroom personnel and all the attorneys became enthralled with the witness and her story. In his examination, Walker brought out that she graduated summa cum lauda, that she was a highly successful business person, that she was married, and that she had two daughters who were in college. She described how she had built an enterprise of 3,000 employees and said that she was on several prestigious boards. And then she said that she was also a former prostitute and proceeded to tell the story of her childhood, of her mother and her mother's death. She told how she had hired many of her fellow prostitutes and how the organization was still employing those who were willing to pay the price, as it were.

Walker asked her to describe the purpose of the Ecumenical Society, and she responded by saying, "The people who come out of prison or from jail really don't have a chance in your society." She pointed to Mr. Nagel. "They come out and they are branded. They have a criminal record; who would hire them? The Ecumenical Society is a society of ex-cons, and we deal with each other as well as with your establishment, Mr. Nagel. I have had to go to my two daughters before I came here and say to them, 'Your mother has been a prostitute.' You can imagine what a shock that was! All their lives I have been a distinguished, well respected, wealthy, prominent person. And now they find out that, in fact, I was once a prostitute. I didn't want to do that, and I have literally thousands of women in my organization who are in the same boat. They are married, they have fine husbands and they have children and they will have to do what I had to do before coming here to testify.

"But it isn't only the trauma to our children. It is even worse for us individually. You may not understand this. I have come to believe with all my heart that there is a God, and that he is a good God, and I have come to believe in Jesus' words that we can be born again. I mean to be a new person. Maybe I can explain it better if I put it in terms of automobiles. For many years I have felt like a new automobile; today I am an old automobile, repaired and remodeled. For many years I have considered myself a brand-new person; today I am the same old person but reformed. There is a big difference. A big difference. And the worst part of that difference is that in your society I am always the old person, and I am either reformed or not reformed. But because I am always the old person I will never have the opportunities and the rights which others have. For the rest of my life I will be known to you as an ex-criminal.

"So far as I am concerned, I don't know where I will go from here. I don't know how much damage has been done to me and to my family. I don't know how the organizations of which I have been a part will react to my disclosure. I don't know what kind of a psychological impact this will have on my children. I don't know what type of an impact it will have on my business. But this I do know: If I must sacrifice myself to prevent these two men from going to prison I will do it and do it gladly. Because if it were not for them I would be nothing, less than nothing. If I can do anything to stop their crucifixion I will do so. I will not be like those who stood by and watched Jesus Christ crucified."

She fell momentarily silent, then turned to Father Leahy and said, "Father I still go to Mass every day." There was now a deafening silence in the courtroom, except for newspaper reporters who quickly left their seats and dashed for the door.

Walker continued questioning Angela. "Can you describe how the society operates?"

"The money we provide is used as capital for new businesses which employ only ex-convicts. It also provides loans for the employees for homes, education, and so forth."

"So, you have formed a sort of economy of your own?"

"That's right. We have to do it for ourselves, and we do."

"Do you still borrow money from the Ecumenical Fund for your operations?"

"No, I have an excellent financial status now. I can borrow money anyplace, and I do because I want to relieve the burden on the fund. However, anytime that we have someone whom we have to train or send to school the Ecumenical fund advances the money."

"Does the Ecumenical Society hold any meetings?"

"We have a Board of Directors which meets once a month. We have what we call a convention twice a year, once in the spring and once in the fall. We have it at various resorts in the United States. All employers and employees are invited to attend, but we never attend as the Ecumenical Society. We always register as a voluntary group and if the hotel wants a name of the organization we tell them that we are a group that just simply wants to have a good time."

"Why do you not meet as the Ecumenical Society?"

"Because, we want the Society to maintain a low profile. After all, we are trying to wipe out our past. We are trying to keep secret the fact that we have criminal records. If the Ecumenical Society, as such, holds a public convention twice a year, it will not be long before we are known as the Society of ex-cons. Obviously, that is something we cannot afford. Of course, with this prosecution and trial we have pretty much been exposed to the world. Our great secret is now in all the headlines and on all the radio and television sets. Our efforts to protect the privacy of people have been nullified by this trial. Even you, Mr. Nagel, should have some idea of what this will do to all the ex-prostitutes who are working for me. I'm afraid lives will be ruined.

"The defendants were ready to go to prison before our secret past was spread throughout the news media. Some of us couldn't tolerate that. We cannot save ourselves at the cost of these men's lives. We would rather suffer more humiliation than see them go to prison. Nothing could be more monstrous than that.

"Another reason we don't publicize is to avoid creating the impression that we are a religious organization. That would stamp us as a cult which we are not! The Ecumenical Society has God as its focal point, as its center. However, it is not a religious organization. It enables Catholics, Protestants, Jews and Muslims to seek God and salvage their lives: in becoming reborn, as the Christians put it, in seeking the perfection of humanity, as the Jews put it, as the achievement of personal purity, as preached by Islam. Mohammed came 700 years after Christ. He recognized both Moses and Christ as God's prophets. It is the same God! But the Ecumenical Society does not seek to combine, mold or infiltrate these separate faiths. It respects each of them and members are free to worship as their faith directs. The Society affirms that in its members' goal of reform, rehabilitation and achievement of relief from criminal proclivities or social faults, God is necessary. And so, whatever our belief or sect, we are urged to turn to God and to work with God in achieving peace of mind. Some of us believe you can't do it without God. The Ecumenical Society is a fellowship among people of all faiths, not a super or different or new faith or creed.

"It is important to emphasize this idea of singleness of purpose among diverse faiths. It is possible to exercise different rituals, different practices and still join together."

"What do you do at those semi-annual meetings?" Walker asked, intrigued.

"We get acquainted and renew acquaintances. Then we share experiences. There are also lectures, usually by members of our organization. Once in a while we bring in outside speakers. There are religious services for those who wish to attend them. Whether we meet on a weekend or during the week, although we generally meet on weekends, we have services. A great many of our members have had the same spiritual experience I've had; we try to maintain that sense of religious commitment as best we can. Almost all the members of the society attend either Catholic or Protestant services and we have Jewish members who attend either at a local synagogue or they form a minyan of their own. Our Muslims hold their own prayer services. And there are also those who have no such experience, and they do whatever they wish. Our meetings are extremely important, because we all have a common bond and we lean on each other and encourage each other. You might compare it with Alcoholics Anonymous. Those meetings are vitally important to the health and welfare of the whole group."

In his cross-examination, Nagel made Burgé admit that a condition of employment in her company was that employees had to contribute 7.5% of their net income to the Ecumenical Society and she contributed 7.5% of the profits of her corporation. For the Ecumenical Society that meant an income of about $11,000,000 from wage earners alone.

God's Mafia

Nagel asked if the Ecumenical Society loaned money to persons known to be drug dealers. Angela responded that it was against the policy of the Society to do that.

"But witnesses have already testified that the Society has done that," Nagel shot back.

"It is also the policy of the Society to take back all those who have gone astray if they do so in penance. Just as the Prodigal son was taken back, so the Society has an open door for those who stray but want to return. And this might happen three, four or more times. In fact, it happens quite often in the Ecumenical Society. After all, the members have not been the strongest of people. For the most part, eventually those who go wrong come back and stay. Apparently, that was not the case with the three witnesses for the prosecution."

"And each time you take somebody back a second or third time he or she is more easily controlled by you." Nagel countered. "Each time it is harder for them to make a living except by working for you under your conditions. Isn't that so?"

Angela Burgé smiled as she answered. "What would *you* do with the person? I know I am not to ask questions but to answer them. However, I would remind you that we do more for society than you do. You just throw them back into prison. And when your prisons are overcrowded you chase them out again. For those we take, we save you money. We pay for the 'in and out' race. And the people are productive when we put them back to work. This is not a charity, Mr. Nagel. This is a business proposition among the members of the Society, for both the employer and the employed. We do this on our own. We don't seek your help. This is our fund, Mr. Nagel. This is our Cosa Nostra. This is God's Mafia, if that is the way you want to look at it."

The witness was beginning to unsettle Nagel. Her words sounded very much like his on many occasions when he had expounded on charity. Still he pressed on. "So, it is not charity. Tell me, then, why do you give away 7.5% of your income?"

"Because we must!"

Nagel was thunderstruck. Those were *his* exact words! He could not avoid turning around and looking at Janet. He expected a smirk, a jeer. What he was met with was a look of pity, of sadness. It was not a look which said, "You see how wrong you've been." He could not focus on the witness. Yet, somehow, he had to stop her, for without being questioned the witness had resumed her testimony. He should have stopped her; somehow he couldn't. "You can only think in terms of exploitation, Mr. Nagel. If our employees are exploited, so are all other employees. There is no difference between our employees and those of any other employer."

"Except that yours must pay 7.5% of their income for the privilege of working." Nagel smiled. He was back on top.

"That 7.5% is not a bribe. It is paid because it is our obligation to pay it."

"Then why don't you deduct it for tax purposes?"

"Because it is not a gift to a charity nor a fee for working. It is not union dues. Nothing whatsoever is promised for that 7.5%."

"I don't understand," Nagel smirked. "If it's not a gift to charity, and it isn't union dues, what is it?"

"It is our commitment to God."

"To God? And who is God?"

"God is the Creator, the Supreme Being."

Nagel felt relieved for the moment. The witness was not motivated as he had been. They were back to this 'God' business, and he could show the jury the flimflam of this operation. "Other people make commitments to God. They do it through their churches. They deduct what they pay. Why is your commitment different?"

Angela had anticipated the questions. "The Ecumenical Society is not a church. It is not a religious order. It does not qualify as an approved gift-recipient under the Internal Revenue Code, but that is not why we don't deduct it. We don't deduct it because, if we did, it would not be solely our gift. The government would share in that contribution. Contribution, or gift, or whatever, we don't want the government's help. We must not accept the government's help. We don't pay this in order to make ourselves benefactors or to aggrandize ourselves. We must specifically avoid that appearance. We pay 7.5% in order to redeem ourselves. We pay it quietly, secretly, humbly, as a penance, as a means of atonement. God knows we have a lot to atone for."

God's Mafia

Nagel did not immediately ask his next question. Janet was staring at him. Furtively, he glanced at her. He could not bring himself to face her. He caught her look of anguish. There was no triumph in her face, no, "I told you so." He realized she felt sorry for him. It disconcerted him and he had to grasp for questions. "Is it not a fact that the defendants made it a condition of employment that you pay 7.5% of your net income to the Ecumenical Society."

"Yes."

"And is it not a fact that this has been the rule for years without exception?"

"Yes."

"So, you pay because you are told by the Society that you must pay, isn't that right?"

"Yes and no, Mr. Nagel. Yes, it is the rule that we must pay. But we don't have to pay if we don't want to. We can quit the Society. Many of us no longer need the Society to furnish us with capital. We have plenty of credit with regular financial institutions. We have excellent financial statements. We still pay 7.5%. We pay it because we must. This is a very odd thing about God's Mafia, even the bosses pay!"

Nagel knew the answer to his next question but he asked it anyway. "Why?"

"The process of redemption, Mr. Nagel, is forever."

Nagel had to go on. To stop now would be to acknowledge defeat. "So, you worship God, but the Ecumenical Society is not a religious organization, is that what you are telling me?"

"Mr. Nagel we must all account to somebody. The person who accounts only to himself is a master who has a fool for a slave! A slave accounts to his master. A free man, to remain free, must account to someone other than himself. The government, which you represent Mr. Nagel, says we must account to it. We do. Your system sets forth written demands called laws and regulations, and they also provide a specific penalty for the failure to abide by those demands. Six months, a year, ten years, life in prison. Maybe only a fine, maybe only probation. Your system actually puts a price on crime. So, if I steal and the penalty is five years in prison and I serve it, I've paid! But your government doesn't keep its part of the contract. After we convicts have paid the price you have set, we still can't be free like other people. You brand us with the label 'ex-con' and you make a record for everyone to see. With five, six and seven million people unemployed, how do you expect us to become constructive, productive citizens? The statistics show we have only a 50% chance. The rest of us are back in prison within 18 months. The recidivism rate for all convicts is even higher.

"In the Ecumenical Society we do not fool ourselves. There is no time limit on our redemption. There is no payment in full. We must go on redeeming ourselves for the rest of our lives. But in our Society, unlike yours, there is reconciliation. The ex-convict is given a chance to become reconciled. He is welcomed like the prodigal son. He is forgiven. There is no reconciliation in your society. You don't permit it.

"We know, Mr. Nagel, that your society cannot do what the Ecumenical Society does. The citizens will not pay the price. The least you could do is stop misleading those who leave prison to believe they have paid their so-called debt to society. You create cynicism, bitterness and more crime. The Ecumenical Society is trying to overcome that for at least a few ex-prisoners. It is not costing you a cent. We are paying our own way. All we ask is that you leave us alone."

The courtroom sat in stunned silence. Nagel knew he was dealing with a highly intelligent, eloquent spokesperson. His biggest problem was himself. She was disarming him. He retreated to what he thought would be safer grounds.

"Is it not a fact that the Directors of the Ecumenical Society are all millionaires?"

"I don't know, but it would not surprise me."

"And they made their money through the Ecumenical Society?"

"I suppose so. They started where I did, with nothing. They would not be successful had it not been for the Ecumenical Society. There are others who are not Directors who are millionaires."

"And the money which made them millionaires came from those who worked for them."

"The money," Burgé responded deliberately and slowly, "comes from the fund which all employers and employees have contributed to. It is borrowed, and it is paid back. There is no exploitation. The Ecumenical Society is not a charity. It is the combined efforts of a group of people who have a common problem and who are determined to solve the problem themselves. We have maintained secrecy because that is the only way we can keep it a private project, a matter of repentance and atonement. If it were public, it would become philanthropy and people would feel, as they do with government programs, that they were entitled to its benefits. That would destroy us."

Nagel knew he had lost. He should stop the questioning, and yet he could not stop. "And this $11,000,000 income each year is free of income tax, right?"

"Right."

"And the Society pays no interest on the money and never pays it back."

"Right."

There was no point in continued questioning. Nagel had had the shock of his life. "No further questions," he announced and dropped into his chair.

Pleased, Walker allowed that he had no more questions.

There was a beehive of activity in the courtroom; people were scrambling, talking to each other. Newspaper men left the courtroom to find phones. Angela Burgé came down from the witness stand and embraced Father Leahy. Then she turned to Reverend Hamilton and did the same thing. Vera Hamilton came through the railing at the bar and embraced Angela. Walker, Hamilton, Leahy, Wingate, Burgé and Schwartz clustered around the counsel table.

Reverend Hamilton, however, was not happy. "I think our troubles have just started. We have a lot of people who are now desperate. What are we going to do about them? Angela, what are we going to do about your people?"

Angela put her arm around the minister. She towered over him. "I will look after my people, Reverend, just as I always have. We are going to hear some awful crying but this had to be done. We'll manage."

SIXTEEN

That afternoon, Walker called his next witness, Joseph Carl. "Do you know Reverend Hamilton seated beside me?" Walker asked him.

"Yes, I do."

"When did you meet him, and how?"

"About 15 years ago at the prison where I was about to finish my second prison term for breaking and entering."

"What was the occasion for the meeting?"

"About a week before we met, I was told by one of the prison officials that a Reverend Malcolm Hamilton would be coming in to see me. I had never heard of him. I was 25 years old. When I was 17, I was sent to prison for three years on a robbery charge. I was out of prison only nine months and I was back again for robbery, this time for five years. At 25, I was about to come out again. I couldn't imagine why a total stranger was visiting me. I intended to see if I could find some of my gang when I got out. I had served my full term. There was no probation and no parole. I would be free as a bird and I had dreamed about how this time I would form my own gang and show everybody how I could survive. I had spent all my time in prison planning my new operation. I was going to commit the perfect robbery so that we would make a lot of money and never get caught.

"Well, Reverend Hamilton came and told me that he'd checked me out and that I had the stuff to make a go of it without robbing stores. I realized he was a minister and I tried to be nice. I asked him what he had in mind. He said that he had a program that would send me back to school without cost where I would have a chance to learn a trade. When I graduated, there would be a job for me.

"I smiled and said, 'What's the payoff?' I said to myself, 'Here's the catch.' Then he explained the Ecumenical Society to me. I said to myself, 'That's a hell of a racket. I can get on the inside and make a barrel of money.' So I was ready for the deal. 'When do I start?' I asked.

" 'As soon as you get out of here,' the Reverend Hamilton told me. Lo and behold, in a week he came back to take me out of prison. He took me to his home. I was a guest in his house. They treated me like a king. Come Monday I was in school. That was something else. There I was, in the tenth grade with kids ten years younger than me. It was a private school, real phony. I couldn't believe what was going on. Before the week was out I was in the headmaster's office. He told me that I was extremely fortunate, that all my expenses were being paid and that all I had to do was work hard, learn and keep out of trouble. He told me that the Reverend had done the same thing for other people and they had all been very successful.

"Well, about this time I started to do some more thinking. This didn't look like a racket to me. It was beginning to look like a reform school. What's the deal? I decided to talk straight with the Headmaster.

" 'I don't get it, Mr. Headmaster,' I said. 'Here I am in this fancy school and you tell me everything is paid for and all I have to do is study and keep out of trouble. I've been told that I'll be expected to go to work for somebody and pay some dues, and I could someday have my own business. He called them donations, not dues, but I know a racket when I see one. I was planning one of my own when I got out of prison. But I don't see this education bit. Where does it fit in?'

"The Headmaster laughed. He said, 'Young man, this is no racket. This is all legitimate. And someday you'll come back here and you will see it for what it is. The chance of a lifetime.'

" 'But why me?' I asked.

"He said, 'Reverend Hamilton told us you have no family. You were raised by your grandmother but she couldn't control you. She died and you were keeping yourself alive any way you could. In checking the prison records, he got a chance to see your school record. From those records he decided you had the "right stuff," as he likes to say. That is why he came to you.'

"Now I was in a real fix. I just didn't understand. This was the first time in my life anybody had cared about me. I still didn't know why any stranger could take me in like this. Anyway, I decided not to run away. After all, this was better than prison and it began to appear that it was even better than anyplace else I'd find if I left. I didn't really have any place else to go.

"Back in my room, I started thinking some more. I remembered when I left prison the first time. I was on parole. I was told to find a job. I went to the unemployment office. They asked me if I had graduated from high school. I hadn't. They asked for my address and phone number. Of course I didn't have that either. They told me to check back with them every day to find out if they had a job for me. I went directly to the welfare office and they helped me out with food and some clothes.

"I had no place to live except for a bunk the welfare office provided in a hut in back of the welfare office. I kept looking for a job. The first thing I ran into was the 'Recall List.' Even when I got a chance to talk to somebody at a plant, warehouse, or store, they told me they had a 'Recall List' which listed all the people who had been laid off. Any vacancies would be filled by people on that list, and there were hundreds, sometimes thousands of names on each of those lists. There was no chance for me to get a job there. At other places there were signs: 'Not Hiring!' But I stayed with it. One day I got to a restaurant and they had me fill out an application. It had a lot of questions on it. One of the questions was: 'Have you ever been convicted of a crime? If so, what was the crime?' When I handed in application, the man looked at it and said, 'Sorry, we can't use you.'

"Still I tried. I had to try if I wanted to keep my bunk or get any food. Soon I realized the whole thing was ridiculous. I wasn't going to be hired by anybody!

"About the same time I made that decision I got a job. It wasn't much but at least it was a job. I worked in a restaurant kitchen doing all the dirty work. I had to keep that kitchen spotless. The manager

God's Mafia

was in there every morning and every night. He looked for dirt and I really caught hell if he found any. But I was now employed.

"Well, the job didn't last long. Food started to disappear from the kitchen. There was a big investigation. We were all interviewed. I was laid off. I wasn't fired. I was laid off and I got unemployment. I swore before everybody that I had stolen nothing. I was told that they were not charging me with stealing. They had just decided to eliminate my job!

"I had a good idea who was doing the stealing. It would have done me no good to say so. It would simply mean more problems. At least I was not charged with any crime and I had a little money.

"I went back to the employment office. This time they told me that I was actually unemployable, that I didn't have enough education and no skills. They told me to go to New York and simply line up at the wharves to be called when needed. I did that. But they had 'Recall Lists' there, too.

"I finally went back to my old haunts and found my old buddies, and we tried to improve our techniques of breaking and entering. We didn't improve them enough and so I was back in prison again.

"And again I was out of prison. I was now getting free the education I needed, and I was living in luxury! I decided maybe I had better take a chance with the good Reverend.

"But that was not the end of my troubles. I still did not understand. My big question was 'Why?' Why was Reverend Hamilton doing this? Maybe some of you would have understood it all very quickly. You must remember that I had never known anyone to do anything for anybody else! 'God' was a word we used in swearing, and I knew there were churches and synagogues and mosques but I had never been in one.

"I finally asked Reverend Hamilton, 'Why are you doing this? What's the deal? At first I thought that you were training me to join a new racket where we would get a lot of money free and use it to make money for ourselves. That would be a real deal. Now I'm not so sure. You'd better tell me all about it?'

"Reverend Hamilton said 'Son, you can only see the bad side of things. That's how you are focused. That's your only frame of reference.'

"I asked him what 'frame of reference' meant. He said, 'It's how you look at things. I tried to describe to you an ideal scheme, a plan, where those who can't get a job because of their criminal records are given the education and training they need to get a job. We expect them to pay money so we can do the same for others. We also provide loans for a home, a car, things they want but can't finance. And all you can see is a racket.'

"You see, at first I saw it the same way Mr. Nagel sees it now.

"Mr. Hamilton tried to explain frame of reference to me, but I didn't understand until much later. He told me that all of us see things through a sort of frame which is made up of many mental lenses. That's why two people can watch the same thing but see very different things. They look at life and, according to their frame of reference, they see different things. That's only natural. 'Those lenses are made up of parts of our respective lives,' Mr. Hamilton told me. Since my life had been one of getting whatever I could for as little as I could, that's the way I saw everything. He told me that his society would change that frame of reference so that the lenses would help me see things differently. It was complicated and still I didn't understand.

"Mr. Hamilton told me that his frame of reference had been laid down by Jesus Christ. He said there were others: the Jewish frame made by Moses and the Islamic frame of Mohammed, among others. They were all helpful in getting a better picture of life. Then he handed me a little book entitled *A Child's Story of Jesus*. He told me to read it and he would talk to me about it later. The next time, he handed me the Bible. I have been learning ever since what life is really about."

"So, Mr. Carl," Walker continued, "what happened after your term at school?"

"Well, I still wasn't qualified for a good job. My benefactors asked what I wanted to do. I told them I didn't know. Father Leahy said, 'Remember our deal. You've got to go to work. You are either going to school or you are going to work!'

"I had done pretty well in school. Reverend Hamilton had my school records before him. 'Frankly,' he said, 'I think you still belong in school. You can do better than become a day laborer. But you've got to decide what you will do.'

"For no reason at all I said, 'I'd like to go to cook's school. I'd like to become a chef.' I suppose that my brief stint in the restaurant kitchen was now my principal 'frame of reference.' And that's where I went. The Society found a school for chefs in Boston and they sent me there. It was not very attractive to me. I had no experience cooking. Most of the students around me had been cooks all their lives. For them it was a sort of graduate school. I was older than many of them, although there were more people my age and older in chef's school than in grade school and high school. I finally found something I could do which would please people. You'd be surprised how much better people like you if you can make their stomachs happy. It was not that I was a better student than the others. In fact, I was no more than average. But in my circumstances I had never actually done anything, made anything which brought praise. You can get a great deal of praise when you prepare a good meal, more, I think, than if you are a very capable lawyer, doctor or engineer. That is, you can be much less competent as a chef and get as much praise as you'd get being a very competent surgeon. A chef's products are things which satisfy humanity's most basic desire. You can make people very happy without being a genius. All you have to do is follow good recipes, and if you happen to stumble on a few novel recipes people are ready to canonize you. You can perform near miracles as a surgeon and not get nearly as much praise.

"In any event, I was getting praise for the first time in my life. That made me feel worthwhile and gave a boost to something I had always had but never able to focus: ambition. I had always been ambitious. I wanted to perfect breaking and entering; that is, entering without breaking. I had wanted my own gang. Now I had something legitimate to apply my ambition to. I wanted my next recipe to be better than previous ones. I wanted to make the entire kitchen more efficient. Within three months after I started chef school I wanted my own restaurant.

"Well, I got through school with a good record. I was not at the top of my class, but I was good enough for a recommendation. I did not have to go to just any restaurant. I asked to be placed with any of the four star restaurants in New York, and I was. There I observed everything. Not just the kitchen, but the entire restaurant operation. The more I thought, the more determined I was to do big things. In this, I was always encouraged by the Society. Somebody there kept track of me, counseled me and directed me to the focal points of the restaurant industry. I knew I could get financing from the Society and I aimed for that.

"I planned an entire restaurant layout, from entry to dining, to kitchen, to office. I made drawings. I compiled a huge book of recipes for everything and the best of French, Italian, German, Oriental and other cuisines. I was having a barrel of fun. I got together with two other people in the Society, Geraldine Barker and Earl Oliphant. They became my partners. Geraldine had trained as an interior designer and decorator and Earl as an accountant. None of us ever got college training, but each of us had been put through specific courses to qualify us for what we were to do, all through the efforts of the Society. We pooled what money we had and we borrowed the rest from the Society.

"We designed a hundred-seat restaurant with a large open area and alcoves along the perimeters for parties of eight or ten. We hired architects. We then obtained from various directories, phone books, and personal contacts with some of the exclusive shops in town the names of hundreds of wealthy people. We learned what we could about them, their businesses, their families, their clubs, their habits. This took time, effort and some money. Our advertising strategy was to use personal correspondence with these people, no advertising in newspapers, radio or television. We prepared newsletters which contained not only our menu and specials but what was happening in exclusive restaurants in Paris, Rome, Milan, Madrid and Buenos Aires.

"Our headwaiter's first job was to know all about the lives and families of these people. Our objective was to develop an exclusive and wealthy clientele. We also did something radical: we set up a 'retainer' system. Each year we took retainers from our customers against which they could charge meals for the coming year. This assured them the number of spaces they wanted and the retainer was adjusted accordingly. We tied up 30% of our space with these retainers, which were based on a discounted price for each meal. Each retainer was for the number of meals the customer wanted to reserve. Our accountant figured that an assured 30% sale, even at a 15% discount, was an excellent deal for the operation. We tried to offer this to celebrities. Word gets around quietly, but quickly, by word of mouth and gossip columns about who eats where. Meanwhile, of course, when you can get 30% of your possible total revenues in advance you have working capital for the year! We could contract supplies in advance at a discount which amounted to about as much as the 15% we discounted our retainers."

"Do you have more than one such restaurant," Walker asked, "and if so, where are they?"

"We started in New York. We now have restaurants in Philadelphia, Boston, Chicago, Los Angeles, San Francisco, Orlando, Pittsburgh, Miami and Minneapolis. We are investigating other cities in the United States and possibly abroad."

Walker, turning to Nagel, said, "You may cross-examine."

Nagel arose and walked to the podium and placed a pad on it. Looking at the witness, he asked, "What is your annual income?"

"About $350,000."

"And is it all from your restaurants?"

"Yes sir."

"How much do you pay your employees?"

"My employees, our employees rather since I have two partners, are paid union scale wages. They are all union members."

"You don't employ through the union?"

"No sir, we employ our own people. They become union members after they have been employed."

"Do your employees pay union dues as well as the 7.5% of their wages to the Society?"

"Yes."

"And the union does not object?"

"No sir."

"So, your employees pay withholding tax, Social Security tax, union dues and then 7.5% to your Society?"

"Yes sir." Carl smiled broadly. "Sir, our employees take home more pay than any waiters in the country."

"Yours, then, is a very expensive restaurant?"

"Yes sir."

"Mr. Carl, I take it that if your employees refuse to pay the 7.5% they don't have a job?"

"That's right."

"And the union approves of that?"

"It has never been challenged at any negotiations."

"Is there not a statute in any state where you operate that prevents such so-called donations?"

"I don't know. Nobody has objected so far."

"Am I to understand, Mr. Carl, that your union contract specifically provides that the payment to the Society, or the donation as you call it, is approved and that non-payment is cause for discharge?"

"Substantially that's what it says. Mr. Nagel, my employees receive more benefits from the Society than they do from their union. They can get help to educate their children, to buy homes, to buy automobiles, to buy furniture and appliances. Most of all, they form friendships with fellow Society members that they don't get with their unions. The Society is what sustains them. They are a fraternity based on more than money. My employees, for the most part, have had the same experiences I have had. They have found God for the first time and they work with God through their 7.5% donation."

Nagel looked closely at his notes then raised his head and asked, "How many people do you employ?"

"Between 800 and 1,000."

"Have you ever been a Director in the Society?"

"Yes sir."

Nagel continued his cross-examination, bringing up all that had been testified to before. He asked Carl that if other organizations demanded payment for protection and were deemed rackets, how was the Ecumenical Society different. Carl had responded by saying "The money we get doesn't go into anybody's pocket. It goes to God."

God's Mafia

When Nagel pressed the comparison, Carl said, "You see, Mr. Nagel, we come back to a frame of reference. My frame of reference is different from yours."

The next witness for the defense was Arnold Rothstein, a thin, well-dressed man about five feet ten inches tall with features which showed considerable wear. His hair was thin, his face wrinkled. He could have been 45 years old; he could've been 60.

Asked to identify himself, he said, "I am Arnold Rothstein. I live at 10467 Wakefield Avenue in Jonesville, New York, where I operate a travel service and insurance agency."

"Are you a member of the Ecumenical Society?"

"I am."

"How long have you been a member?"

"Twelve years."

"What is your educational background?"

"I have a bachelor's degree from Columbia University."

"Mr. Rothstein, have you ever been convicted of a crime?"

"Yes sir."

"Have you served time in prison?"

"Yes sir."

"Perhaps you could tell us about your experience with crime?"

"I was born in New York City. My parents were, and still are, the sole owners of Modern Garment Co. which is engaged in the business of manufacturing ladies apparel and wholesaling it. I was one of those who is said to have been born with a silver spoon in his mouth. My parents are multi-millionaires. I have one brother and two sisters. I am the youngest. My brother Myron is the oldest child. He is now president of the family company. My sisters' husbands are employed there. I was my mother's baby. I am five years younger than the younger sister. Everybody said I was spoiled. My brother is fifteen years older than me. When I was in my teens he was already the executive Vice President of the company. Nobody urged me to prepare for work. I was, as I said, the baby, everybody's baby, the darling in the eyes of my parents and my sisters as well. As for Myron, he was the one who was to look after the company, keep it competitive, keep the money coming in. My father never paid much attention to me. To my mother

I was both a baby and show piece. I was expected to reflect my family's place in the community. I was entitled to be the playboy. My father didn't seem to care, and Myron tolerated me as an extra expense. My sisters were delighted when I made the papers with my polo playing. I became good enough in tennis to get public attention and that put our name on the sports pages as well as the fashion and society pages. I was handsome; I dressed very well. I went to the best schools and managed to graduate from Columbia, the only college graduate in the family. That was part of the show piece bit. I dated a lot of young ladies and that made the papers as well.

"I never had a job! I was never asked to enter the family business. It was not thought necessary. I would always be taken care of. I never knew how the stock in the company was held. In fact, it was held in a trust in which my brother was the trustee together with the Madison Trust Company. I never knew the provisions of the trust. Although I was over 21 and a college graduate, it was not deemed necessary that I be informed. I guess I was expected to be the eternal playboy.

"Each member of the family received a semi-annual dividend from the company, which was more than enough to take care of our daily needs.

"When I was 16 and in prep school, I had my own private apartment. I haven't lived with my parents since then, although I have moved from time to time. Without really realizing it, I was becoming separated from my family. As I grew older, my parents did not include me in their social gatherings except on holidays or very special occasions. My brother and sisters had their own social sets, and I developed my own social set. Then a strange thing happened to me. I was part of a so-called 'singles' set, and that set was composed of people like me, rich with nothing to do except play. And we sure played! There were no restraints. The parties ran all night. The girls were not from our class, if I might use the word. They were ambitious social climbers or they were paid performers. We men knew what they were and we treated them accordingly. Paid them well. The social climbers were also paid, sometimes in cash, sometimes in such positions as our influence could place them.

"After years of this, everything began to get stale. What was once a thrill was no longer a thrill. Group flights to Rio de Janeiro or Buenos Aires or Paris or Hamburg, cruises all over world, night-long orgies, even these became stale. So far as my family was concerned, the only time they noticed was when I made the news for one reason or another, very often for the wrong reason. They thought it was funny and, anyway, every prominent family has its playboy.

"There came a time when alcohol and drugs were the only things that could turn us on. Although not all my new friends used liquor and drugs to excess, I did. After all, who cared? What else was there to do? Anyway, nobody was getting hurt.

"But a liquor and drug lifestyle costs money, a lot of it. And the more I bought the more I needed. Pretty soon it got so I could not afford the drugs. I tried to continue my habit on credit, believing I would always have money coming in and would one day own a part of the company. The dealers let me have credit. But when I didn't pay they worked me over and dumped me in the streets, unconscious. I was taken to a hospital where I was identified by documents I had on me, and the hospital called my brother. He came to the emergency room alone. He did not tell my parents or my sisters. I told him I had been accosted in the street, robbed and beaten, but the hospital informed him that nothing had been taken from me. He pressed me for the truth. I stuck to my story, told him that I assumed money had been taken from my wallet. Perhaps my assailants had been scared off before taking my possessions. I had no way of knowing.

"My brother was kind to me. He was skeptical, but he did not berate me or threaten me. He told me that it might be best if the family was not informed of what had happened. I was happy to comply with that suggestion.

"I was soon out of the hospital and back in my apartment. I had no serious after-effects from the mugging, but I still owed the money. If I used my dividend to pay the debt, I would not have money to feed my habit and if I used the money to 'fix,' I could not pay my debt. Under no circumstances could I go to my family for the money!

"By this time I had no more pride. I had to have cocaine. Nothing else mattered. I was absolutely desperate. So I decided to do what had been done to me. Of course, I was not thinking straight. I mugged an old lady and tried to take her jewelry, but I was not a good mugger. The old lady resisted. Instead of just letting me have her purse and necklace, she began to pound me with her purse and her fists. So I hit her. I hit her hard, broke her glasses and damaged her eyes! To make matters worse, two bystanders grabbed me and held me while somebody else called the police.

"The woman lost her sight in one eye and the other had limited vision. Not only was I in jail for aggravated assault, but there was also a $10,000,000 lawsuit against me. I served three years in prison, which dried me out, but the $3,000,000 judgment against me was not easily wiped clean. The story made all the newspapers in the country, of course. This was not the kind of publicity my family wanted. I had shamed them terribly."

Nagel listened intently to the testimony, absorbed. But now it occurred to him that there had been enough testimony from others. He would try once more to stop it.

"Your Honor," he said as he rose from his chair. "I object to this biographical rendition. It is really irrelevant."

Walker asked the court to deny the objection. "Your Honor, the defense must show that their enterprise is not a racket. This witness is in the process of showing what the Society is and does."

Judge Kowalski used his gavel and announced, "Objection overruled."

The witness continued. "The trust which held the family fortune was so structured that neither creditors nor court orders could reach it to obtain any interest held by me. Moreover, the sentence provided that I must pay for my keep while in prison. Rather than fight that part of the sentence and in order to avoid the civil suit the trustees simply cut me off completely as they had a right to do.

"At the end of my prison term, I was determined not to seek out my family. They had virtually abandoned me while I was in prison. My brother came to see me six times in three years. None of the others bothered to see me at all. I got no holiday cards. No birthday cards. All of my drinking buddies forgot me. I did a lot of thinking in prison, but the future was all black. Not only did I have a prison record, but I had a $3,000,000 judgment against me and so long as that judgment hung over me I would get nothing from the trust. As I look back it probably would have been possible to get a court order permitting me to keep a certain portion of my dividends but such an order would have kept me in poverty in any event. It might also have been possible for the trust to have settled the judgment and deducted it from my share. My brother contacted the victim's attorneys, but they wanted no less than $2,000,000 and the company simply could not afford that. Moreover, the family now considered me an enemy, and one who never contributed anything anyway. Strangely, only my brother had any feeling for me whatsoever. My father felt I had let him down, and my sisters were embarrassed by my very existence. My mother went into a semi-trance when my name was mentioned.

"When I came out of prison I put on the suit I had worn when I went in and started looking for a job. Needless to say I didn't find one. I really tried. I read all the classified ads. I was willing to take anything, but my name was mud. A man who had been on drugs and who'd attacked an old lady was not going to find employment, so I robbed a grocery store just to get enough money to buy food. I was arrested again and went to prison as a second offender. And, of course, the name Rothstein got plastered all over the papers again. I was more determined than ever not to seek out my family. For their part, my family disowned me completely. In addition to everything else, they were upset that I did not come crawling to them when I left prison. I served another three years, then I started all over again. This time my brother came to the prison to get me. He gave me $1,000 in cash and rented a room for me for six months. I thanked him and told him he would never have to do that again.

"I was now virtually a street bum. I tried hard not to drink at all. I stayed sober because I had to in order to get a job. But with two convictions I had no chance at all. I conserved that $1,000 to have more time to look for work. I could put together a good résumé. However, private prep school and Columbia didn't mean a thing. My only occupations in life had been alcoholic, drug addict and convict. I began drinking again to shut out the world. The money was soon gone and so was my apartment. I started sleeping in the streets. I managed to get food as best I could and I hounded the unemployment office. The alcohol on my breath killed me, although nobody mentioned my drinking. When the food stamps came in I managed to use them to buy beer. Then I would go to the restaurants' kitchens and beg for discarded bread and table scraps. I was nobody. My brother, if he looked for me, would not have been able to find me, and I guess the rest of my family hoped I had rehabilitated myself and found a life. That's what they liked to believe, because they did not read that I was back in jail. At least that is what I concluded. I could still see our merchandise in store windows and in advertisements in newspapers and magazines, but that was a different world which no longer had anything to do with me.

"In roaming around the back of the restaurants I was lucky to find a cook who felt sorry for me. One day he told me that he was an ex-convict and a member of the Ecumenical Society. He offered to submit my name for consideration for admission to the Society. I later learned this was one of Mr. Carl's restaurants. The cook introduced me to the manager of the restaurant, told him my name and that I was a Columbia graduate.

"I was interviewed by Mr. Carl himself when he came to New York. He presented my name to the board and the next thing I knew I was in a alcohol/drug rehab program. I dried out a second time. The next man I met was Mr. Schwartz. That was a life-saving experience for me. I am a Jew. My family is Jewish. But my family never identified themselves as Jews and they never practiced Judaism. I had never seen the inside of a synagogue or learned one thing about Judaism except what I had seen on television or in the movies. It was not so much that Mr. Schwartz tried to persuade me to re-establish my Jewish heritage; it was his general attitude toward life. Previously I'd thought that accumulating wealth was selfish and sometimes even immoral and that one atones for that by his charities and philanthropies, but this man insisted that acquisitiveness was a part of self-preservation and that I owed it to my self-respect to become independent. He told me that I wouldn't really be free until I'd become independent. He said that the quality of freedom is greater when one can provide for his own security than when one's security is dependent upon the state. In fact, when the state provides security completely no one is free. There is no such thing as freedom without responsibility. 'You are free,' Mr. Schwartz said, 'when you are the master of your own destiny. You are less free as your destiny becomes identified with the state. Of course,' he said, 'for the vast majority of people, there is no chance to build such security. At that point, the choice is between cooperation among individuals or mandated cooperation by the state.' He showed me how the Ecumenical Society was an attempt to build security by those who could not get work on their own or through the state."

Arnold Rothstein paused, and Walker was about to ask another question when the witness spoke up again. "Ben Schwartz also talked to me about charity. He said charity is Biblically inspired and morally mandated. The problem with charity, he said, was that it has become the ultimate and final responsibility when it's really only a temporary help, a Band-Aid, aspirin. To the extent we conceive that to be the ultimate manifestation of our obligations, it is a disservice. It is a disservice because it perpetuates poverty, social imbalance, social disorder. Just as a Band-Aid will not cure an infection or aspirin treat a disease, charity does not cure poverty. The real obligation is to be concerned to the point of seeking solutions and cures instead of palliatives. To be sure, there will always be the poor, those who can't cope, and they will always receive charity. But for a vast number of people there is the possibility of freedom and independence if they are not permanently debilitated by charity."

"So, what did you finally do for a living?" Walker asked.

"I started in the travel business. I borrowed from the Society and bought a travel bureau. I then solicited all members of the Society and prepared tours which they thought they would enjoy. In two years I had the business in such shape that I paid off my debt to the Society, not the $3,000,000. In providing travel insurance I learned a great deal about the insurance business and I borrowed more money and bought an insurance agency and then merged that agency with two others and am now paying off the debt I incurred in those purchases."

"How many people do you employ?"

"Probably 100 altogether."

"Do you hire ex-convicts?"

"Almost exclusively."

"And what is your present relationship with your family?"

"A few years ago, my name became rather well known as some kind of Jewish missionary. I became so fascinated with the heritage I had neglected that I set out to reach other Jews who did not have a religious up-bringing. I tried to induce as many as I could to share with me their histories. Most of their parents had come from immigrant families, but unlike other ethnics they never bothered to really identify themselves or to celebrate their heritage, even though most of them had come to this country because they had been persecuted in the countries from which their forefathers had emigrated. It was not so strange to learn that whereas they were identified as Jews, separate from the countries of their birth, when they came to these shores they became Americans first and foremost, contrary to the claims of hate mongers who would have everybody believe otherwise.

"In my service to that cause I often made the headlines. My family began reading about me. Most of the comments were good. One day I called my brother Myron. I told him I wanted to hold a reunion with the family. He said he was pleased to hear from me and he arranged the get together at my parents' home. They were all there; father, mother, brother, sisters, in-laws, grandchildren. It was stiff at first, but I was determined to soften it up. Before the meal, I arose and told them I was a new person. I had come back to apologize for the sorrow I had brought upon them and I asked for their forgiveness. My dear brother immediately got to his feet. He could hardly hold back his tears. With a choking voice he said that whatever may have happened in the past it was for me to forgive them, for they had abandoned me when I needed them most. They were all grateful that I had come back out of the depths by myself and I was now the hero of the family.

"I picked up a glass of champagne and I offered a toast to the future. I got my family into a synagogue and we became a real Jewish family. Now I am married and, at the advanced age of 42 years, I await my first child."

"You may cross-examine," Walker said to Nagel, but before Nagel could commence the court ordered a 15 minute recess. The courtroom buzzed with quiet conversations. Rothstein came off the witness stand and joined Frank, Janet and the defendants at counsel's table.

Myron Rothstein came from the audience and Arnold introduced him to the others.

Walker asked Myron how long he had been at the trial. "From the very beginning," Myron replied. "I'm becoming educated. I feel like I'm entering a new world."

Walker reached for Myron's hand. "Hopefully, we all are," he said with a broad smile.

Father Leahy was close by and heard the conversation. "It's not a new world, Mr. Walker," he put in, also smiling, "it's simply a new frame of reference, or, perhaps, an old, neglected frame of reference."

In cross-examining the witness, Nagel elicited from Rothstein that only one in ten of the prisoners he interviewed were hired. He took only those whose records in prison and school and whose general demeanor indicated they would make good employees.

"So, Mr. Rothstein, you are like a gold miner. You take the nuggets and throw out the slag."

"You can put it that way, Mr. Nagel. But we are just like any other employer. We try to get the best. We are not out to get incorrigibles and reform them. We try to get people who will be good employees and who will fit in with the philosophy of the Ecumenical Society, people who acknowledge they have made a mistake and who are willing to start over and cooperate with others who are trying to do the same. It's strictly a business deal but it requires a moral commitment. New hires have to be able not only to help themselves but help others, not as charity, not as a social obligation, but as part of a team pulling together under the guidance of God.

"The genius of our program, Mr. Nagel, is the introduction of economics into the process of redemption. What Father Leahy, Reverend Hamilton and Ben Schwartz have done is to face what social reformers have never been willing to face, that in order for people to redeem themselves they must have the financial means to do so. All social programs in history have called upon the wayward ones to 'shape up' on threat of further punishment. They have been willing to provide short-term aids like unemployment compensation and welfare but no real niche in the socio-economic structure. That just doesn't work. We know that. In this century we have learned that socialism and communism — which promise security if one just obeys orders — don't work. Our program offers the opportunity for redemption with dignity not only for one's own salvation but for the others on the team."

"You reach less than 1% of the prison population, isn't that true?"

"Mr. Nagel, that's a cheap shot. Right now we have 6,000 members. It's taken 30 years, and it hasn't been easy. It's been terribly expensive; your establishment would never pay for it. We hope we can reach 100,000, 200,000 prisoners. We are sure there are a lot more people in prison who can be recruited. We just can't handle them now. We don't have enough employers. In recent years we've grown more rapidly. I hope we can do more."

Nagel looked to his two associates, Draefus and Wicker, seated beside him. They had nothing to offer. He stole a look at Janet. She was staring at him without expression. He was aware that she had hardly taken her eyes off him throughout the trial. He felt he must continue.

"Mr. Rothstein, is there any standard by which the board determines who will be helped and for how much?"

"No, there is none."

"The board has unrestricted discretion. Is that correct?"

"Yes, that's correct."

"Is there an appeal from the board's decision?"

"No."

"Is the board elected? If it is, who elects it?"

"The board is elected by the employers. Six members serve staggered terms, with elections held every two years."

"So, no standards are applied: there is no appeal from the board's decision; and the employees have no right to vote for the director, right?"

"That's right."

"That's a bit autocratic, isn't it?"

"Not more than with any bank's board of directors. A bank board's decision is final, and there is no appeal, and the directors don't have to give you a reason why you were turned down. As for standards, we don't have any because we want to be free to help anybody. We don't consider only the financial statement of the petitioner. Our criteria include compassion. We approve a petition absent a very strong reason not to. A bank is concerned about its fiscal soundness first; we are concerned about the needs of the petitioner first. That's why we can help when a bank cannot; we are not a bank. If we operated like a bank the petitioner would not need us. In fact there would be no need for us at all. We always give credit where a bank would not."

Nagel pondered getting into the "God" business. He was about to ask, "Just who is God?" when Draefus nudged him and pushed a legal pad toward him. On it was written, "STOP."

Nagel looked up. "I have no further questions."

The court asked Walker if he had any further questions. Walker didn't. The judge then said, "Tomorrow is Friday, which is the day when I hear motions in many matters. Monday is a legal holiday. This has been a long day. It is five o'clock, past our usual adjournment time. This court is now adjourned until Tuesday at 9:00 a.m.

SEVENTEEN

Nobody had anticipated what happened next. The headlines in the afternoon papers blared: "Ecumenical Society Association of Ex-Prostitutes." The sub-head read: "Owner of multi-million dollar business defends employment of ex-prostitutes." And the stories went on to quote Angela Burgé's testimony. The story in the local paper was factual and accurate. It added a query: "Is it a reform group or a criminal syndicate?"

The following day's papers ran a tragic story under the banner: "Five Ex-Prostitutes Commit Suicide." The story linked the deaths to the criminal trial and summed up the case against the minister and priest charged with establishing and maintaining an extortion racket. The full story revealed the testimony of Angela Burgé and the defense's claim that there was no racket, only a means by which former criminals were offered an opportunity to reestablish their lives.

In the office of the attorney general, Nagel, Draefus and Wicker were in conference. "We neglected to have the jury sequestered. They have read the papers. This is information which would not be admissible at trial. What do we do about it?" Nagel asked.

Draefus said: "The question is whether we ask the court to give the jury additional instructions."

"Such as what?" Wicker asked.

"The judge could tell them to ignore the newspaper articles."

"Before considering that," Nagel said, "we must determine how this news is likely to affect the jury. Will it build sympathy for the defendants?"

"The articles I have read," Draefus said, "seem to reflect the dilemma the jury must resolve: Did these people commit a crime or were they pursuing their duties as clergymen?"

Nagel agreed. "That is what Kowalski thinks is the issue, and he's the judge. Remember, however, that we have never conceded that to be the issue. Our case is simple: Do the facts make out a case of extortion? Have these defendants aided and abetted the drug traffic? Can you force employees to pay you money on the threat of losing their jobs? It doesn't make any difference what you do with the money after you've got it. Suppose this was the Methodist church and the money was used in accordance with church operations. Does that excuse the forced taking?"

Wicker shook his head. "I'm afraid, Paul, that your example doesn't fit. The record shows that we are not dealing with a church. We don't have a religious organization. This is really a sort of cooperative and the deal is that everybody keeps supplying capital if they are to continue to be members."

"Is it really a cooperative? It's not organized as such under the law. So far we have heard of no particular procedures for the allocation of benefits. There are no dividends. Hey man, this money is given to God!"

"And used by the Defendants," Draefus added, "and their Board of Directors as they wish."

"Yes," Nagel said. "Does it matter what is done with the money? So far as I know, it doesn't make any difference what you do with the money if it is originally taken illegally. Is this different? The process described by Angela Burgé did not sound like extortion to me. I don't know what it is, but I'm afraid that jury may very well conclude it is not extortion."

"Paul, I'm afraid I agree with you," Wicker said sullenly.

"Just a minute, you guys," Draefus objected. "Don't go jumping off the track. Suppose that we had heard the Burgé testimony at the same time we got the statements from our witnesses. Would you have taken the responsibility for refusing to prosecute? Remember RICO. It is intended to stop racketeer money from going into legitimate businesses. Extortion is a violation of RICO. A bunch of ex-cons are taking money from people who can't help themselves and putting it into existing businesses and starting new businesses. Remember we got this case from Washington."

"Why didn't we get more information from our witnesses?" Wicker wanted to know.

Nagel chuckled. "You got enough from them to seal their bargain with you. Murray might have gotten life. He was saving his skin by telling the FBI what it wanted to hear. That's the trouble with plea bargains. I guess, gentlemen, that this one is for the jury."

Draefus suggested they get back to the question of the newspaper and media stories. "I think they are a great benefit to the defense. They furnish a reason for the secrecy other than hiding a crime. Whenever there is secrecy, it is automatically assumed that it's for the sole purpose of covering up the criminal aspects of the case. This record shows that was not the purpose of the secrecy. The secrecy was really a part of the legitimate reform program."

"So, what do we do about it?" Nagel wanted to know.

"Nothing," Wicker said. "If you ask the court to instruct the jury to ignore the news stories, you will simply increase the benefit to the defense."

"Any comment, Draefus?"

"None."

"Very well," Nagel concluded, "so be it."

The conference broke up, and Wicker and Draefus left the office. Nagel sat hunched over, twirling a letter opener in his hands, thinking about Janet Wingate. The glances exchanged in the courtroom came to his mind. She actually felt sorry for him! She wasn't angry with him. He would always miss her terribly. He was glad he had told her he loved her in spite of the bizarre circumstances. He would tell her again, if he ever got the chance.

In the office of Frank Walker, a different conference was taking place. Janet, Ben Schwartz, Reverend Hamilton, Vera Hamilton and Father Leahy were in a somber mood.

"It isn't worth it," Father Leahy was saying. "This whole business is not worth the lives of five women, five mothers with children and

God's Mafia

husbands." Reverend Hamilton rose from his chair and went to Leahy's side. He put his arm on the giant's shoulder and stood there but said nothing.

Walker broke the silence. "I don't think anyone could have foreseen this."

"That's not so, Frank," Hamilton retorted. "Pat and I have been afraid of this all along. And we remain afraid. These people, particularly these women, have tried so hard to renew their lives. Nobody is more ashamed of their past than they are. They are not Angela Burgé and are not that strong. They are weak. They always have been. They have mustered the strength to start over, but now, in spite of all that effort, they are back where they started. Is it surprising that some couldn't face it?"

Father Leahy agreed. "There are others, I am sure, who are in despair. I'm told that some men have disappeared, probably the former pimps and male prostitutes. You can guess where they've gone. Right now there are thousands who need care. We can't reach them all! They are scattered all over the country."

Nobody had any solution, not even a way to approach the solution. There was complete silence. Then the telephone rang. Walker answered. He said into the phone, "Wait, I'll put you on the speaker phone. I have everybody else here. It's Angela." Walker turned on the speaker phone.

"I'm glad I reached all of you." Angela's voice was strong, confident and assured. Just what the group needed. "I'm calling to tell you that I've been on the phone with Nelson. The directors have been assigned to cover all the employers. They are to call them and the employers are to call all their employees. Those who are not working will be called in. I'm calling all my people from all over the country. They are coming to the Halbury Hotel here in Indianapolis on Sunday. I've offered to pay for those who can't afford it. I've arranged a phone hook-up between the hotel and each employer's office. I will be talking to my people in the auditorium of the hotel and everyone else will pick it up by phone. I'm going to explain to them what we are doing and why they must keep calm, cool and collected. This will all work out. I'm going to tell them that the secret is dead, that we are coming out and we are coming out with our heads held high.

"Ben, I'm going to need some money to pull this off. Bob says he can provide it if it's OK."

Ben said, "The board must have approved it if they are participating."

"They have OK'd it, if you and Reverend Hamilton and Father Leahy approve."

Janet and Walker listened with bated breath. Father Leahy approached the speaker phone. "God bless you Angela. You can do it."

Hamilton called from across the room. "Thank you, Angela. Thank you for your strength."

"Don't worry about money," Ben said, "Just be sure you feed them lunch when you get them together. We're behind you all the way."

Janet shouted, "Don't hang up. I want to say something." She took a step or two toward the phone. "Angela, you are right. We've got to come out and tell the world how proud we are of ourselves. We are better than many others. We've come the hard way. No more hiding, no more secrets. Let the gossips talk. This is the only way, Angela. I'll be in Indianapolis and I'll get the defendants down there, too."

Father Leahy asked, "Angela, what are we doing about the suicides?"

"All the suicides are my employees. They're all mothers. I've already sent staff members to each of their homes. They are to report back to me as to the circumstances of each family. My staff is to tell the families that there is life insurance and other things we can do for them, and that we will approach the Society for any extra help which may be needed. The life insurance policies are all old enough so they cover suicide." That ended the phone conference.

"What a woman!" Walker exclaimed.

Janet went to her father's side and took him in her arms. Then she reached over and pulled her mother into the embrace. "That woman has won your lawsuit, Frank. And she will solve this problem too."

With such short notice, it was impossible to even guess how many would show up at Angela's meeting. She made reservations for 700 meals with an option to increase it to 1,000 on 12 hours notice. The meeting was set for Sunday three days from now. On Sunday morning by eleven o'clock, 1,200 people, almost all women, appeared. No rooms had been reserved, only the main auditorium. Some of the attendees had made their own reservations at hotels around town. The women were greeted by members of Angela's staff, but Angela herself was not there to greet them. They were told to make themselves comfortable and to arrive at the auditorium at one in the afternoon.

People of all colors — black, white, yellow, brown — gathered at the appointed time. All were chattering furiously. Some were angry. Of all people to betray them, their leader and boss! How could she let them down? Some answered, "Because she must do it"; "We can't hide forever"; "Now is the time to come out." There was no consensus, but there was plenty of worry.

For years these women had been respected in their communities, their churches, their clubs, their children's schools. Now they were faced with the worst possible humiliation. Already there were reverberations. The news stories had identified their employer, had publicly proclaimed that the employer hired only former prostitutes. Eyebrows of friends, neighbors, and acquaintances had raised. One could almost see and hear the gasping in disbelief, the outright shock. Nothing could be worse, not even death! And five had already chosen death.

The promoter of this gathering was not as self-assured as she had sounded over the telephone. She was sure she was right in promoting 'coming out,' but how could she be sure the public would respond favorably? The news since her testimony had shown some reaction which she considered favorable. But a lot of it was not favorable. She began to wonder if this was the thing to do. That was why she had not alerted the news media to the gathering. It could be a huge disaster. But there was no turning back now. She must follow through.

Burgé ascended the small podium, stood behind the lectern and spoke into the microphone. She first asked that all the doors to the auditorium be closed. "I've asked all you to come here today because we are in the midst of the worst crisis of our lives. We must face it together not with those who don't know our history. We know our history. We know what a struggle it has been for all of us. Here today we are of one background, a background which runs from the misery of the streets to homes, families and love. We have come along the same path together, fighting the same fight, overcoming the same odds. We are a family. We have come to love each other because we have succeeded together. And we are proud of what we have done. Don't let anybody tell you different. Nobody has fought the fight you have fought and won it, at least not by themselves. Together, working with each other, on our own, without any help from the government or from charities we have pulled ourselves out of the gutter and into the mainstream of life. They said we couldn't do it, but we did. We are now proud women, proud mothers and wives, citizens. We will not be shamed! We will stand before the whole world and let everybody know that we have earned the respect we deserve. We must not run for cover. We must not wince or retreat. Let them see the worst and we will show them the best. We don't ask admittance to society. We are part of society. We don't ask for pity for the life we once led. We ask for respect, for by ourselves we have left that life once and for all. We are role models, for if we can overcome what we have overcome, the rest of the world must be inspired to overcome their little problems.

"We cannot go on hiding forever. We cannot sneak into holes while the two men who saved us are put into prison. It will be our crowning achievement that after we have saved ourselves we have saved those who provided our chance to save ourselves. That's why we're here, to tell the whole world who we are, what we are and that we are as good as anybody else. We will not let them crucify our saviors! We will fight to save them. We will match our courage with the courage of those who would crucify them. Today, in this hall, we will rejoice, not bemoan. We will give thanks that God has given us the strength to fight, to overcome and to save those who saved us.

"I've asked the hotel to bring in what we will call an indoor picnic lunch. Now let's celebrate. And we can celebrate. Already our founders, the two defendants, are heroes, regardless of what the jury decides. Already the world knows what they have done. And we, each of us, all of us, can celebrate because we have been a part of it. Stand up, stand up tall, everybody."

The words were still crackling around the auditorium when everybody leapt to their feet, cheering, clapping, laughing, crying, hugging each other, shaking hands. One of the black women began singing, "We Shall Overcome," and soon the entire assembly was singing. Angela Burgé stayed on the podium and as she watched she didn't quite know whether to shout and laugh or cry. As she looked about, she grew angry at herself for not inviting the press. As she was bemoaning that fact, a black woman climbed to the podium and approached Angela. "My name is Rose Blythe, and I'm with the *Telegram*," she said. "I've watched these proceedings. I want to write about it. I want to send your message all over the world."

Angela threw her hands in the air and then took the woman in her arms. "God bless you," she shouted. "Where were you? I didn't see you."

"Well," said Rose, "I happened to be in the hotel and wondered what was going on. I had to tell the people who closed the doors that I was an employee. The next time you put on something like this you must give the press notice. Can I interview you? Right now?"

At that moment, through one set of doors came Father Leahy, tall, handsome as ever, smiling with both hands in the air. As he entered, a shout went up and the women ran toward him, surrounding him. Within moments, Reverend Hamilton came in through another set of doors. A group of women surrounded him and pushed him and Father Leahy to the podium where Angela and the reporter were talking. Angela was in tears. First Father Leahy and then Reverend Hamilton embraced her. Then all three faced the crowd and the roar could be heard throughout the hotel. Rose Blythe got off the podium and took photos of the three and then of the entire room. She ran up to Angela. "I'll see you later. Right now I'm sending story and photos over all the wires."

The story Rose Blythe sent out made every major daily throughout the world. Rose had turned it into a great human interest story, the story of women pushed into prostitution who with the help of a couple of clergymen, had regained respectability and happiness. Editors of the various papers seized upon the story and editorialized their concern that a statute clearly intended to fight organized crime could be used to make criminals out of such dedicated men who were really helping to solve the crime problem. Only the small mind of the prosecution, so intent on making a name for itself would so harass innocent people. There was virtually no support for the view that Leahy and Hamilton had utilized a philanthropic guise to extort money and to make millionaires of themselves out of the hard luck of hapless women.

Nagel read the big story as well as the editorials. Why hadn't the writers contacted him? What kind of reporters or editors would base their article on the representation of one side only? He was angry. He would call the editor of the paper he had read. Did newspaper men really believe that prosecutors would distort the law just to put people in jail in order to make a name for themselves? The Department of Justice and the FBI were not craven institutions. How could they think that way?

More important, however, the jury had read all this. What was to be done about that? Now he simply must ask the court immediately to tell the jury to ignore such reports and consider only what was said in the courtroom. He had to take the chance that this might call the story to the attention of jurors who had not read the papers, or heard it on radio or television.

EIGHTEEN

On Tuesday the effect of the publicity on the jury was discussed. The judge decided to instruct the jury to put out of their minds whatever they might have heard or read over the weekend, to consider only the information they had learned in court.

The testimony continued with Walker calling Ben Schwartz to the stand. He asked the witness to identify himself and to inform the court if he was acquainted with the defendants. The witness did not seem like the Ben Schwartz who was known to his friends. This was a somber, serious, distant person, so different that it startled those in the courtroom who knew him. In a very formal, quiet manner he began to testify.

"My name is Ben Schwartz and I came to Fairfield about 25 years ago. I have known both defendants since then, and I am fully acquainted with what they have done. I have joined in what they have done and if they are guilty, so am I. I have never been in prison in the United States. I am not an ex-convict, but the Ecumenical Society has done for me what it has done for the people who have testified. I have spent some wonderful years in Fairfield and with these two defendants. I am Jewish and I was pleased that even though there were no other Jews in town the community took me in with open arms. I was never asked where I came from, but now it is time to reveal my own secret. Where did I live before I came to Fairfield? My prior residence was the Auschwitz concentration camp in Poland." Father Leahy's mouth dropped open. He lowered his head and closed his eyes. Malcolm Hamilton stared wide-eyed at his old friend. Vera Hamilton raised her eyes to the ceiling. Tears came to Janet Wingate's eyes.

Alfred J. Fortino

"Before Auschwitz my home was in Berlin. I was born there, and my family was part owner in an international investment house there, one of the older investment houses in which there were very few partners and in which my family had a considerable interest. I was educated in schools in Berlin and I graduated from Heidelberg University with a degree in Economics and Banking. I was 17 years old when I graduated. I worked at the family bank, married and had two children, a boy and a girl. Throughout Germany's bad times, my family was secure. We traded briskly in the international market, mostly in foreign currencies. My father was a partner who taught me what he could. Then came the Nazis. Early on, before they came to power, my father saw the handwriting on the wall. He began to move a great part of our estate into Switzerland. He told me we must do that while there was still time. After my parents died, I continued moving our securities into Swiss banks. I went to Switzerland while Jews could still leave the country, and I provided the bank with photos and fingerprints to make sure that our funds could be identified and our family identified. We moved no more than 70% of our total assets, because we had to leave something for the Nazis to find. When the they came to power, they seized our bank but they kept it intact because they wanted to learn how it operated. My friends died of broken hearts mostly, but my family survived and I kept hoping for some miracle. The time came when the Nazis needed me no longer. As much of our property as they could reach they took, and then they shipped us out of Berlin. They took my family away from me and I was shipped alone to Poland. I never saw my family again.

"I was moved around and I finally ended up at Auschwitz. And that, my friends, was hell. My family had always been devout Reformed Jews. We worshipped at a synagogue as long as we could, and then we had worship services in our home. I lived through Auschwitz, witness to the horrible debasement, humiliation, degradation, and eventual murder of my fellow Jews. I survived but in a horrible physical state. I was kept alive by my faith. I don't know how I was still alive when we were freed. I wasn't completely alive, but I was sufficiently alive to be taken to a hospital. My problem wasn't so much physical as mental. I was ashamed to be alive! I was ashamed that I had survived.

I could not think of my family at all. I didn't know if they were alive or dead although I was pretty sure that they were dead because I saw how Jews were killed.

"Of course I tried to find them. It was impossible. I got in touch with the bank in Switzerland, was able to go there, and from there I was able to come to this country. I had studied English from grade school through University. I have always spoken English without a foreign accent. Chance brought me to Fairfield, except that I wanted to live in a small town where I could become inconspicuous. I did not have faith that this country could endure a wave of anti-Semitism. I was pretty sure that I would be faced with it here as I had been in Germany. I did not want to become a part of the New York establishment or the New York investment houses. I found this little business in Fairfield, bought it and I have been here ever since. But I was ashamed to be alive, and I was not very happy. The future for me was bleak. I made many friends in the town and among them were these two defendants. I think I shocked them one day. They were telling me how in their work as pastors they were sad that so many good people who got into trouble with the law were never able to overcome that failure even after they paid their debt to society and emerged from prison. They concluded that people convicted of crimes were never permitted even to repent. Far too many who deserved a chance never got it. And they also concluded that there was no way in which this society or any society could really take them back. They believed that ex-convicts had to pull themselves up by their own boot straps, make their own way. There would never be enough money or enough jobs to help rehabilitate them. It would be necessary therefore to build a kind of economic society for ex-convicts. This they had done in discussions between themselves and, apparently, after a lot of reading. It was a philosophical discussion. One day I asked: 'How much money would it take to start this kind of organization?'

"They had no idea how much it would take but knew it would take an enormous amount of money. I suggested that maybe it wouldn't be necessary to have all the money at once and that I might be able to get them started. They never asked me how I could manage that, and I didn't tell them that my family had been wealthy and that

Alfred J. Fortino

although we lost 30% of everything 70% was still intact and that I had access to it. I offered them $50,000 for starters."

"They took that money and they put together a simple trust. They had no overhead because they did all the work. The money was invested, and at first I provided the financial advice. It was second nature to me. The first year there was little more to do than preserve and nurture the $50,000. The second year I gave them $100,000. With $150,000 they got things going. In giving I was reborn, as they say. That was a long time ago and now you see what has developed. I am very proud to have been a part of it. I am grateful for the chance to be alive again."

Walker asked, "Can you estimate how much money you have donated to the Ecumenical Fund?"

"I only contributed during the early years when they had no other sources. I probably did that for three or four years. Over that period of time I probably contributed half a million dollars, maybe $600,000."

"Have you ever received anything in return for your donations?"

"Not in money."

"Have Reverend Hamilton or Father Leahy ever received any money from the fund?"

"Only for expenses, because they do not have enough funds of their own to make trips and to help others. But they have never been paid anything for their services."

"Do you know if there are any paid personnel?"

"Oh yes there is a considerable staff at the New York office and most of them are on salary or hourly wage."

Walker turned to the court and said, "I have no further questions of this witness."

Nagel decided there was no point in cross-examining Schwartz. "I have no questions," he announced.

The Judge left the courtroom and the bailiff escorted the jury out. Janet ran over to Ben Schwartz and threw her arms about him. She didn't say anything, just held him for awhile. They were about the same size and he embraced her as well. Before Hamilton and Leahy could reach Schwartz, he was surrounded by newspaper reporters. Ben raised both arms. "Gentlemen I told it all from the witness stand.

That is your story." But it was not enough to satisfy the press; they wanted to ask him about his family and the early days of Hitler's reign. They wanted to ask him about Auschwitz. They wanted to ask him about his physical condition. How had he survived?

Ben Schwartz raised his arms still higher and he spoke in a loud, clear voice in order that he might be heard above the din. "Please hear me. You have been writing about this case for weeks. You have insisted and the government has insisted that people divulge their innermost secrets, that they must tell it all. I have lived among you for 25 years and this is the first time you have heard me tell my story. Why do you suppose you have not heard it before? Can't you understand? There are things that people would like to forget, things that people want to brush aside for their own sanity and their own health. Like the others, I have had to reveal it all, and I have done so because I wanted in this record the fact that there can be a hell on earth, a man-made hell, a hell that results when the government is run by bureaucrats who are absolutely right in their own minds beyond the shadow of a doubt even to the point of destroying those whom they should serve. When a society insists on making criminals of people who seek to find their own way, you have created a new prison. You will not give them a chance in your society. You put a brand on them. Your idea is to build more prisons, increase punishment. These people are trying to say to you, 'We understand. We do not expect you to rehabilitate us. We will rehabilitate ourselves. Just give us the chance.' The story of this case is not my story, and it is not the exposé of those who have testified. It is the exposé of your life, of your society."

With these words, Schwartz hurried to the exit and left the courthouse.

Walker next called Robert Nelson, a man of average height and weight, thinning hair combed straight back, a fine-featured face with blue eyes and white teeth. He sat down and seemed to make himself comfortable.

"My name is Robert Nelson, I'm 51 years old and reside in New York City."

"What is your marital status?" Walker asked.

"I am married but have no children. My wife lives with me in New York and she works for the New York Public Library."

"Do you have any connection with the Ecumenical Society?"

"For the past 15 years I have been the Executive Director, albeit with no operational functions. Ms. Louise Windsor manages the affairs of the group. My time is taken with devising and implementing functions to be utilized in advancing the purposes of the organization, in organizing departments or committees to enhance the function of the organization and in writing policies for the organization."

"What is your educational background?"

"I am a graduate of the New York public school system and the City College of New York. I have a Ph.D. from Princeton in philosophy."

"A Ph.D. in philosophy?" Walker was a little surprised. "I thought that the degree doctor of philosophy meant that you had a doctorate in one of the physical or social sciences."

Nelson smiled. "Well, my Ph.D. is in philosophy. I studied the philosophies of many wise people and I emerged thoroughly confused."

Everyone laughed but Nagel, Draefus and Wicker. Walker waited until the laughter subsided before continuing. "Well, let me ask you, did you have an area of expertise? What drew you to your present employer?"

"I would have to say that prior to my employment with the Society I never had any expertise. I read and studied whatever came to mind. I tried to observe the world in general and enjoyed doing it. I was unemployed when I applied for this job and so intrigued by the job description that I was more interested in talking to the people who conceived and dared to promote the idea than I was in landing it. In my interview for the position, I met the defendants in this case and Mr. Ben Schwartz. They seemed to like what I told them, and they hired me. Mr. Schwartz guaranteed my salary, which was more than I was making, since I wasn't making anything. I have wondered ever since why they hired me. I have found it to be the opportunity of a lifetime, and I have been most grateful."

"What is the Ecumenical Society?"

"It is a voluntary association of persons with a common handicap who try to help each other to overcome that handicap. In that respect it is much like Alcoholics Anonymous or Weight Watchers. However, whereas one can stop drinking or over eating on his own, one cannot employ himself or go into business without capital. Therefore, the Ecumenical Society goes the extra mile, so to speak, in providing a job and financial assistance.

"The Ecumenical Society does not try to solve the crime problem. It seeks to solve the problem of the ex-convict who is willing to pay a reasonable cost for the help. It is not the claim of the Society that the social order causes crime or that the criminal system is at fault. The first thing a member of the Society does is to admit he and he alone is at fault, much as the alcoholic or the overeater. The social order does not have enough money to do for ex-convicts what the Ecumenical Society does, nor should it. There is no reason why law abiding citizens should subsidize the treatment and rehabilitation of those who have robbed or killed. As a matter of fact, the Ecumenical Society cannot do that either. It cannot even do it for one percent of the convicts. The reason the program works is because it is really based on the same principal as insurance. One contributes as one must but receives only as he needs. Everybody in this courtroom insures their homes or their automobiles or personal property. Only a small fraction ever collect. Nobody complains about that. Everybody is happy to have the protection. Nobody complains that they never get back the premium they have paid.

"Our premium is not extortionate. It is based on the ability to pay. If one makes $18,000 per year the premium is $1350, a little more than $100 per month. Most people pay more than that for fire insurance on their home or on their automobile. If one makes $25,000 per year it is only $1,875 per year, about $150 per month. And look at what he or she gets: a job, the ability to borrow to buy a home, educate children, meet medical expenses, etc., at a time when they can't even get a job!

"Of course the initial expenditure by the Society when it brings a person in is without cost to the individual. Sometimes that involves a lot of money. It may involve several years of education or rehabilitation. In every case in which considerable money has been expended by the Society the recipient paid it back many times over in later contributions. If that person makes $300,000, or $400,000, then they pay $22,500 or $30,000 per year."

Walker had no further questions. Nagel rose to cross-examine. "Mr. Nelson, you have not told us the nature of the Ecumenical Society. Is it a corporation, a partnership, a syndicate, a limited partnership, an association?"

"In our income tax returns we are treated as a voluntary association. However, we pay income taxes the same as a corporation."

"Do you have by-laws?"

"We have what we call 'Rules of Order' by which we conduct meetings. These also cover election of directors."

"Don't you have any procedure by which you account for the money you take in and spend?"

"We retain professional CPAs and attorneys. They prepare financial reports and statements. Each calendar year we account for what we received and how it was spent or invested."

"To whom do you send this account?"

"To all the employers and employees who have contributed."

"Are your officials bonded?"

"Yes sir."

"Who owns all this money?"

"The Society."

"But the Society is really nobody. The members don't own it."

"All the assets of the Society are in a trust at the Central Bank in Fairfield. There is a trust document which provides that the trust is for the benefit of the Ecumenical Society."

"But no human being can claim ownership, is that right?"

"That's right. Everything belongs to God."

"And who is God?"

Nelson looked at Hamilton and Leahy and smiled. "Mr. Nagel, when you asked that of Ms. Burgé she told you what God is, not who He is! She said 'He is the Creator, the Supreme Being.' There is no answer to the question, 'Who is God?' When Moses asked God that question, the answer was, 'I am who I am.' That's in Exodus, Chapter 3, Verse 13. It was the philosopher Spinoza who said that when one asks 'Who is God?' he is no longer talking about God. God is beyond human identification. God simply is!"

"So, God is a figment of the imagination!"

Nelson smiled again and gave a knowing look to the defendants. "Mr. Nagel, I do not come from a religious background. In my home, religion was never anything more than a philosophical or historical discussion. I am now a believer. What I have observed in this organization has convinced me. Previously, I was like you, believing religion to be either myth or gossip. There was no proof that God existed. In fact the proof is apparent every day in every one of us. You call it a figment of the imagination. By that observation you imply that God is a concoction of our making, that there is no reality which we can identify as God. I ask you, 'What is the law which you press upon us so assiduously in this courtroom? Is it anything more than a figment of our imagination? Can you see the law? Can you touch it?'

"You might respond by saying, 'It's in the books.' Well, so is God. We know the law by its stewards, its legislators and judges, its lawyers. And that is the only way we know God, by His stewards. The great failure of mankind is that over the centuries people have fought people over the claim of who are the true stewards, a disastrous betrayal of God by man. In this country, for example, this senseless struggle for anointment has gotten to the point where we prefer not to recognize God at all, lest it should appear that some particular sect is the true steward. The days of the Crusades, of the so-called infidels, are still with us. And God's work remains undone.

In separating the church from the state we have managed to separate man from God."

Both Draefus and Wicker were becoming uneasy. This was developing into a theological, philosophical, discussion which Nagel could not win. But Nagel felt he had to press on. Walker, on the other hand, was enjoying the proceedings. All the testimony was argumentative and objectionable, but Nelson was winning the argument; why object? He didn't.

"Mr. Nelson," Nagel asked, "do you really think that those of us who seek to enforce the law are without conscience or ethics?"

"We are not talking about conscience or ethics. Conscience and ethics are always parochial. What conscience and ethics might dictate is not necessarily what God demands. A thief may be prompted by his conscience to share his loot with his fellow thief, but his conscience is not strong enough to deter him from stealing. Likewise with ethics. I'm reminded of the story of the little boy who asked his father what was meant by ethics. His father told him that ethics was something no man could be without. He said, 'Suppose I am in business with a partner. One day when I am alone a customer buys $5 worth of merchandise and gives me a $20 bill. I make a mistake and give the customer change for a $10 bill. Now comes the question of ethics: Do I tell my partner?' "

"Then what are we talking about, Mr. Nelson? It is not conscience. It is not ethics. What is it?"

"Morality."

"How do you distinguish between conscience and ethics on the one hand and morality on the other?"

"Conscience and ethics are devised by man. Morality is devised by God."

"So now you separate God from man. You have just testified that God is in each of us. Which is it?"

"I do not separate man from God. Man has within himself both morality and conscience. He eases the burden of morality by substituting his conscience for God's morality. Soon he comes to consider God's morality archaic, irrelevant. In this he is encouraged by the declared policy separating the church from the state, as though the church were God. God's mandates are now purely a private matter between God and the individual, dedicated solely to the salvation of the individual. The relationship between government and the individual is gauged by 'social consciousness,' a messy mixture of individual consciences.

"The government has tried mightily to achieve a society of peace and tranquillity. We have piled new laws and regulations on old, as government intrudes more intensely into our lives. We are now seeking to regulate in fields we never dreamed of regulating in the past. In this state, within 40 years we have increased the size of government at least ten times. Forty years ago the governance of this state was managed through offices in the capital building and in one other office building a block away. Today there are 14 office buildings at least six stories high which surround the capital. There is a secondary complex of an additional ten office buildings located about ten miles away. In addition, the state leases 24 other buildings in and about the capital. Of course, there are many more office buildings throughout the state. Within these buildings we have 24 separate state departments, 95 boards, commissions and agencies and over 300 other separate divisions.

"In 1950, the Federal Register, which publishes the rules and regulations of the various Federal agencies, published 9500 pages. Today it publishes over 67,000 pages. Until 1944, this state had not published a compilation of the state rules and regulations. The State Administrative Code was adopted in 1944. By 1974 it was publishing 7000 pages per year. Now there is a whole volume published monthly!

"We have indeed accepted the standard proposed by John Dewey when he said, 'So long as the lowest insect suffers the pangs of unrequited love this is not the perfect society.'

"Has all this brought us peace and happiness? Hardly. We have simply become more contentious. In this state in 1941 33,000 civil cases and 5200 criminal cases were filed. Today there are over 230,000 civil cases and 57,000 criminal cases. Almost 70% of the civil cases involve divorce, paternity, child custody and child support. All other civil cases, including automobile negligence, other damage suits, product liability, malpractice and so forth comprised only 30% of the entire state-wide docket.

"Our prison population, throughout the entire nation is growing at the rate of 7.5% per annum. Over 5,000,000 of us (2.7% of our population) are in prison, on parole or probation."

"The population has grown, hasn't it?"

"It has, at a rate of $9/10$ of 1% per annum."

"And whose morality would you apply, Mr. Nelson?"

"The Society doesn't apply any. It respects them all. The tragedy of institutional religion throughout history has been that the various sects have spent all their time and effort fighting for recognition as the chosen way. So much so that this country has decided to ignore the morality factor completely. Where we need morality the most, in governance, in education, we deliberately cast it out. Morality, as delineated by God's stewards, is said to have no place in the very core of our existence. Why? Because we are afraid we will offend some code other than one of our choosing! In the Ecumenical Society, we respect all codes of morality, so we keep God at the center of our lives, of our organization. The irony of this is overwhelming, for it was the search for morality which not only founded this country but which was at its educational base. Harvard was founded to 'advance learning and perpetuate it for posterity, dreading to leave an illiterate ministry to the churches' as stated in its original documents. William and Mary College in Virginia, Yale, Princeton, Brown, and Rutgers were all founded under religious auspices. William and Mary by the Church of England; Yale, Congregational; Princeton, Presbyterian; Brown, Baptist; Rutgers, Dutch Reformed. Georgetown was the first Catholic University. It was founded in 1789."

"Mr. Nelson, nobody is disputing what you say. The history you recite is well known. Is it your claim that when these three complainants say they were forced to give money on pain of losing their businesses, their property, that they had a moral obligation to pay that money?"

"Yes sir."

"And that is by your Society's standards?"

"No. It is by the standards of the complainants."

"But they deny they had any obligations."

"I'm sorry. I did not hear them say they had no obligation. I heard them say they paid because they had to do so in order not to lose their businesses, their property. They did not say they had no obligation to pay. We all paid because we had to, because we must. You see, Mr. Nagel, you and the statute say there is no obligation. That is because your law does not recognize a moral obligation. I assume you don't either."

"Mr. Nelson, is it your position that the government should legislate morals? What would you do with RICO to give it a moral basis?"

"If the government were to legislate morality, all we would get would be disaster. From the beginning of history, all such attempts have failed miserably. The Ecumenical Society does not impose any moral code. It merely helps people find their own moral roots. Most people have some moral roots. Only a few are amoral, that is with no sense of morality whatsoever. It is almost impossible to bring them around.

"The problem, Mr. Nagel, is one of bringing people to a better frame of reference, a frame of reference which puts our lives into a social, historical, objective perspective. For even the most moral among us, the frame of reference is always in terms of ourselves. We ask God to help us individually. It is difficult to overcome this paradigm. In his inaugural address John F. Kennedy, said, 'Ask not what your country can do for you; ask what you can do for your country.' The Ecumenical Society admonishes, 'Ask not what God can do for you; ask what you can do for God!' That's what the Holy Spirit, the Holy Will is for. It is only when we are all stewards of God that we will encounter the millennium. We will never do it without Him. Man cannot do it alone!

"Another philosopher, Emanuel Kant, provided the answer to your question, Mr. Nagel, when you asked me to distinguish morality from conscience and ethics. He seized upon the concept of the Holy Spirit, also referred to as the Holy Ghost, and called it the Holy Will. That is, he said it was something more than a channel by which the individual asks God for help. He called it the repository of an innate sense of right and wrong, not just for the happiness of the individual, whereby the individual avoids doing those things which, if we all did them, would make life impossible. It propels one to seek happiness for humanity as a whole, regardless of whether that brings happiness to the individual. He called this the 'Categorical Imperative,' an absolute standard which dictates what we must do. This obligation is categorical, that is, absolute, without condition, unquestioned. It is imperative in that it is absolutely necessary, urgently needed and compelling in its logic. It is mandated by God and has been enunciated by Moses, Jesus, Mohammed and others.

"Mr. Nagel, do you actually believe that constructs like mathematics, physics, chemistry, and science in general, along with and concepts such as love, happiness, compassion and fear, are generated by a mass of nerve tissue, an enlargement of the spinal cord, otherwise known as the brain? Kant's observation on this question was brief and concise. 'I can reason,' he wrote. 'Therefore there is a God!' "

"And so your directors are God's true stewards?"

Nelson chuckled. "As is His Honor, the court, this jury and you, Mr. Nagel. Potentially we are all God's stewards. And the world will be better when we are better stewards.

"Mr. Nagel, the 7.5% which we have talked about so much is not a donation, or a gift, or dues. It is part of our Categorical Imperative. There is no quid pro quo."

The courtroom was silent, and the silence persisted as Nagel fumbled with his notes. He seemed stunned. He looked at Janet, afraid her expression would be contemptuous, although her face invariably reflected compassion. She was sorry for him, and looked as though she was ready to offer him support. He glanced down at the podium. His notes were in disarray. "I have no further questions," he said.

"The defense rests," Walker announced.

Nagel then asked for a 15 minute recess to consider rebuttal testimony. Nagel, Wicker and Draefus sat silently in the District Attorney's office. Draefus spoke first. "There's no way we can respond to that. If we call back our witnesses, we have no idea what they will say. They may confirm what Nelson has said."

Draefus and Wicker looked to Nagel. He had not said anything at the conclusion of the proofs or in the office. "We've lost this lawsuit," he said at last. "No rebuttal will save it."

Another silence. Finally Wicker spoke up. "The only rebuttal must be our final argument. Maybe the jury won't buy the defense's story. They are practical people. Philosophy is not their cup of tea. They may very well see this as a grand scheme to make a lot of money."

Back in the courtroom, Nagel announced that the prosecution had nothing further. The judge looked at the clock. "It is now 11:30. This case is adjourned until nine o'clock tomorrow morning. I expect counsel in my office at that time to discuss instructions."

Walker had long since worked on instructions and there was very little that he could do to change them. The next morning in the judge's chambers the issues in the case quickly came into focus. Walker claimed that the entire record portrayed innocence on the part of the defendants: there was absolute absence of criminality; there was no

God's Mafia

violence, no threats, no extortion. The reason for the secrecy had been explained, and he believed that the court must instruct the jury that under those circumstances that a verdict of not guilty should be forthcoming.

Nagel's position was quite the opposite. The jury must be instructed, he argued, to look at the facts. Criminality, he said, was not something sought in demeanor. "It is apparent in what has been done. In this case," he said, "the fact remains that ex-convicts were exploited. A group of men and women decided to exploit convicts who could not get work and extract from them enormous sums of money which would make them wealthy. The fact that this was done subtly, without violence, does not mean that it doesn't constitute racketeering. The whole thing is a clever cover-up and if these people could get by with it, a pattern would be established that, in the future, could be used by organized crime." That this was done on a massive scale, Nagel argued, was clearly shown by the fact that $20,000,000, or more, had been accumulated in this fashion. "This amounts to extortion. It's no different from the operation of the Mafia. The Mafia took care of their 'families' just as these defendants provide for their 'members.' It's a classical mob operation, cleverly disguised. The mere fact that the record does not show that these defendants obtained money does not mean that they are innocent; whether they got anything makes no difference. In any event, it isn't necessary, under RICO, to show that they received any money or any other benefits."

Walker contended that no extortion had been shown in this case. "To constitute extortion there must be a threat of harm. Violence or the threat of violence is a necessary element of extortion."

Nagel disagreed, saying that any denial of any benefit such as a job was enough to create the crime of extortion. "It's obvious," he argued, "that the fear of losing a job prompted the 'donation.' No one voluntarily gives up 7.5% of his pay. The fact that this might amount to no more than $100 per month, or $150 per month, is no defense." The amount was small enough to make it possible for the victims to pay but large enough to make the extorters wealthy.

Judge Kowalski remained impassive. He made no comment and thanked the lawyers for their instructions. The lawyers and the judge returned to the courtroom. The jury was called in and Nagel stood before the jurors to prepare his closing argument.

"Ladies and gentlemen of the jury," he started, " I must admit to you that this is the cleverest cover-up I have ever encountered. What better way to cover up racketeering than under the cloth of the church? Yet this is what has happened. You must not be misled by all the sweet talk from witnesses for the defense showing what wonderful people they are and what good they have done with the money. We are not here for sentimental reasons. We are here to determine whether a law has been violated and whether the defendants have conspired to violate that law. If it were a defense in a criminal proceeding that one charged with a crime had given to charity, every defendant who had ever been tried would be able to put up a defense because in the course of a lifetime probably the greater percentage of one's time has been spent in doing the things that are legal, and even in aiding people from time to time. I say to you that this is not a valid defense in this case or in any case.

"The case is simple. Under the Act entitled Racketeer Influenced and Corrupt Organization Act, we charge that these defendants conspired to violate the law prohibiting the sale of narcotics in that they funded narcotics dealers. The mere fact that the dealers testify that the defendants did not know that they were using the funds for that purpose is irrelevant. You must determine whether the defendants knowingly contributed to the sale of narcotics in view of all the circumstances in the case. The circumstances are that the defendants knew that the people they gave money to dealt in drugs. Yes, they tried to disguise this by saying that they were giving these people a second chance, and a third chance, and a fourth chance to redeem themselves. Well, it is up to you, ladies and gentlemen of the jury, whether or not to swallow that story. There isn't any question about the fact that the defendants obtained vast sums of money by exploiting helpless people. This is extortion, because it puts people in fear of losing their jobs if they don't contribute and because it is part of an ongoing scheme. There isn't any doubt about what was done here. It is admitted. There is an accumulation of money; there has been an organization which has persisted for 30 years in obtaining these funds. This proves beyond a reasonable doubt that the defendants were part of a conspiracy to build up an organization which produced great wealth. This was the easiest racket around. Here were vast numbers of people just out of prison and desperate to work. They would do anything for a job. The defendants and their cohorts took advantage of their predicament, exploited these people, and forced them to pay tribute in the form of kickbacks in order to hold onto their jobs. The money was put into a revolving fund principally for the benefit of the owners of the businesses. The owners became extremely wealthy. Ladies and gentlemen of the jury, I do not see where this case differs from the typical Mafia case. And they can't hide it behind the garb of a priest and a minister.

"The Defense claims they are not guilty because the money was used to educate, to train, to rehabilitate ex-cons and even to finance various projects for them.

"Look closely. These goodies were passed out by the directors as they saw fit. There were no standards by which a request was measured. There was no appeal from the decision of the board. There was not even a procedure to be followed in applying.

"Does this sound like a bona-fide cooperative or association? No, it sounds more like a Mafia crime family that rewards dedicated 'soldiers' who obey orders. There was always plenty of money left over in a fancy trust account in a small town bank controlled by whom? By these two defendants.

"Finally, ladies and gentlemen of the jury, even if you look at this Society just as the defense would have you see it, and for the purpose for which they claim, the rehabilitation of ex-convicts, does that mean they are not guilty? No, for they have taken money from people by illegal means, forced them to give money in order to keep their jobs. The fact that they use some of that money to help some of their 'family' does not excuse them. The regular Mafia takes care of its own 'family' as well. Plenty of money was left over to enrich the operator. It's all part of a very clever set-up."

Nagel went into details and specifics, but in essence that was his case. As he turned from the jury to meet Janet's eyes, he saw no compassion in her face this time. She was angry, livid! He shuddered and returned to his chair, not in triumph but in weariness.

Now Walker addressed the Jury. "Can there be any question in anybody's mind that the defendants in this case, instead of being racketeers as the prosecution claims, are dedicated men who were trying to save the lives and souls of people desperate to find their way? The record is replete with the good that these men have done. I don't have to go through every phase of it for you; you heard it all. To send these men to prison would be the most horrible miscarriage of justice imaginable. These men didn't extort money from anybody; they didn't threaten to break the legs or shoot or maim those who did not pay. The money wasn't paid for protection; It was paid to sustain an organization and an economy, which created employment for people who could not get it elsewhere. The money was used to provide loans so that people could buy homes and cars, so they could educate their children. The money was used to rehabilitate ex-convicts by retraining them, by sending them to school, even to college, and professional schools. The money was used to provide these people with new skills so they could sustain themselves. Is there any question that this was a humanitarian, moral program which did more good than the system established by the law?

"Bear in mind that the only charge here is that the defendants were engaged in a conspiracy to steal money. Well, you heard what the organization did, and if you determine that the real purpose of this organization was to salvage people, to rehabilitate them and to do that in the name of God, then your verdict should be 'not guilty.' You must determine the purposes and aims of these men, whether they were racketeers who were trying to profiteer, or men of God who were trying to do the will of God and to help their fellow man."

Walker implemented his arguments with specific instances from the testimony. He retold the stories of Angela Burgé, Joseph Carl, and Arnold Rothstein and he described the meeting the employees of Angela Burgé held in Indianapolis. "The tragedy," Walker concluded, "is that these men find themselves in court defending themselves against charges of being racketeers. That is a monstrous accusation and the only reasonable verdict you can bring is 'not-guilty.'"

On the crucial issue in the case, Judge Ron Kowalski informed the jury that "under the statute here involved, it must be shown that

God's Mafia

the defendants engaged in a conspiracy which promoted racketeering as defined in the statute. The distribution of drugs is an act which is prohibited in the statute and a conspiracy to promote that is racketeering. The attempt to force payment of money in order to hold a job comes within the statute and constitutes extortion. The accumulation of money is some evidence that it resulted from racketeering unless it can be shown that there are legitimate reasons for it and that it was for a legitimate purpose. You have the obligation to view all the circumstances in this case and you have the right and the obligation to consider the case the defendants have presented. In this case, it is a valid defense if it has been proved to you that the defendants' objectives were as they have described them. Ordinarily, a person charged with a crime can not come into court and show the jury what a nice fellow he is. His conduct comes into play only when the court is considering what punishment to administer. But when one is charged under RICO and a case like this is presented, the jury must consider the actual motives of the defendants. The acts committed by these defendants come squarely within the statute, particularly their obtaining funds from their employees under threat of losing their jobs or their financing. However the motive in obtaining such funds from employees must be considered. You must decide whether you can believe what the defendants claim to have been their motives. As for the charge that they encouraged the sale of narcotics, there is the testimony of the persons convicted of the sale of narcotics that these defendants did not know that the money was being used for the sale of narcotics. You have the right to consider the testimony of those people, even though they have committed a crime, but you must also weigh their testimony and see what weight you would give to it. You must determine from all the surrounding circumstances as to whether these two defendants, in spite of the testimony of the convicts, knowingly contributed money for the promotion and the sale of narcotics."

The judge was much more detailed in his instructions, but that was the essence of his charge. He then asked that the bailiff be sworn to take custody of the jury, and the jury was escorted from the courtroom.

Walker was satisfied with the charge of the court and believed that there would be an acquittal. Nagel also believed there would be an acquittal. The judge believed that there would be an acquittal. Obviously these men did not convey their impressions to each other or to anyone else.

The jury deliberated for the rest of the day and at 5:00 p.m., when the bailiff brought them back to the courtroom, the foreman announced that the jury had not been able to arrive at a verdict. The judge told them they would resume deliberations at 9:00 a.m. the next day.

Nagel hurriedly called his staff together and told them to meet him in the DA's office immediately. Walker asked the two defendants, Schwartz, Janet, Angela and Nelson to meet him in his office at 7:00 p.m.

In the DA's office Nagel, Wicker and Draefus sat around the old table in their suit coats without speaking. Someone had prepared a pot of coffee, and Wicker poured three cups.

"Well," Draefus said, "at least we got it to the jury."

"No way was the judge going to take this case away from the jury," Wicker said as he slowly sipped his coffee.

"You know," said Nagel, "it doesn't matter much which way this case goes. We got problems."

"Yeah," put in Draefus, "if we win, we got the press telling the world how horrible the criminal system is for convicting these martyrs. If we lose, we're a stupid bunch for bringing this suit in the first place."

Wicker said "Paul, you really dragged your heels on this thing. We were quite disgusted with you. Previously, you were the guy who always wanted to get the gangster. This time, you weren't sure. What were your doubts?"

"I just could not see the defendants as gangsters. That damned secrecy persuaded me to press ahead. I figured if they were innocent, they'd talk."

"And it never occurred to us that there might be a serious problem with privileged conversations," Draefus said as he poured more coffee.

"Or that a defendant charged with a felony would rather go to prison than betray a confidence. If you think you're dealing with crooks, you don't give them credit for a sense of obligation," Nagel said.

Draefus held his cup in both hands and stared at it as he spoke. "It sure looked like a well-crafted racket to me."

Nagel put down his cup and rose to his feet. "And maybe it was, and is. Maybe it's so good they've even got us persuaded. Let's go home, gentlemen." With that the party broke up.

That night, Nagel couldn't sleep. He tossed and turned restlessly. Janet Wingate came to his mind over and over. He saw her face when they dined. He saw it in the courtroom. He recalled the knowing glances that had passed between them throughout the trial. Her eyes appeared to read his mind, but her eyes, even in court had been kind, not angry, not resentful. During all his castigation of her father, she never displayed anger until the very end. He wondered if anyone had noticed how often he had glanced at her. In the loneliness of the night, he wondered if he had betrayed his innermost feelings to everybody in court. To be sure, with each compassionate look from Janet he had felt more and more drained, intellectually and emotionally. She appeared angry with his closing argument and he felt badly about that. He had only done what he had to do.

For the first time in his life Paul Nagel was seeking an escape. What a horrible trap he had constructed for himself! A question nagged him. "Did I really believe what I said to that jury?" This question plagued him. It gave him no rest.

In Walker's office that evening the consensus was that they had won, but there was also apprehension. Walker had always had some reservations. How would the jury overcome the "extortion" charge? Consent of the donors was clearly no defense. The statute which forbids the deduction from wages for charitable purpose was a mere misdemeanor under state law, however, the mere fact of obtaining money by putting one in fear of losing his job was a violation of RICO regardless of whether the state statute made it a felony or a misdemeanor. And there was no need for violence or harassment or threat. Case law made fear of economic loss sufficient and the three who had pled guilty to drug dealing testified that they were afraid that if they didn't donate they would lose financing and their businesses. Maybe that was what was giving the jury trouble!

Janet was also preoccupied. "How could he?" she kept asking herself.

Walker noticed that something was wrong. "What is it, Janet?"

"Nothing. Just thinking."

"About what?"

"How could Nagel talk that way to the jury?"

"He was stating his case as best he could. That's his job, Janet."

"But he knows what he says is not true."

"That's what you think," Walker replied.

"That's what I know! And so does he!" Janet flared.

At the next session of the court, the jury was quickly assembled and the judge announced that the jury's verdict might soon be forthcoming, so everyone involved should be available by phone at the attorneys' respective offices. Then the defense team went to a conference room in the court house and the Nagel team went to the District Attorney's office.

At 3:15 the bailiff reported that the jury wanted to confer with the judge. The judge refused and then the jury requested that the court reconvene.

After the lawyers and the parties had assembled, the judge asked the jury be brought in. He addressed the jury: "Ladies and gentlemen, you sent me a message that you wanted to talk to me. You may ask any questions at this time."

A man rose from among the jurors. "I'm foreman, Your Honor. We want to report that there is absolutely no possibility that this jury can arrive at a verdict. It would be a waste of time to keep us here."

The courtroom went silent. Nobody spoke. The judge looked away from the jury, to the bailiff and then to the counsel table. "I'm afraid, ladies and gentlemen, that it is not possible for you, after only a few hours' deliberations to announce that you are not going to agree and that you wish to be relieved, if that is what you want."

"That's what we want," said the foreman.

"I must remind you that you must deliberate until you have arrived at a verdict. That is your sworn duty. We cannot hold expensive trials and then, because you are tired and don't want to play this game any more, let you go home. It is not that simple."

"Judge, we are satisfied that we are not going to change anyone's mind on this jury. We all have definite views and we are not going to convince those who disagree with us to change their position."

The judge was silent for a moment. He called Walker and Nagel to the bench. "Anybody got a good idea?" the judge asked.

Each of the lawyers was caught as flat-footed as the judge. Everyone had anticipated a not-guilty verdict.

"Judge," said Nagel, "in spite of what the foreman says, you have no choice but to send them back to their deliberations."

Walker agreed. "We have had juries tell us they are split, and we have sent them back to continue deliberations and generally they come up with a verdict."

"Judge," Nagel offered, "I suggest you tell the jury to go back to the jury room while we consider their request."

"That's not a bad idea," the judge said and, after sending the jury back, asked counsel to join him in chambers.

Nagel was the first to speak. "Your Honor, what concerns me is that if you send that jury back and force them to deliberate against their will, we may have a real problem on our hands. This case has been in the news all over the country. With what happened today, whatever verdict is brought in after further deliberations the press will interview the jurors at great length and get stories about pressure, arm-twisting, wanting to go home and intimidation by the court. You can bet your last dollar there would be motions to set aside a guilty verdict and the press, if not the government, will try to reopen the case if the verdict is not guilty. This case is too big to have it in such a state!"

The judge was silent. Walker knew, of course, that a hung jury would create an extremely difficult situation for his clients. They would never know where they stood. A sword would always hang over their heads. He said nothing, but privately he thought that a guilty verdict would be disastrous.

Finally the judge said, "Gentlemen, I have no choice but to make them continue. There has not been enough time to declare a mistrial."

The men returned to the courtroom. The jury was again put in the box. "Ladies and gentlemen of the jury, I've conferred with the lawyers, and it is my decision that you must continue to try to arrive at a verdict. There is nothing more I can tell you unless you have a question."

"How long must we try?" one of the jurors called out. This was not an easy question to answer. In fact, it was a very delicate question. To tell them they had to deliberate until they reached a unanimous verdict could push those wanting to get it over with to do anything to end it, and they might well say so afterwards. To tell them that they should "give it another try" might simply continue the impasse.

Walker had witnessed many scenes like this. It was common. Nobody had worried about what the jurors might say later. They were always told to continue deliberations. The judge tried another tack. "Folks, we're all tired. I know that you're all tired, too. I cannot tell you how to decide this case or how to go about it, except as I did in my original instructions. I can't tell you to try for two hours or two days. I can only tell you to go back and try again. Go over the testimony you have heard. Try to follow my instructions. If you need help, just ask the bailiff to bring you in to ask any questions you may have. That's all for now. Bailiff please take the jury to the jury chamber." Then turned to the lawyers. "Gentlemen," he said, "it might be well if you remain here. There may be questions."

Both Nagel and Walker thought the judge had handled the matter as well as possible.

Nagel caught a glimpse of Janet as he turned from the bench. She was distraught, and he felt badly about that! As he walked toward the rail she approached the gate and her eyes caught his. This time she was stern. She quickly looked away. He knew instantly that it was his final argument! That had done it. She would never speak to him again!

Time dragged on. At five o'clock, the offices in the federal building closed, but the court remained in session. At six o'clock, the juryroom bell rang. Everybody jumped to attention. The jury was asked back into the courtroom. The judge ascended the bench asked, "Have you arrived at a verdict?"

"No," responded the foreman. "We are unable to agree."

The judge asked the foreman to be seated. He then addressed the jury as a whole. "Do you all agree that you cannot agree?" There was a nodding of heads. "Does anybody feel differently from the foreman. If so, please stand." Nobody stood!

The judge then thanked the jury for its diligence and patience. "I know this has been tedious and tiring and a considerable sacrifice for each of you. You should not feel you have failed because you could not arrive at a verdict. I'm sure you tried and that is all we can ask." Then the judge turned to the defense table. "You are advised that this matter is still pending and you are at liberty pursuant to your respective bonds which are hereby extended to the date of the new trial. You are free to leave."

The bailiff rapped his gavel and announced that the court was adjourned.

Nagel continued to sit in his chair while Wicker and Draefus put books and papers into cases to be carried to the DA's office. Walker and Janet cleared their table without saying a word. Angela Burgé, Ben Schwartz and all the other defense witnesses silently mingled among the spectators.

The jurors left the court house as quickly as they could. Outside the courtroom they encountered the media and reported that from the very outset of deliberations eight had stood for acquittal, four for a guilty verdict. Throughout the debate that number had never changed. Nor had the identity of the individual members of each group. Each group had chosen a spokesman in anticipation of this encounter with the press. The majority had decided very simply that there was no criminal intent, that these defendants had, in fact, rendered a great service where the government had failed and to have sent them to prison would have been a travesty. The "guilty" group said that the majority was simply "soft-headed," that they had not paid any attention to the testimony or to the law. "We were trying two men for what they did to three people who testified for the prosecution, and in each case it was clear to us that the defendants had loaned money to people they knew to be drug dealers, and they extorted money from them. The rest of the witnesses had nothing to do with the case. They liked being extorted, apparently. In a trial for burglary you can't bring in people to testify they were not robbed."

One of the reporters turned to the spokesperson for the majority. "What do you say to that?"

The spokesperson pursed his lips. "The minority overlooked the fact that the defendants were charged under RICO and under that statute the Government must show a pattern of racketeering. The testimony of the defense witnesses demonstrated that there was a pattern, but it was not a pattern of racketeering. It was a pattern of helping people help themselves. There was absolutely no criminal intent."

The minority spokesperson was quick to take issue. "We saw this case as one in which three people were loaned money used in the drug traffic. The defendants, in the guise of an Ecumenical Society, extorted money from these people and put that money into legitimate business, precisely what RICO was enacted to stop. We didn't fall for all the 'God' stuff. God is often used as authority to violate the law. Look how much money these people are making. This is the smoothest racket I've ever heard of. As far as criminal intent is concerned anytime somebody breaks the law it's pretty certain they intended to break it. You can't let them say 'excuse us, we didn't mean to break the law.' You have to look at the facts, and it doesn't make any difference that a priest and a minister are involved. Before the law, they are like everybody else."

"What about all the ex-cons who got jobs and careers and a new life?" the reporter asked.

"What does that have to do with the question of whether the law was broken? The law says one can't extort money from somebody else and use that money to start legitimate businesses. Stop and think for a minute. What are these people who are supposedly 'saved' doing? They are paying protection money just as in any other racket. How is this different from so-called organized crime? There isn't any difference! This is organized only too well but it is criminal still! This whole thing is so clever it has fooled the majority of the jury. But it hasn't fooled all us!"

The reporters were writing as fast as they could and the TV cameras were recording it all on film.

A female reporter spotted Angela Burgé and hurried over to her, her cameraman in tow. "Ms. Burgé, what are your intentions at this moment?"

"Our intentions are to do what we have been doing for over 30 years. We have not been convicted of anything. We are not guilty of anything. There about 6,000 of us in this, and we are proud of what we have done."

"Do you plan to continue business as usual?"

"Indeed we do. In fact we have no choice but to do that. You can't bring something like this to a sudden halt. What's more there's no reason to bring it to a halt."

"Do you speak for all members of the Society?" another reporter asked.

"I have not been delegated to do so, but I'm confident that I do."

When the interviews with members of the jury were televised, the statement of the spokesperson for the minority was very impressive, much more impressive than that of the speaker for the majority.

When Nagel heard it that evening he was startled by the effect of the jurors' statement when spoken outside the courtroom. He was now sure that the public would accept his view of the case. This was almost the opposite of the public response after the defense had started putting in its proofs.

Walker was not as shocked as Nagel when he watched the same newscast. The views of the spokesperson for the minority of the jurors were the views he feared the jury as a whole might adopt. He twinged as he heard the words of the dissenter. He was afraid that this view would predominate in a new trial. He considered himself biased because he had become an admirer of the two defendants and because he was more prone to look at the case from a wider perspective than the ordinary citizen. He had been impressed by the great results the defendants' program had obtained, but this would soon be old news. The 50% who returned to prison under the current system as contrasted to the 15% under the defendants' system might not impress another jury as much as the money made by the directors.

NINETEEN

On Saturday following the end of the trial, Janet was in the law office at 8:30 in the morning. Frank was at the coffee shop. As Janet thought about the television report and the statement of the minority juror, her worries were renewed. She too had thought the case had been won. Now it had to be done all over again. Somehow, it was not likely to go off as well the second time. It was an old story now. No matter how careful they would be in selecting a jury, it would be old stuff. There would be no secret to reveal to the pleasant surprise of everybody. The secret was now gone. Everybody knew about the Ecumenical Society, and the case for the prosecution had been brilliantly stated on television sets all over the country. This time, the burden would truly be upon the defense to prove their innocence, no matter what the court instructed the jury. She paced the floor of the office from the library to the waiting room. Her anxiety grew by the moment.

When Walker walked into the office he told Janet that things were rather quiet at breakfast. The shine had worn thin. People were pleasant and courteous but there was no longer any great enthusiasm. In fact, nobody had asked any questions. Henceforth, it would all be anti-climactic. Janet expressed her concerns, and Walker tried to assuage them. He said that in spite of the temporary setback, the real ace in the hole was that the jury might find the defendants guilty but a prison sentence would seem to be out of the question.

"Small consolation," moaned Janet. "A life's work would still go down the drain. The Society will go down, too. Everything will be lost." Her mind turned to Nagel. She shook her head. He didn't win either. Sarcastically, she whispered, "I hope you are happy, Paul."

God's Mafia

The daily newspaper was thrown against the front door loud enough to be heard in the library. Walker retrieved it and brought it into the library. He perused it and read aloud from the editorial page.

> "The hung jury in the Leahy/Hamilton case brings to mind the necessity for calm, unemotional viewing of such public trials. The indecision of the jury indicates the dilemma in today's society. One is suddenly brought down to earth after an airborne ride on the winds of emotion. Have these dedicated men gone too far? Perhaps it was not such a grand exercise of love and compassion after all. Perhaps it was just a matter of being opportunistic and clever. In any event, we must withhold judgment until another jury hears the case."

Walker put down the paper and sat in silence for a moment. Finally he said, "There's no use commiserating. We have work to do."

"What would you suggest we do?" Janet did not even look at him as she spoke. She stared out the window.

"We go back to page one. Let's see if there is something we missed." With that, he reached for a legal pad and began writing as a means of refocusing his mind. Long since he had learned that ideas often emerge after one writes a lot of nonsense.

At the same time, Nagel, Wicker and Draefus were in the AG's office. "I hate retrials," Wicker observed to no one in particular.

"Somewhat like reheated hash," Draefus agreed.

"The worst part," continued Wicker, "is that your mind holds what was in the first trial and you forget to put it into the second trial record where it must go for sure. Just think about trying to pick a second jury. That will take days and days, maybe weeks," Wicker exclaimed.

Nagel asked, "Will the court simply set a date for the new trial or must we arrange it among all the parties?"

"I imagine he will ask us what dates are mutually agreeable. He has always been pretty good about that." Wicker was now reheating the coffee.

"I think we'd better call Washington," Nagel said to him.

"Why?" Draefus asked.

"They have no idea whether this is to be retried or when," Wicker added.

"This case has acquired national stature. After all, Washington pushed us into it when we were hesitant," Nagel said. "I don't want them to second guess us. If we try this case again and we get another hung jury or mistrial, they'll be the first to point fingers."

"That raises another interesting point," Wicker interjected. "We had 75% against us the first time. How do we plan to win them over? Remember we all believed we had lost and 75% of the jury agreed with us. Do we consider that fact before we do anything?"

"Just how do you dispose of this case short of a retrial?" Nagel asked. "Do you call Frank Walker and say, 'Forget our lawsuit, we're dropping it'?"

Silence, then Wicker said, "Maybe it is best to call Washington. They're the bosses. Let's give them the chance to decide what we do and how we do it."

"I'll do that Monday," Nagel said. "Frankly I don't know what we can do until we talk to Washington. Let's all go home."

"We'll leave it up to you, Paul," Wicker said as he left the office.

On Monday, in the judge's chambers, his secretary, Betty Sloane, was reviewing the docket with the judge. "Judge Kowalski," said Ms. Sloane, an attractive, middle-aged woman who had been his secretary since before he ascended to the bench, "the Leahy/Hamilton case upsets our calendar. If you plan to try that case soon we'll have to revamp the calendar immediately."

The judge asked for the list of cases scheduled for trial. "I suppose the big case should have priority. However, some of these other cases have been around a long time. I'm not going to schedule the Leahy/Hamilton case. Let's send a letter to counsel telling them to arrive at a stipulation on a possible date and have them submit it and we'll try to fit it in."

A letter to that effect went out.

When Walker received the letter from the judge he put it aside. He was surprised that counsel for defense should receive such a letter.

Ordinarily the court would send out a notice for another pre-trial conference. Walker surmised that the court did not intend to push this case to trial, hoping somehow it would go away, which of course it never would. There was no way this case could stay in limbo very long.

Casually, Nagel mentioned to Tom Thornton, the local district attorney, that he thought Washington should be consulted. Then he called the Attorney General's office in Washington on Tuesday and he got through to a deputy in the criminal division. Nagel had planned his approach carefully. He called attention to the divided jury and said "We'd like to receive some direction from your office as to our next move."

"I don't understand," the deputy answered. "We expect there will be a new trial as soon as possible. This office has not given the matter any further thought. What other options are there, unless the defendants would like to plead to some lesser offense."

"That's not very likely," Nagel responded. "Our question is whether we should press the matter any further."

"Are you suggesting we drop it?" The deputy's voice was shrill.

"Sir, eight jurors are against us at this first trial. As you know, we got blistered badly by the media, and the defendants came through the trial like heroes. What are you going to do with them if you get a conviction?"

"We won't do anything. The judge will do it. I don't get it, Nagel. What's the problem?"

"Well, sir, this case has not turned out to be what we thought it was. There's too much equity on the side of the defense. Like I said some people consider them heroes."

"I would say," said the deputy sharply, "that if what you say is true you must not have investigated the case very thoroughly before you filed. This office is not about to pull your chestnuts out of the fire, Mr. Nagel. This is your baby. You run with it or drop it. We are staying clear."

Nagel was angry. "You guys were pretty gung-ho originally. When I held up, you pressed the hell out of me. Now you want to turn and run and let me fall on my face!"

"Mr. Nagel, we assumed you knew what you were doing in the first place. Don't lay this baby on us. You do what you think you have to do. We are going to put out a statement that your office will decide what to do. It is a local matter in which Washington will depend on the good judgment of the people on the ground. Obviously we won't say anything until you have announced what you are going to do."

Nagel slammed the phone down. "Damn" he muttered to himself. Then he thought of the local District Attorney. After all, Nagel was only an Assistant Attorney General. The man in charge locally was the man who had been appointed District Attorney. Since Washington was passing the buck to the district, the District Attorney would have to call the shot!

Since Nagel was the senior in the local office — the District Attorney by contrast was probably the youngest lawyer in the office — he would go directly to Mr. Thornton, the real District Attorney. As the senior man, he had ready access to the boss.

"What can I do for you," Thornton asked as soon as Nagel stepped into his office.

"The Leahy/Hamilton case," Nagel replied. "I called Washington to get their perspective on a new trial and they told me that this office must decide what's to be done."

"What do you mean? We have a new trial coming up. What's the problem?"

"The problem is as follows: First, do we actually go to retrial; second, do we amend our indictment; third, do we indict 50 or 60 more people?"

None of these questions had in fact been discussed by the staff. They just came to Nagel's mind as he responded to the DA's question.

The DA was truly baffled. None of this had been remotely referred to. Not having entered into any previous discussions, he was hesitant to say much of anything."Well," he said finally, "what does the staff recommend? What do you recommend? After all you are the point man in all this."

"I'm trying to tell Washington, and they won't listen, and now I'm trying to tell you that staff will do whatever the policy makers tell us to do. We do not think the staff should decide the future course of this case."

"Mr. Nagel, it is my understanding that we presently have two men under indictment. It is now a matter of disposing of that case. That appears to be purely an administrative matter to be processed in accordance with court rules. Now, all a sudden, a great national issue arises. Just because a case gets a lot of publicity does not necessarily make it a great public issue with overtones affecting policy. Let's not make this a national issue. Let's just conclude this case as quickly as we can. Nagel, you're the guy to call the shots on this. You've been closer to it than anybody. I'll back you up in whatever you decide."

"Including possible withdrawal of the indictment?"

Thornton paused. "Why that?" he asked dumbfounded.

"That's been discussed by the staff."

"Why?"

"Because we have heard the case tried and have seen the witnesses and because 75% of the jury ruled against us the first time."

Now the DA's mind was in a whirl. After all, he had told Nagel it was his baby. Should he force a trial over staff's recommendation? "Yes," he said. "including dropping the case if the staff thinks that is the thing to do."

"All right," said Nagel, "we go from here." He walked to the door. Thornton watched him, satisfied that the responsibility was where it belonged.

Nagel left the DA's office and went to his apartment where he threw himself on the bed and stared at the ceiling. Driving home he'd been in a complete daze. Now he wondered how he had made it. He could not recall any of the familiar landmarks. Now, however, the thoughts which germinated in his mind were in full focus. The fate of two people was totally in his hands! The lives of two other people were at his mercy! Somehow, that thought had not bothered him when he had prosecuted other cases. Never before had he felt the responsibility as deeply as he felt it now. In fact, he could not remember when he had given a second thought to the destiny of those he had prosecuted. This time he not only felt the burden, he longed to escape it. To think, at the very moment when he did not want such a choice it had been forced upon him. He reviewed his actions the past few days. The talk with his colleagues, how he had steered the conversation away from prosecution. Why had he done that, particularly when the media was coming over to the prosecution's side? When the prosecution's case was set forth by the minority juror, it seemed to win over the public. At least it gave the prosecution credibility. Why was he talking about withdrawing the indictment? Why? He recalled his colleagues' words about no jury sending these two men to prison; that they simply were not criminals or racketeers. And then he recalled Janet, the way they had exchanged furtive glances throughout the trial, how he had felt emotionally naked before her. And then came his final argument when she became angry with him. That final argument! Had it persuaded four jurors?

Finally, Nagel found himself condemning RICO. It was an abomination. That was the problem. Innocent people could be found guilty. But wait, when had he ever felt that statute had caused a miscarriage of justice? He could not recall any. The statute was serving its purpose.

But not this time, he thought. This time he was trying to put some men into prison who were, in fact, rendering a great service. After all, who was he to prosecute these men? Were they not men who were persecuted because they were doing good? Were these not precisely his clientele, the innocent people whom the system continually wronged? All his life he had fought for the downtrodden, for those left behind by society. Were not these two men the champions of an abused segment of society? Had they not, in effect, been willing to sacrifice themselves in order to save those who had been ill-treated by society? That was it! That was it! And Janet, her role has been to demonstrate that fact to him. Yes, she was proof in herself that these men were not criminals. If she supported them they must be all right! Nagel came back to reality and he shook his head. Was love for a woman overcoming his better judgment? Agog in confusion, he got up, left the apartment, got into his car and drove off, without knowing where he was going.

As he drove his car through the countryside he felt sufficiently isolated to think. In a moving car he had ultimate privacy. He had no telephone. He was truly alone in the sense that he could be totally honest with himself. And on this day of days he felt he needed to be absolutely honest with himself. This led him back to Janet Wingate. It was she who had asked him if he was playing God. He finally began to understand the implications of that question, for at this moment he was given a sort of license to play God! He held the fate of two men, and probably two women, in the palm of his hand. And he was finding that he did not like the role. Moreover, until Janet Wingate had mentioned it, he had never thought of himself as a would-be God. In fact, he had never liked the idea of God! Today, as he drove through the countryside he began asking himself, just what did he believe? Profounder still, whatever he believed, where did the belief come from? He thought of the testimony of Robert Nelson. Great minds, after searching history and their own minds had postulated God, assumed that there had to be a God. He got the impression from all the testimony he had heard at the trial everyone has either a God or is his own God. At least one has, deep inside, a feeling that there are certain standards, certain beliefs even certain assumptions. Isn't that what he had? He had been proudest of the fact that he always tried to be totally objective, that he would never permit personal desire to color his thought or judgment. He had tried to keep his beliefs to himself lest he be thought a windbag of slogans and shibboleths. He had sought all his life to be absolutely honest. Had this been his Categorical Imperative?

Suddenly Paul Nagel could not find a single standard by which to measure his honesty. What was the truly honest thing to do at this moment? Suddenly he must decide what he thought a jury should decide. But that thought evaporated quickly. For it was he who had decided that a decision had to be made before a jury would be permitted to make the decision. That's absurd, he thought. Then, again, was it absurd? Is that not what a prosecutor does before every case? Yes, but in that decision the duty is to apply the known facts to the law and decide if there is a prima facie case. In this case there was no doubt that there was a prima facie case. So, what was his function? That was the system. First the prosecutor, then a grand jury or a magistrate and finally a jury must deem one guilty. But now he was thinking how could he be so presumptuous? What gave him the right to determine these men's future? Somehow that was now a very troubling question when it never had been before.

Another scene appeared in his mind Paul Nagel, chief trial counsel, 18 years' service, excellent rating, always respected as a dedicated public servant, absolute integrity, no monkey business, no deals, straight arrow, no nonsense. He followed the law; there was no room for sentiment, no politics. Even those who didn't like his straight-laced approach admired and respected him. But now, in the space of one day he was chasing around trying to "pass the buck."

He pounded the steering wheel. "Why don't you call it? Call it! Don't waffle! Don't be like the rest. You are Paul Nagel!"

He lowered his head. It almost hit the steering wheel. What was the matter with him? He drove back to his apartment. It was now dark. He realized he had not eaten. He realized he wasn't hungry. He dropped into an easy chair and leaned back. Then he raised it. Both his hands gripped the arms of the chair. "They are not guilty!" The words came out automatically. There seemed to be no thought connected with the words, no legal rationale. Nothing. "They are not guilty." As he repeated the words he suddenly felt relieved. A weight had been lifted from his shoulders. That was it. It was simple. Those two men did what they did not for illicit, greedy ends; they did it pursuant to conviction.

Those men were of his own mold! They were men of principle. This is what he had tried to be all his life. They had their God to encourage them, to console them, to guide them. Even now he was having to do it on his own. Very well, he would do it on his own, and let the chips fall where they may. After all, everybody had left it up to him. And so he would 'call the shot!' Smiling, he went to bed.

The next morning Nagel called Wicker and Draefus into his office. "Well," Nagel said, "both Washington and our DA have washed their hands of the case. It is our baby. We are to decide what to do with it."

"How do you like them apples?" Wicker groaned. "When it gets rough the boys on the line must put their necks out."

God's Mafia

Draefus said, "It doesn't surprise me. Essentially, this is a political organization. Paul, as you know, we have been behind you all the way. We await your word."

"Gentlemen, the bottom line with me right now is that in the last analysis a verdict of guilty would be the worst possible result we could obtain. Picture it; the two are found guilty. No matter what the sentence might be — prison or fine or probation — the Ecumenical Society would come to an end. Twenty million dollars would be forfeited, 30 years of hard work would be lost. And what would be gained? The possibility that real criminals might use the same format to operate a real racket, I'm satisfied that we could beat such a sham."

"Simple, isn't it?" quizzed Wicker. "Maybe all good answers are simple. How do you want to proceed?"

"I'll call Walker and tell him we are dropping the case." Nagel reached for the phone. Walker was not available. His secretary would have him call back. With that, Wicker and Draefus left Nagel's office.

❖❖❖

While Nagel had been busy with his torment, Frank and Janet were themselves suffering. All previous discussion among them and Hamilton, Leahy and Schwartz had resulted in a determination that there was no way to avoid a new trial. For the prosecution to drop the case now was impossible in view of the switch among the media. The public, at least as reflected in the press, radio and television, desired a resolution by jury. To withdraw the case now would raise many imponderable and nasty questions which it would be best to avoid. To simply let the case die, to which the judge had obviously opened the door, would be even worse. Finally, Walker spent a great deal of time looking for some error which might permit him to get the case dismissed on legal grounds. The court had made no error of that magnitude so far as Walker could determine.

Janet meanwhile, was in the law office reviewing the statements of other potential witnesses not used at the first trial. Such testimony, she felt, would be largely redundant.

That afternoon, Walker returned to the office from court to find

Janet at work in the library. She was pouring over the files of statements.

"Find anything new," he asked her.

"No," she replied.

"I guess it's a retrial. Same witnesses, same format. Let's hope we get the rest of the votes this time." Walker sat down and stared straight ahead. "Right now, I'm also wondering what's going through Nagel's mind."

"Frank, you'll never guess what's going on in that mind. I doubt he's sure what his own next thought will be."

"Oh no! That's not Nagel. You may be sure he knows what he wants and how to get it."

Janet put down the legal pad she was holding. "My guess, Frank, is that he was shocked by what he heard from the witness stand. He is not so stupid that he does not realize his problem is worse than ours. He knows my father and Father Leahy are innocent, but his pride and ego won't let him admit it. He'll do anything, say anything, to maintain that precious record of his. Mr. 'Straight-arrow' can be very devious, believe me."

"He's just trying to do his job," said Walker. "He can't drop this case if he wanted to. A lawyer is in this situation more often than he likes to be. The entire country wants to see the end of the mystery."

At that moment the phone rang. The secretary was out after the mail and Janet answered. "Walker Law Office," she trilled.

"This is Paul Nagel calling from the DA's office. Is Mr. Walker available?"

Flustered, she coughed. "Yes he is," she squeaked. "Hold on and I'll put you through to him." She put the call on hold and called Frank. "It's Nagel."

Walker put down the paper he'd been reading. "Get on the other line, Janet."

"Hello Paul," Frank said. "I suppose you want a date for the new trial." Frank was convivial. "Funny, but I was thinking about taking a long vacation. I figured you just might see the light with 15 to 30 days to mull this over."

"Frank," Nagel replied, "you can take a vacation and you can take

God's Mafia

as much time as you like. There's not going to be a new trial."

Frank and Janet were stunned. They looked at each other. Walker laughed. "Paul, this is really no time for practical jokes."

"This is no joke, Frank. I'm dropping the case."

Walker couldn't believe what he was hearing, but he had to pretend that it wasn't a great surprise. "Paul," he said, "I can't let you just drop the case. Withdrawing the indictment at this time does nothing for either side."

"Would you rather try it?" Nagel asked.

Janet looked at Walker in disbelief. What was he saying!

"No," Walker responded. "If you withdraw the indictment, my clients won't know where they stand. There has been no vindication. The question will still hang over their heads."

"What do you have in mind?" Nagel asked.

"I think the way to clear this matter up once and for all would be for you to announce to the court that you do not wish to proceed and I'll make a motion for a verdict of 'not guilty.' That will clear the air once and for all." Janet listened apprehensively for Nagel's answer.

"I think your point is well taken," Nagel conceded: "I'll write the judge. You make your motion. I think the judge will get the picture."

Janet broke in, pitching her voice low. "Paul, this is Janet. I want you to know that I appreciate this and the defendants appreciate this. I also want you to know both Frank and I know very well that this was not an easy decision for you and that you do it because of your own sense of what is right. And now, Paul, I'm going to hang up and cry. Thank you, thank you, thank you."

Nagel never expected to talk to her. He put the phone down ever so slowly, drinking up her last words. She had sounded so sultry.

Janet dropped the telephone, dashed over to Frank and wrapped her arms around him and sobbed.

"My dear this is not the time to cry. This is the time to shout for joy. Quick, let's call your father, Father Leahy and Ben and get them over here." In order to preserve the surprise, Walker asked his secretary, who had now returned, to put in the calls.

Within ten minutes they came in. Mrs. Hamilton was with them.

"Mother, Dad, all you," Janet exclaimed, tears pouring down her cheeks, "it's all over. The court is entering an order of 'not guilty.' It's over. There is to be no trial! We are vindicated. We can live again. Thank God!"

Father Leahy smiled but did not display exuberance. "What happened?" he asked.

Walker responded. "Nagel called minutes ago to tell us that he was dropping the case. I told him we would not settle for that. I insisted on an order of acquittal. I'm making a motion for that and he said he will not oppose it."

"Nagel did this?" Father Leahy could not believe what he was hearing.

Janet spoke up. "Of course, this could have been directed from Washington but I feel in my bones Nagel is responsible. He learned we were innocent during the trial."

Vera Hamilton approached her daughter and took her in her arms without a word. Reverend Hamilton found a chair and seated himself.

Walker reached for the telephone. "I'm calling Nelson now to call those who testified and to send out a brief memo to others. We should not anticipate the judge's order. It will not come for a couple of days. But we can't delay contacting the organization either."

TWENTY

Both Nagel and Walker presented the proposed order of "not guilty" to the judge the day after their phone conference. Judge Kowalski read the order. He looked at Nagel. "Paul," he said, "I've known you long enough not to challenge you. I assume you have cleared this with the local DA as well as with Washington."

"I have," responded Nagel.

"And they washed their hands of it?" the judge asked with a smile.

Nagel sat silent. Walker waited for him to respond, but Nagel said nothing. The judge couldn't stop smiling. "Paul, both Frank and I have known you a long time. Let me call it: this is your handiwork, isn't it?"

Paul Nagel blushed. He refused to look at them. There was another period of silence. Frank thought to break the spell. "If the court will sign the order, I'll file it immediately."

The judge signed the order, handed it back to Frank and said, "Thank you, gentlemen," Nagel and Walker walked out of the judge's chambers together. Walker turned to Nagel, held out his hand and said, "Thank you." Walker then went into the clerk's office to file the judgment and Nagel went to his office.

The next morning, newspaper headlines announced the strange end to the case. The brief account summarized a statement released by the office of the district attorney to the effect that, in the opinion of the prosecution, a retrial was likely to result in another hung jury, and the prosecution did not feel it was in the interest of the public to pursue the case further. Oddly enough, the tumult died down without further discussion, editorial or otherwise.

Walker assembled his cohorts, Janet, the Hamiltons, Schwartz and Father Leahy in his office. "I just want you to know that the person responsible for the favorable end to our trial was Paul Nagel. He engineered the end of the case, he and he alone!"

Shocked silence greeted his announcement. Janet finally spoke up. "I'd like very much to thank him again. I've already thanked him once, when he first called."

One week later the local paper had another story. The headlines read: "Leahy/Hamilton Case Prosecutor Resigns." Immediately, Janet called the DA's office and asked to speak to him. She was informed he was not in. She called his apartment. He was not there. She again called the office and asked to speak to Wicker or Draefus. Draefus took the call. "Where can I find him," she asked.

"Sorry, I can't tell you that," Draefus responded.

Janet pressed further. "Do you know where he is," she asked. "I have a matter to discuss with him."

"Yes, but I'm not at liberty to tell anyone. However, I am to tell you that I am your contact on the trust."

"Can you deliver a message for me?" Janet was not even thinking of the trust.

"Yes, I can do that."

"Please tell him that I said he cannot forever hide from others, and that he cannot forever deny his own soul. He must let the rest of the world know that he is a wonderful person and that he should let God help him."

There was a moment's silence. "Ms. Wingate," Draefus finally responded, "I will be most happy to give him your message. I've written down your words and I'll convey them to him."

TWENTY-ONE

Two weeks after the end of the trial Janet Wingate called the law office and asked for an appointment. Recognizing her voice, Frank's secretary said, "Mrs. Wingate I can put him on the line right now. I'm sure he'll be happy to speak to you."

"I don't want to speak to him. I simply want an appointment — as soon as possible."

The secretary became concerned. "Is this an emergency?"

"Not exactly, but the matter has been unresolved for months and I'd like to get it resolved."

The secretary set up an appointment for the following Monday at 11:00 a.m. The secretary told Walker about the appointment, and when he expressed surprise she told him what Janet had said, that she was anxious to resolve a matter which had been pending for several months. Walker was surprised that Janet would have something on her mind. She had said nothing to him about such a matter although they had seen each other at least three times during the past two weeks.

When Janet came into the office Walker held the door, closed it behind her and promptly took her in his arms. "What's your problem now?" he asked.

"Sit down," Janet said and waited for him to seat himself while she remained standing. "I wish to discuss a sort of understanding about which you talked to me at some length but never brought to fruition."

"Oh?" Walker had no idea what she was talking about.

"Yes. I refer to the matter of marriage, if you will recall. I'd like to get the matter resolved as soon as possible."

Walker sighed with relief, then laughed. "Well," he said jokingly, "I must tell you that I have given that matter considerable thought in recent weeks. As you might guess there are a lot of things to consider before one enters into a long-term contract."

"Well, Mr. Walker, as I've already informed you, I don't like delays, procrastination or fuss over details. I have with me today the following."

She enumerated:

1. Application for marriage license.

2. Outline for an ecumenical marriage with the following participants beside the two of us:

    a) my sons who will give away the bride
    b) my father who will conduct the ceremony
    c) Ben Schwartz who will read from the Old Testament.
    d) Father Leahy who will read from the New Testament.

    They will select the passages.

3. I have with me a suggested card announcing our marriage which I hereby submit for your approval.

4. A suggested menu for a dinner to be held in your library for the wedding party, to include some of my fellow workers at the bank, Bob Nelson and Angela Burgé.

5. I'll let you pick a best man and he can attend the dinner.

6. I'm asking Mrs. Smith, my boss's wife to sing two solos.

7. I have arranged for airline tickets to Orlando, Florida, and have arranged for a week's stay at very exclusive, private accommodations.

8. I have made a list of the clothes we will take with us.

9. I will drive my car to the airport and park it there. On our return you will drive the car.

"Do you have any objections to any of this? If you do, please state your objections now."

Walker allowed a few moments to permit Janet to catch her breath. "If you have finished will you please be seated?" Janet sat down, put all the materials she had brought with her on his desk and then leaned back to await his response.

Sternly Walker said, "It did not occur to you, I see, that I might have some ideas for a marriage in which I was to have a part."

"Sir," Janet replied, "You had at least two weeks to announce your desires. It should have occurred to you that it was your responsibility to come to me, reaffirm your request for marriage and induce me to accept your proposal with suggestions for a fancy wedding, a gorgeous gift and a fascinating honeymoon. I concluded that I might wait a long time and you might never do anything. Therefore, I took matters into my own hands. As a proper young woman, I cannot afford to be stood up."

Walker shook his head. "I'm afraid that I'll not have much to say about anything in the future, least of all my wedding."

"And I'm sure that will suit you just fine. I have reconciled myself to that fate. That's what one gets when one marries an old bachelor."

❖❖❖

And so the marriage of Frank Walker and Janet Wingate took place in the small chapel in the Presbyterian Church of Fairfield. Reverend Hamilton performed the ceremony. Jasper and Brent gave away the bride. Ben Schwartz read from the Old Testament. Father Leahy read from the New Testament. A brief reception for the wedding party and a few friends was held at the law office. Among those in attendance were Janet's boss and his wife, Mr. & Mrs. Smith, a few bank employees, Angela Burgé, Bob Nelson, Mr. Carl and Mr. Rothstein. There was no best man.

Immediately after the reception, the bride and groom drove to the airport, a distance of about 100 miles. Janet drove, and they had not traveled far before she started talking. "My dearest husband," she began, "I propose that on this trip we start a love affair that bars no holds. I further propose that nothing shall ever come between us. Your first and primary job is to be my lover. We shall keep 'bed time hours' as you have kept office hours. I never want to regret again that I have not loved enough. Our affair will be fulfilled if it lasts six weeks or 50 years! Is that agreed?"

As had happened to him so often in the past, Walker was stunned. What a woman! He could only utter: "Agreed. I take it that this is an amendment of the marriage vows we just took."

"Not an amendment, a footnote to provide details. Getting married, Frank, just seals the deal. Now we discuss the details of the deal. I'm just trying to tell you the details I think are most important."

"I think I understand, counselor. You are really interested only in the more physical aspects of marriage." Walker chuckled as he spoke.

Janet glanced over to him. "I've been taught, Frank, that at the point of love-making the physical becomes spiritual and, if there is real love, the more physical it is the more spiritual it is. The human orgasm, my dear husband, is the only place when the physical can become the spiritual. That's why it is the supreme joy."

"I take it, then, that I must keep all this in mind when I make love to you?" He could not help chuckling.

"No. You keep it in mind before and after love-making, during love-making, my dear man, you shall perform and your thought is to be only on performance, physical performance. I trust you understand?"

"I think so. I'll try my best."

At the airport in Orlando a rented car awaited them. In it were written instructions. "This tells us how we get to our destination," Janet explained. By this time Walker had given up trying to keep track of things. He simply got into the passenger side of the front seat. The luggage was put in the rear.

Janet soon pulled into the driveway of what was obviously a private home and a rather impressive place. Walker's bewilderment increased.

"This is my boss' winter cottage," she explained. "A week's stay here is his wedding gift to us."

Janet had a key. She opened the door. Nobody was about. "We have this absolutely to ourselves for one week." Walker noticed a large enclosed swimming pool behind the living room. Janet went directly to it and put her hand in the water. "Yes, it's heated," she said. "What about a dip before we dine? Let's get the luggage in."

They went to the car and brought in the bags. "I didn't bring a swim suit," Frank remarked, trying to sound off-handed but blushing furiously.

Janet opened her trunk. "Neither did I," she said. "We'll just have to do without them." In a flash, she was nude and running toward the pool. Walker stared, unable to speak. He was no longer chuckling.

Janet dove in. When she came up, she shouted, "Come on in, the water's great."

"Coming," Walker managed to say.

He removed his clothes and hesitantly walked toward the pool.

"Come on. Dive!" Janet splashed water at him. Frank dove and came up in front of her. Her arms were around him instantly and she kissed him. He was in a daze.

Janet swam away, with Frank in splashing pursuit. She made it to the edge, climbed out and ran into the bedroom. Moments later, she reappeared, wearing a robe and carrying a towel and a robe for him. She helped dry him, helped him on with the robe and led him to the kitchen. Opening the refrigerator door, she pulled out several pans, one of which she placed in the oven.

Walker was still in a daze as they ate a pleasant, simple meal. When the meal was over it was dark. Night had fallen. "You go on to bed," Janet directed. "I'll clean up here and join you in a few minutes."

When Janet arrived at the bedside she shed her robe and stood before him naked. Walker was in bed in his pajamas.

"Will you kindly remove those garments," she said as she pulled back the bed covers. "Remember, nothing is to be between us."

Walker got up and removed his pajamas. This time he smiled, let out a shout and jumped back into bed where Janet awaited him.

In this manner, the marriage of Frank Walker and Janet Wingate was consummated.

TWENTY-TWO

With the now famous trial ended, the life of those associated with the Ecumenical Society changed radically, as did the Society. The news media swept down on the members. They were deluged with requests for interviews, statements, pictures, biographies. They were offered large sums of money for endorsing products. The biggest problem was the mail and telephone calls. There were tens of thousands of letters. Calls plugged the telephone lines. Everyone wanted to join the Society. They wrote lengthy letters extolling their virtues and included letters of recommendations from many sources. The operation of the Society came to a standstill.

In the midst of all this, Reverend Hamilton received an urgent telephone call from Nelson. Could, he, Leahy and Schwartz come to New York for a meeting with the board next week? When Hamilton asked why, Nelson simply replied that some urgent decisions had to be made immediately and these would concern the very existence of the Society. "It's a different world," Nelson reported. "Everything has changed. For the past six weeks we have done nothing but handle phone calls, letters, interview requests. We have not been able to conduct regular business. Nobody expected this."

The office in New York was in upheaval when the three men arrived. Bags of mail were piled in the outer office; new employees crowded the room; A bank of new telephones were being answered by operators whose sole job appeared to be answering phone calls. The men were escorted into the inner office where the board of directors was already assembled. Angela was there, of course. A strange man was seated next to Nelson.

"I'm sorry for the general mess you see around here," Nelson said. "We have not been able to keep things in order. We're trying though. Before I get into a recital of our problems I want to introduce Mr. Ronald Baker. Mr. Baker is a vice president of O'Reilly, Hendicks and O'Shea, Investment Bankers. He is here to make a proposal to solve our problems and he might as well make his presentation before we consider whatever other proposals may be suggested. Mr. Baker."

The small, sallow-faced bespectacled man with a bald head encircled by short-cut gray hair, cleared his throat and said, "I'm not surprised to see the congestion in this office. My firm took the liberty of calling several foundations to ask if they would join in a consortium which would make annual donations to the Ecumenical Society. The unanimity and the enthusiasm of their response is a reflection of what the country generally thinks of your Society. It was an overwhelming response. We will have no trouble doubling the amount of money which you currently receive from your members, possibly tripling it without raising one finger to obtain it. There would be no fee for this. The only requirement would be that they be identified as sponsors of your organization and that they could issue that fact in the material they publicize about their own operations. It will be necessary, of course, to have you as a qualified recipient of charitable contributions by the IRS but there should be no trouble at this point.

"The idea in this proposal is to lighten your load in obtaining money and to permit you to do more than you are doing now. There would be no outside controls or regulations.

"It should be obvious that you can no longer operate as you have in the past. Your client base will grow very fast. You will need more people, more equipment, more of everything. You are no longer a secret organization. You cannot limit yourself as you have in the past. Every individual in prison, every correctional system in every state, every court in the land now knows about you. And they will want to use your services. It should be a win-win situation."

Nelson asked the first question. "We have never tried to qualify as a charitable organization with the IRS. We never considered ourselves a charity. We hand out the money we receive, or we invest it. It produces, hopefully, income; we get interest and dividends on this money. How do you propose to qualify us as a non-profit organization and a charitable institution?"

"You won't need that interest income and those dividends. You will have all the money you need from contributions. You would not even have to assess your beneficiaries for money. More important, we think there would be many wealthy individuals who would be glad to contribute annually.

"The thought which has prompted this proposal is that yours is the only idea which has come close to providing an immediate solution to our overcrowded prisons. You have made it clear that the present scheme to go on building more prisons is futile. But of course your program is an infinitesimal effort. It must be multiplied a thousand times in order to do what ultimately must be done. There will be no government money, state or federal, in this enlarged operation."

"Do you think that a qualified foundation can provide capital for the formation and operations of a private business?" Schwartz asked.

"The foundations would not be doing that," Baker replied. "They would simply make donations to the Ecumenical Society which would already have qualified itself as a recipient of foundation funds. You would use the funds to organize businesses for profit."

"I seriously doubt that we could ever be accepted by the IRS as a charity qualified for deductible donations or donations from a foundation so long as we used the money as a means of obtaining profits," Nelson said.

"Then you would just stop organizing businesses. You would simply be a placement agency for your members, putting them to work in businesses already in operation."

"We already have a United States Employment Agency with offices in every city in the country," Schwartz said.

"We will urge Congress to provide a tax incentive to employers who hire ex-convicts," Baker offered.

Nobody responded to this last comment. After a rather prolonged silence, Father Leahy asked, "Have you made any inquiries in Washington on the possibility of getting such legislation?"

God's Mafia

"No. In fact that just occurred to me as you raised the question of IRS approval."

"Is there anything more you would like to tell us Mr. Baker?" Nelson asked.

"Obviously, a great many details remain to be discussed. I want you to understand that my firm does not stand to profit from this. We were so impressed with what you have done that we made a few preliminary inquiries and then came to see if you might be receptive to the idea."

"Does anybody else have any questions?" Nelson asked. No one did. "Mr. Baker, please tell your people that we are grateful that they have given as much thought to this matter as they have, and that we appreciate your presentation here. We will give the matter consideration and get back to you."

With that Mr. Baker excused himself, and Nelson turned to the board. "I thought I would let you hear him directly before we get to the rest of our agenda, because if we were to enter into something like he is proposing we would have a means of solving the many problems I'm about to present to you."

Reverend Hamilton opened the ensuing discussion. "Obviously, Mr. Baker was talking about something entirely different from our program. We would simply be swallowed up in a huge operation which would be a private annex to the corrections departments across the country. We would be useful only in giving some measure of notoriety and maybe some prestige to the new program. I certainly have no objection to such a program. However, it is not what Father Leahy, Ben Schwartz and I had intended. At least, I hope they agree with me."

Father Leahy said. "Mal, we probably should be careful about what we say here. It doesn't make any difference what we tried to do or what we intended. I'm sure none of us has any pride of authorship. It is for the Ecumenical Society to decide what it wishes to do."

Nelson looked to Schwartz. "Ben, you know what all the people here think of you. What are your thoughts?"

"I'm afraid I have a little different attitude about this," he said. "I'll be blunt and tell you that the scheme will never work. First of all, you will never get IRS approval. And if you did get it, the new organization would indeed be a flagrant violation of RICO! It would become an easy way to raise capital for any fool enterprise that wanted to escape all the regulations on capital formation! The Securities and Exchange Commission would tell Congress to get somebody else to protect the public. I just can't feature legitimate foundations providing free capital for private industry by merely passing it through the Ecumenical Society. Ex-convicts can do that with their own money, but foundations cannot do it with money held in trust. The regulators would never permit such capital formation without very close scrutiny, scrutiny that we would never have passed in the corporations we developed."

Angela Burgé did not wait to be called upon. "Whatever some well-intentioned capitalists want to do to help solve the problem we have struggled with is fine. They can go ahead and start their own program and we will wish them well. The Ecumenical Society is comprised of a group of people who have pulled themselves out of the gutter by the grace of God and by the grace of God alone. I hope we never forget that. Moreover, this organization will be sustained only so long as each member is compelled by his or her own will to maintain the organization. Mr. Baker and his people are good people who are trying to help. Indeed we could reach many, many more people. But they are proposing something which will become either a branch of the corrections system or another giant charity. In very short order it would become an entitlement, not by the government but by a charity which exists by the grace of the government. It will not be self-help by the grace of God. It will do nothing for one's soul, for one's self respect."

Reverend Hamilton supported Angela. "She has hit upon both the spirit and the genius of the Ecumenical Society. It does not fit with what has been presented to us today."

Werner Kaiser said, "I agree with all of you. My question is, 'How are we going to escape this kind of takeover either by somebody like Baker and his well-intentioned foundations or the government?' We knew why we were keeping our operations secret. We knew what would happen if it became public and now we have it! We are now getting thousands of applications to join our group. There is no way we can handle that. Do we dare take just a fraction of those who apply?"

"Why not?" Wilma Smith asked.

"Because you are now a public institution in spite of yourself," Nelson said. "Everybody is looking over your shoulder. You are under as much scrutiny as General Motors, IBM, or Coca-Cola even though you are tiny. Think for a moment. The government tried to prosecute us as a bunch of racketeers. Now we are approached by 50,000 ex-cons for a job. We take 50. In spite of our protests that we are not a charity, that is how we are perceived by the public. If we are not a charity we are racketeers as originally charged.

"If it happens that some new organization is formed along the lines described by Mr. Baker, rejected people could join that organization. Now, think some more. Why would anyone pay 7.5% of one's income to join us when they can go to a much larger outfit free?"

In a contemplative mood but in a voice loud enough for all to hear, Schwartz said, "It is worthwhile to save the Ecumenical Society. It is a miniature of what the whole world needs to save itself. The people of the world, sooner or later, must do what the members of the Ecumenical Society have done. They have conducted themselves to do what was necessary to preserve their Society. They have done this by adopting a frame of reference which has always kept in focus not just their own immediate welfare but the welfare of the entire Society. They have done this by force of a Holy Will within each of them, once that will was awakened by the prodding of two men. Whether you call this the holy ghost, the holy spirit or the holy will, it is part of each of us which must be rekindled if any society, large or small, parochial or catholic, municipal, national or universal, can survive. This is the Categorical Imperative of which Kant spoke. The key is that it is a participatory process. Everyone sacrifices some. Everyone plays as a part of a team. It is this process of creation which saves people. It is not the process of giving. It is not charity.

"What has been proposed today, although well intended, is something entirely different. There is no creation. There is no joint participation. There is no all-encompassing frame of reference. There is only charity. That is not enough.

"Although I would not for a moment accuse Mr. Baker and his associates of any ill motives, I'm reminded of a program called 'National Socialism' in Germany. There, too, the individual had only to fall in line, follow orders. There was a job for everyone but only a few were creative. The masses were not permitted to participate in the creation. A monster resulted, and believe me, if the spirit, the ghost or the will, is not holy it will not have the power needed to do the job. A moral dimension, not a political, legal or economic one is required."

A motion was made and adopted authorizing Nelson to advise Mr. Baker that after careful considerations of his proposal the board did not feel it could participate in the suggested program. The Society stood ready, however, to offer any assistance it might give in any organizations his associates formed.

A long discussion followed the disposition of the Baker proposal. It was finally decided that a notice would be published in the national media acknowledging the receipt of thousands of letters and that promising each letter would be answered in due time and that each application for employment would be given consideration and appropriate response made. It was felt that in due time the pressure of the mail would slacken. It was further decided that the Society would be operated as in the past.

The mail did in fact taper off. Meanwhile interviews were arranged for the few who were deemed worthy of consideration. No other organizations were immediately formed. But all knew that sooner or later it would happen.

❖❖❖

Almost two years passed. The Ecumenical Society gained wide reputation; its work increased and its efforts were further applauded. Frank and Janet Walker carried on their lives. The boys were happily growing up with their new father.

One day, Janet's secretary told her that a Kathleen Wilenski was in the office to see her. As the lady walked in Janet noted a distinct resemblance to Paul Nagel. While Janet pondered the similarity the lady said, "I'm Paul Nagel's sister. I would like a moment of your time."

"Please be seated," Janet managed to say. She had not known Paul had a sister.

In view of the circumstances of his departure, Janet hesitated to ask about him. She had a second look at the lady. She was about Paul's age, an attractive, well-groomed brunette. "I am here," she said, "because you hold a trust which my brother established for a young man some time ago. Mr. Draefus, of the attorney general's office in Crystal, referred me to you."

"Yes," Janet responded, "there is such a trust."

"I'm told by Mr. Draefus that the young man has two years to go and he will be through college."

"That's right," said Janet.

"Mr. Draefus was unable to tell me what happens to the trust when the boy finishes college."

"If he wants to get more education, the trust can be used for that. If he does not, then the balance in the trust is to help him start in some kind of job or business. Why do you ask?"

"Mrs. Walker," the lady stammered, "I was warned by Mr. Draefus not to tell you anything. I was simply to ask what I wanted to know. Mr. Draefus did not know the answer himself. He said that he had had very little to do in the matter because you looked after the young man yourself."

Janet now knew something was wrong. "Where is Paul?" she asked.

"I'm not supposed to tell you."

"You mean that you expected to come in here and ask about the trust and not tell me about Paul?"

"That's right."

"You can't do that Mrs. Wilenski! There is something wrong with Paul. I must know about it." Janet was loud and demanding. She had not asked the question casually. She had asked it anxiously, worriedly. "Where is Paul? What's happened to him? Please don't give me a bad time. I must know."

"Paul had a terrible automobile accident about a year ago. He is paralyzed on his right side."

"Where is he?" Janet insisted.

"He is in San Francisco."

"Where in San Francisco?"

"In the county medical unit."

"As a public patient?"

"Yes."

"Oh God, Mrs. Wilenski, please tell me more."

The woman was surprised by Janet's reaction. Why should this trust officer, the daughter of one of the defendants in her brother's famous case be anxious about him? She replied deliberately. "I'll tell you all. He is a pauper. He has nothing and I can't help him. I came here to see if there might be some money available from the trust. Medical bills have taken everything he had, which wasn't much. I learned about this trust when I asked Mr. Draefus if he knew of anything my brother might have that I didn't know about."

"How is he?" Janet was now more composed. "I mean his physical condition."

"He is confined to a wheel chair. His mind is all right. He can talk, but he cannot write. He has had rehabilitation. He might have some more, but he will never walk."

"Will he be able to go back to work?"

"We don't know that right now."

"Who has looked after him?"

"Nobody. I'm almost 2500 miles away. I have a family. I spend as much time as I can on the phone with him but obviously that's not much."

Janet got to her feet. "I must go out to see him."

Now Ms. Wilenski's curiosity was getting the best of her. "Why should you do that?" she asked rather bluntly.

"Because I must."

This made no sense to Kathleen Wilenski, but she hesitated. Strange, she thought, that this woman could be the trustee of her brother's trust! She asked the question foremost in her mind. "Is it because he might use some of the money in his trust?"

"No," Janet said. "Look, Ms. Wilenski, it may surprise you but your brother and I were very good friends before my father's trial. I was very fond of him and I still am. I can't bear the thought of his being in the shape he is in without anybody to help him."

"I'm sorry," Kathleen choked. "I didn't know, of course."

"Kathleen, I am married and I have two children. I'm tied down just as you are, but I must see him. I must help him."

"Why?" Kathleen pressed.

"Because I care about him very much. In many ways, Kathleen, I have known your brother better than you have. He has nothing because he gave everything away. He helped every person he could. He never thought about himself."

Kathleen Wilenski lowered her head. A tear came to her eyes. "I guess I'm not surprised," she said. "Why hasn't he told me about you?"

"Because he is who he is," Janet answered despairingly. "If he had been different, all our lives would have been different, including mine." she took a breath.

"Kathleen, your brother loved me, but he couldn't tell me until it was too late."

"Too late? What do you mean?"

"That's a long story, Kathleen, and it's no longer relevant. All I know now is that I must help your brother. I must go out to see him."

Kathleen Wilenski didn't know what more she could say. Deep within, she was happy that at long last her brother had fallen in love and with a very fine woman, even if it was "too late," whatever that meant.

"Kathleen, we must stay in touch. You and I must help your brother. He has spent a lifetime worrying about others. Only we are left to worry about him. Please give me your name, address, and phone number. I'm leaving as soon as I can for San Francisco."

Mrs. Wilenski wrote out the information and gave it to Janet. "You have my address and phone number, I assume," Janet said.

"I do."

Then Janet came around the desk and took Paul's sister in her arms. "I'll call you from San Francisco."

"Janet, I'm so grateful to you. I'm so happy I came to see you. I almost didn't. You don't know how much it means to me that there is somebody else who cares."

After Paul's sister left Janet's office, Janet called Frank. She told him about her visitor and about Paul Nagel. She did not tell him she intended to fly out to see him. That could wait until she got home.

TWENTY-THREE

Janet rushed home after work and prepared a quick meal. When Frank arrived home he went to the kitchen and kissed Janet as he always did. Soon they were all seated at the dinner table. The boys dominated the dinner discussion. Janet excused them when they were finished and prepared to tell her husband of her plans.

"You were very glum tonight, my dear," Frank said before Janet had the chance to organize her thoughts. "I understand that Paul Nagel is helpless. He is alone, and you are planning to fly to San Francisco to see him."

Janet looked at her husband, startled. Then she laughed. "My darling, you are the most thoughtful man I've ever known. How could I be so lucky?"

"I'm sure Nagel was very much in love with you. I could see it all over him. What's more important, he has always been a gentleman and has always thought about others. Now he has no one with him, and he is crippled."

"It's worse than that, Frank. He is broke. He is now a public charge. He gave away most of what he had. Whatever insurance he had is used up. There just isn't anybody else. His sister has tried to help him, to see what can be done for him."

"I understand," Walker replied sympathetically.

"My darling," Janet responded, "I thought I was going to have a bad time with you about this. You are a dear."

"Janet you really are an open book. I can read your mind. In fact, I read your mind while you talked to me on the phone. We must also remember that Paul dismissed the case against your father. He took the responsibility for that, which is why, for your information, he resigned from the DA's office. I learned that from Draefus."

"Why did he do that?" Janet asked.

"I don't know. He didn't tell Draefus; Draefus deduced it. Paul was crushed by the case, not because he didn't get a guilty verdict but because he'd decided the defendants were not guilty."

"But he made such a strong final argument to the jury," Janet said, confused. "I was mad at him because I also believed he thought my father innocent, yet he still made an impassioned plea for a guilty verdict."

"That's why he resigned, Janet; at least that's my guess. He was in an impossible spot. He did what he had to do, though he didn't like doing it. It left a bad taste in his mouth. He didn't think he could go on in that position. I'm no psychologist, but I think I'm right. He was in love with you, and he was never sure whether that was what prompted him to drop the case. I know that guy well enough to believe his high-mindedness got to him, and he thought the only honorable thing to do was resign."

"Why haven't you told me this before, Frank?"

"Because it was all guesses and suppositions. Under the present circumstance, I think you should know my thoughts. I thought it might be helpful if I were to go with you but I really think this is something you must work out yourself."

Janet hardly knew what to say, but her thoughts were clear. "I have a dear, dear husband who really thinks about me and my happiness!" She rose from the table, went to him and embraced him.

Walker continued thinking aloud. "Have you given any thought about how we can help Paul?"

"Not really. I guess I've not gotten beyond going to him and seeing him. But, of course, something must be done. First, I've got to find out just how bad off he is."

"Think about the Society employing him in the New York office. He can get the best medical help there, and I'm sure he can help Nelson. Remember our thesis, 'No charity, just self-help.' "

"Thank you, Frank. Thank you. I'm sure Nelson can use the help. They are swamped."

Janet hoped Kathleen had warned Paul that she was coming, and Kathleen had done just that. She had also gotten from Janet when Paul was to expect her so when Janet saw Paul for the first time in San Francisco he was more prepared than she. He was fully dressed, shirt, tie and suit. He was in his wheel chair but he had a huge smile on his face and his left hand was out to take hers. "Hello, Janet," he said.

Janet awkwardly took his hand, smiled meekly and replied, "Hello, Paul." Instinctively she wanted to hug him but she did not think that appropriate. She pulled up a chair and seated herself close to him.

"It is so very nice of you to come," he said, still smiling. "Kathleen told me you were coming."

Janet felt that Paul was going to keep this on a causal, polite, platonic basis. Somehow, that disappointed her. Seeking to keep the meeting on his terms, Paul said, "How is everything with you? How is Frank?

"I'm just fine. Frank keeps his nose to the legal grindstone."

"I didn't learn you had children until after the trial. How are your boys?"

"Growing every hour," Janet replied, trying to smile. "Tell me about yourself, Paul."

"All there is what you see. There are people all around me who look after me. It's really a nice place."

Janet concluded that Kathleen had told Paul that between them, they were going to look after him. She wondered how Paul felt about that. She decided to talk about Kathleen. "Your sister Kathleen and I had a chance to get acquainted. And we are going to get better acquainted. She is a very nice person. I like her."

Paul smiled. "Apparently she likes you, too. With just one visit, you two have become buddies."

"One visit and we both realized we were going to look after you, Paul."

"You both have plenty of others to look after."

"We each have somebody to help us with our families. We're going to look after you."

Paul now became somber. His smile faded. "Janet, you must not do this! You must not get involved with me."

"Very well, I'll not get involved with you. What are your plans for the future?"

"First, I'm going to get back in shape and then I'm going back to work."

"Where are you going to work?"

"Look, Janet, there is nothing wrong with my mind. I can get a job with any law firm in the country."

"And of course you would never consider a job I might suggest!"

"Oh, now you're going to tell me you came out here to offer me a job?"

"Maybe. Depends on whether you are the same bull-headed, hard-nosed, stubborn, ornery character you once were or are now a little more sane."

"You haven't changed much either. OK, so I need a job and I'm not in a position to be very choosy."

"That's better. I'm going to ask two people to come out here to talk to you about a possible job. They may even make you an offer. I hope you will take a few minutes to listen to them."

That evening she called her husband from her hotel room.

"Did you reach Nelson?" Janet asked Frank.

"Yes, and I talked to Ben. They will both arrive there at 3:00 p.m. tomorrow."

"What do you think about our chances?"

"You will be very pleasantly surprised. Those two have been doing some things lately that have not even been reported to Dad or Father Leahy."

"What's going on?" Janet asked.

"I'd rather they tell you. Suffice it to say they will actually need Paul."

"Hurrah," Janet shouted over the telephone. "By the way, how are my Indians?"

"*Our* Indians are fine. They don't miss their mom anymore. You know how that is. But your husband misses you dreadfully."

"I miss you too, dear. I'll call again tomorrow."

Janet arranged for rooms at a San Francisco hotel, and she managed to get Paul Nagel there for the conference. Leaving him at the hotel to freshen up, she drove to the airport to pick up Nelson and Schwartz.

"What's the big deal?" she asked as she drove the rental car from the airport.

"It's a rather long story. We will tell you about it when we talk to Nagel. Do you think he will be interested? What's his condition."

"I'm sure he will be interested. I'm not sure of his condition. I've not been able to talk to his doctor. He certainly appears to be all right mentally. He is badly handicapped physically. He can't walk and his right arm is useless. I will find out from the doctor if physical therapy will improve his physical disability."

In the hotel suite — two rooms with an adjoining small office — the four of them sat around and talked. Janet was surprised at how cordial it was. Nelson opened the discussion.

"Janet, you remember hearing about Ronald Baker, the investment banker who came to us and offered to provide full financing through donations from several foundations. You know that we turned down his proposition. Well, since that time the situation has changed. We don't have time to recruit. We got so many applications we have all we can do to handle them. Many of them have looked very good and those we interviewed have shown promise. We decided, you may remember, that we would continue as always, taking very few people and working them into the system.

"Several weeks ago I called Ben, and I suggested he join me in brain-blitzing our problem. The question was, 'Can we cope with this increased demand without going completely charitable?' Well, we decided to go back to Mr. Baker. We simply asked him if the many foundations he had talked to would lend us money instead of giving it to us! At first he was shocked, and he said he could not see how that would work. If we would not accept gifts why would we want to borrow? We told him it was because by borrowing we could keep the Ecumenical Society independent. We assured him that they could review each loan proposal on a bank-loan standard and could turn us down on any one loan. We also told him that we would keep our pre-

God's Mafia

sent capital of $20,000,000 in liquid form such as government and corporate bonds and we would supply the equity for each loan, about 20% and borrow the other 80%, bank standards at bank interest rates. That would immediately expand our operation five fold, giving us a base of $100,000,000. We suggested that a consortium of foundations be formed of 20 to 40 such foundations so that the risk would be minimized for each one. We would administer the consortium and send quarterly distributions to each foundation.

"Baker bought our idea and he already has 15 foundations which will participate. He thinks he can double that. All a sudden, our problem is creating enough businesses to employ our increased membership. We are setting up a separate department for establishing new businesses, whereas in the past we asked members to form whatever enterprise they chose. We will now advertise offers to entrepreneurs with new ventures and furnish capital and employees upon their joining the Ecumenical Society. We can show them our record of employee performance, and the few successful enterprises we presently operate. In instances in which we may need more equity capital, we can use Baker's firm for public issues.

"We want to capitalize on our present notoriety, but we know the dangers of publicity. We can lose our moral base. For that reason we are also setting up another department which will intensify the training and education of recruits. I hate to use the word, 'indoctrinate,' but I can't find a better one. We will indoctrinate no particular creed or belief, but we must indoctrinate the moral dimension, the proper frame of reference. We will try to merge our moral imperative with our business requirements. We will take the time to explore all this and reduce it to a code. For those who have no God, they will abide by a code which we have taken from God. We intend to use our moral leaders, Leahy, Hamilton and Schwartz as our counselors, but we will staff the department with young people.

"Paul, we want you with us in this endeavor, as general counsel."

Before Paul could respond, Ben Schwartz said, "Paul, I think this has tremendous potential, but it won't work without the complete dedication of all concerned. You are capable of that dedication."

Janet looked at Paul. "This is the alternative to charity you and I talked about so often. This is the chance for you to be a part of something which will provide more people with the opportunity to help themselves, to avoid charity, to avoid welfare and public subsistence. You can't turn it down."

Paul Nagel smiled. "I don't intend to. When do I start?"

Janet took Paul's left hand into hers. "You see, Paul, Someone is guiding you to the place of your dreams." Then she kissed him.

"Thank you, Janet. Thanks to all of you."

Janet made two telephone calls when she got to her hotel room. the first was to Kathleen. She told her what had happened. "I'll see to it that he is settled in New York," Kathleen offered.

"You will want to help him settle in, Kathleen, but the Society will make all the arrangements." Then Janet called her husband. Her message was simple. "All is well. Paul is taken care of. I'm coming home. Please be at the airport to give me a big hug and a kiss. Please have my sons there, I have big hugs for them, too." Then she climbed into bed and slept without dreaming but with a big smile on her face.

END